Praise for Sarah Price

"Sarah Price once again engages her readers in a tender drama that leaves you wondering if two very different worlds . . . the Amish and the English can collide and still leave us with beauty. After Alejandro Diaz, a famous Cuban singer, crosses paths with Amanda Beiler, an Amish girl in the middle of NYC, the beauty begins. Alejandro's world becomes Amanda's, and Amanda seeks her own path in the light of Alejandro. Fantastic and well written . . . mostly beautiful."
—Dianna Bupp, founder of All Things Amish on Facebook

"*Plain Fame* has a unique story line that will keep you up late at night hiding under your blanket with a flashlight, trying to squeeze in one last page before you head into La La Land. Yes, it's that good! I love that I loved these characters so much. They are as different as night and day . . . an Amish girl and a famous pop star brought together by an unfortunate accident involving a limo. Or was it unfortunate? Some may say it was fate pulling these two together like a magnet to metal. The only thing for certain is that their lives are about to be forever altered . . ." —Sue Laitinen, book reviewer for DestinationAmish.com

"Once again Sarah Price does not disappoint. I have enjoyed every book that I have read by her. *Plain Fame* is a little different from your normal 'Amish' novel. Readers who don't normally read Amish novels will like this one, as it, in my opinion, is more about how fame affects someone rather than being just an Amish novel." —Debbie Curto, book reviewer from *Debbie's Dusty Deliberations*

"Amish Christian romance like none other—Sarah Price opens both her characters and her readers to new worlds. This love story could easily become a classic as two lives from opposite cultures collide, creating intense conflict and romance. *Plain Fame* was my introduction to Sarah Price and the beginning of my Price addiction."

—Lisa Bull, blogger of *Captured by My Thoughts*

Plain Fame

The Amish Classic Series

First Impressions (Realms)
The Matchmaker (Realms)
Second Chances (Realms)

For a complete listing of books, please visit the author's website at www.sarahpriceauthor.com.

Plain Fame

Book One of the Plain Fame Series

Sarah Price

Waterfall
PRESS

Text copyright © 2015 Price Publishing, LLC

Published by Waterfall Press, Grand Haven, MI

www.brilliancepublishing.com

Amazon, the Amazon logo, and Waterfall Press are trademarks of Amazon.com, Inc., or its affiliates.

ISBN-13: 9781503945371

ISBN-10: 1503945375

Cover design by Kerri Resnick

Printed in the United States of America

Fame is a strange thing.

Some people work their entire lives to acquire it, willing to give up their privacy and personal lives in order to satisfy the curiosity and fantasies of their fans.

Still others find themselves unwillingly in the center of the limelight, despite wishing to remain anonymous. Their privacy and rights are stripped because they become celebrities.

This book is dedicated to the people who fall into both of those categories: the singers, performers, artists, and entertainers who give so much of themselves for our own enjoyment.

They change our lives. But we also change theirs.

Rejoice, O young man, in thy youth; and let thy heart cheer thee in the days of thy youth, and walk in the ways of thine heart, and in the sight of thine eyes: but know thou, that for all these things God will bring thee into judgment.

Ecclesiastes 11:9 (KJV)

About the Vocabulary

The Amish speak Pennsylvania Dutch (also called Amish German or Amish Dutch). This is a verbal language with variations in spelling among communities throughout the United States. For example, in some regions, a grandfather is *grossdaadi*, while in other regions he is known as *grossdawdi*. Some dialects refer to the mother as *mamm* or *maem*, and others simply as *mother* or *mammi*.

In addition, there are words and expressions, such as *mayhaps*, or the use of the word *then* at the end of sentences, and, my favorite, *for sure and certain*, that are not necessarily from the Pennsylvania Dutch language/dialect but are unique to the Amish.

The use of these words comes from my own experience living among the Amish in Lancaster County, Pennsylvania.

Chapter One

New York City was as crowded as ever, and traffic was backed up for miles. Alejandro leaned his head against the plush headrest of his private limousine and shut his eyes for a few moments. After weeks of traveling, he was tired. Tired of living out of quickly packed suitcases, tired of hotels, tired of the lack of privacy. He missed the heartwarming sun, the long sandy beaches, and the quiet of his own home in beautiful Miami. He made a mental note to remind his assistant to stop scheduling these trips for a while. He just needed some time to recuperate, to take a step back, to reexamine his life, and to recharge his batteries.

"*Ay, mi madre,*" he said to himself. Then, leaning forward, he tapped on the glass that separated him from his driver. "*¿Qué está pasando? ¿Por qué hay tanto tráfico?*" He couldn't imagine why there was so much traffic at this hour. It wasn't even noon, but it was well past the morning rush hour. Yet the streets were packed, bumper to bumper. Even more frustrating were the pedestrians, ignoring traffic signals and crossing when they shouldn't. That was adding to the traffic. Alejandro sighed. He was going to be late.

The driver glanced back and shrugged his shoulders in the casual manner of a typical New Yorker. "Traffic, my man. It's just traffic."

"Dios *mío,*" Alejandro complained under his breath. "We are going to make it in time, *sí*?" His voice was deep and husky but thick with a Spanish accent. To the knowing linguist, he was Cuban. To the average American, he was just another Hispanic.

"Yeah, yeah, don't sweat it," the driver said.

Don't sweat it, Alejandro repeated to himself and shook his head. Spoken by a man who drives a limousine for a living, he thought. "If I'm late . . ." he said but chose not to complete the sentence. In reality, so what if he was late? It was only a meeting with Richard Gray, the largest music producer in America. But it was Richard Gray who had contacted him, Alejandro Diaz. It was Richard Gray who had requested the meeting, a lunch meeting, and that took all of the pressure off Alejandro's shoulders. He was in control of this one. He was being sought after by the big man.

The stretch limousine lurched forward, and the driver started to finally regain some speed. The traffic seemed to be breaking up somewhat, permitting the driver to make up some time, and Alejandro began to relax. They'd get there on time. It was only twenty blocks from the hotel to the restaurant where the meeting was to take place. But they still had to pass through Times Square and Seventh Avenue by Madison Square Garden.

"Don't these people work?" Alejandro grumbled as he began fiddling with his cell phone. Three texts from his manager, and two from his agent. He was lucky. It was usually triple that amount. A slow day. Must be a Tuesday, he thought grimly. The only slow day of the week. And still, he had meetings and appointments and e-mails and text messages. When had life started to get so crazy? he asked himself.

He heard the crash before he actually recognized the jolt for what it was. The driver had slammed on his brakes, the car screeching to a halt, but not before the thud on the hood of the car made it apparent that something had been hit. Alejandro fell forward, despite the fact that the limo had not been driving over twenty miles an hour, if that. When he picked himself up from the floor and sat back on the black leather seat, he tried to assess what had happened.

"You all right back there?" the driver asked, his voice shaking and his face pale.

"*Sí, sí,*" Alejandro said, trying to calm himself. An accident. What were the odds of that? And why today of all days? He glanced around but didn't see another vehicle in front of the limousine. "What happened?"

"Hit someone. A jaywalker," the driver replied before picking up his cell phone and dialing 911.

The crowd was already gathering around the front of the car. People. There were always crowds of people around when he wanted them, but especially when he didn't. This was one of those moments. Alejandro exhaled loudly. Now he'd definitely be late. There was no way that he could get out of the limousine in this crowd without being recognized, and that would be the kiss of death. He could see the headlines already: "Viper Strikes Pedestrian in Manhattan."

He tried to do a quick calculation of how the next hour or two would pan out. The police would come and want to interview him. The crowd would gather, the traffic would be thick, and it would become a mob scene. He'd have no choice but to get out. Alejandro sighed, reaching into his suit pocket for his black sunglasses. If he had to get out and face the crowd, better to do it early on rather than look like he was avoiding it. And when the inevitable lawsuit happened, it would look better if he had seemed concerned. With that, the decision was made.

The driver turned around, just about to say something when he noticed Alejandro reaching for the door handle. "What are you doing, sir?" There was panic in his voice. "You can't get out, sir. They'll notice you. There will be a mob!"

Alejandro nodded. "Exactly. But if I don't, that will be even worse than if I get out now." It would be a different headline then: "Viper Indifferent to Struck Pedestrian in Manhattan." That would never do; so, ignoring the concern of his driver, he pulled at the door handle and flung the door back, careful to not hit anyone who was standing nearby.

It took a second, maybe two, for the beginning of the murmuring to trickle through the crowd. He heard it, the gentle hum of recognition. Whispers, looks, people pointing, and then the name: Viper. They were already talking about him. Out of the corner of his eye, Alejandro could see the cell phones lifted above the crowd so that people could take photos. He knew better than to react. Instead, he ignored it and hurried to the front of the car. He pushed past several people, making certain to say, "Excuse me" as he did so. Manners, his mother had always taught him. No matter what the situation, a man had to be civilized and mannerly. He wondered where running over pedestrians in New York City ranked in Alecia's list of mannerly behavior.

When he finally made his way to the front of the limousine, he noticed two men leaning over a woman.

"Is she all right?" Alejandro asked, pulling at his pants as he knelt down beside them.

"She's hurt bad," one man said, glancing over his shoulder at Alejandro. He frowned as if recognizing him but returned his attention to the woman.

"But is she responding?" Alejandro asked. He reached out for the woman's hand. Holding it in his, he was glad to feel her fingers twitch and clutch at his hand. He looked at her quickly. Her face was rolled to the side, and her eyes were closed. The color had drained from her cheeks, so her brown hair, pulled back from her face, gave a sharp contrast to her pale skin. There was no blood, and for that, he gave a quick prayer of gratitude to God. But she was lying in a crumpled heap, one of her legs twisted in a crooked fashion underneath her light-blue dress, over which she wore a black apron. "My driver called for an ambulance. I wouldn't recommend moving her until they get here."

The driver was standing on the other side of the woman. "They said five minutes." He looked around at the traffic. It was even worse now since the limousine was blocking the intersection. "Like to see how they'll manage that."

As Alejandro continued to hold the woman's hand, he became well aware that people were beginning to take photographs. He frowned and motioned toward the driver. "Give me your jacket."

"What?"

"Your jacket! To cover her. They're starting to take photos," Alejandro snapped, trying to keep his voice down so that he was not overheard.

The driver quickly shook his black jacket off his shoulders and handed it to Alejandro. Carefully, he laid it over the woman, hiding her face from the people who were taking pictures with their cell phones.

"Is she dressed in a costume?" the driver asked.

Alejandro looked up, caught off guard by the question. "Costume?"

"She looks like Dorothy from *The Wizard of Oz.*"

"She's Amish, you idiot," someone said from the crowd that was now forming on the sidewalk.

Alejandro wanted to ask what "Amish" was but didn't want to draw further attention to himself or to the situation than what was needed. Right now, all the media could say was that his driver hit the woman and he, Alejandro Diaz, had stayed by her side until the ambulance came. The police would soon arrive, question him, and then he'd be on his merry way to his meeting with Richard Gray. The worse thing that could happen was some minor damage to his bad-boy image.

The woman fluttered her eyes, trying to make sense of what was happening as she began to awaken. The color started to return to her cheeks. Her chocolate-brown eyes tried to make sense of all the people staring at her from above. "Where am I?" she asked.

"Oz, according to that guy!" someone from the crowd quipped.

Alejandro glared over his shoulder at the man who was laughing, then looked back at the woman from behind his dark sunglasses. "You've been hit by a car," he said gently. "Don't try to move. Help is on the way, Princesa."

But she didn't listen. When she tried to lift herself, she winced and fell back down to the street. "My leg," she whimpered, collapsing against Alejandro's body. He was still holding her hand, and she clung to it, her head buried against his leg.

Alejandro lowered his voice. "You're going to be fine, but wait for the medical people. You can't move, Princesa." He stared at her face, tanned with some freckles over the tops of her cheeks. She was fresh looking, like a country girl. The driver was right. She did resemble Dorothy with her blue dress. Except she had a white heart-shaped covering for her head that had been knocked off and lay in the middle of the street, a tourist stepping on one of the strings.

When she looked at him again, her dark eyes trying to make sense of what was happening to her, he felt a jolt. For as young and fresh as she was, she was also remarkably beautiful in a natural way that completely took him by surprise. Her tan skin glowed in the sun rays that trickled through the skyscrapers. Her dark hair was pulled back from her face, a few loose strands curling down her neck. No makeup or fancy hairstyle. Just a plain beauty that caught him off guard.

"My family," she whispered, moisture at the corner of her eyes.

"May I call someone for you?" His voice was soft, almost a whisper so that the people surrounding them couldn't hear, as he tightened his grasp on her hand. He was surprised when she clasped it, her grip strong, and he found himself staring into her face, once again amazed at how beautiful she looked.

Despite the clear pain that she was in, the young woman was still stoic and dignified, hiding her discomfort. Yet when she tried to shake her head, a single tear trickled down her cheek. "We don't have a phone. They need to know," she said, her voice trailing off.

No phone? Not even a cell phone? He frowned but didn't inquire further. He could hear the sirens in the distance. He imagined the police would arrive first, and from that point on, he'd be questioned, then able to leave. Another thirty minutes, he thought. Forty-five, tops.

"What is your name, Princesa?"

"Amanda," she whispered. "Amanda Beiler."

Alejandro nodded, aware that she had a slight accent. He couldn't quite place it. It wasn't European, and it certainly wasn't from South America. But it was different from the other American accents. "If you tell me your address, I'll make certain that a message gets to your family."

She clutched his hand, and he leaned forward. "Creek Road in Lititz, Pennsylvania." She paused, shutting her eyes as tears started to well at the corners. "They think I'll be home tonight for my chores."

He laughed softly and caressed her hand with his thumb. "You won't be home for chores tonight, Amanda Beiler. But you'll be just fine." He paused before adding, "I'll make sure of it." She was the image of innocence and clearly a long way from home. While he knew nothing about Lititz, Pennsylvania, he suspected it was far from Philadelphia or Pittsburgh. And certainly not close to New York City. "I promise," he heard himself say.

He could hear the mumbling behind him. The crowd was beginning to liven up. If people hadn't recognized him before, he knew the word was now floating through the flock. He could sense the energy as more people began to peer over the heads of others, trying to see him, trying to take a photograph of him. The cell phones were in the air snapping shots of Alejandro kneeling beside the Amish woman on the streets of Manhattan. No, he corrected himself. Photos of Viper with the Amish woman. Alejandro wondered which one would wind up on the entertainment channels and the tabloids later on this evening.

The police arrived moments later, their cars making a way through the crowded streets, avoiding the pedestrians who didn't seem to care that they were breaking the law by darting across the road. Once the police had parked their cars, ignoring the other drivers who began honking their horns at being blocked and delayed, two policemen began to push the crowd back, creating a buffer so that the ambulance would be able to get through when it arrived. Another police officer approached Alejandro, quickly assessing that he was a good person to start interviewing.

"What happened here, sir?"

Alejandro glanced up, peering at the officer from behind his dark sunglasses. He tried to pick his words carefully, knowing that too many people were probably recording the scene. What he said now would most likely be replayed over and over again, on television, on interviews, and in court when the young woman sued for having been hit by his driver.

"I'm not exactly certain," Alejandro said. "I just know that she was hit by the limousine."

The officer peered at him for a moment. It was the moment of recognition. "Aren't you . . . ?"

And so it begins, he thought wistfully. Avoiding the question, Alejandro glanced at the woman. "No disrespect," he said. "But she's in a lot of pain, Officer. Do you have any idea when the ambulance will get here?"

To Alejandro's relief, the officer leaned his chin over to his shoulder, speaking into his walkie-talkie. While the officer was trying to get a reading on the location of the ambulance, Alejandro turned his attention back to the young woman. "Amanda?" he asked softly. "Amanda? You hanging in there, Princesa?"

She nodded slightly. The color drained from her face again, and tears began to fall down her cheeks. "I just wanted a pair of sunglasses," she said, her words barely audible.

"What?" Uncertain that he had heard her correctly, Alejandro leaned down, trying to hear what she was saying. "What did you say?"

She reached for his hand again, holding it tightly in her own. "While I was waiting for my train," she whispered. "I was crossing the street for a pair of sunglasses."

He didn't have an opportunity to ask her about what she had said. The ambulance was pulling up behind them, the horn beeping for people to get out of the way. The officer in charge motioned for Alejandro to back away so that the paramedics could bring the gurney closer.

Respectfully, he moved back but stopped just a few feet from where she was stretched out on the road. He noticed the white cap lying on the ground a few feet away and stooped to pick it up. Clutching it to his chest, Alejandro watched as the paramedics worked, quickly taking her vital signs and asking a rapid barrage of questions. Within minutes, Amanda Beiler was gently lifted from the streets of Manhattan, placed on the crisp white sheet covering the gurney, and whisked away to a hospital.

Alejandro stared after it, too aware that his cell phone was vibrating in his pocket and the officer was asking him a question. But his mind was elsewhere. This young woman, dressed in such plain clothes and with such a pure, fresh look on her face, lingered in his memory, and he found that he could think of nothing else. She was alone in Manhattan and clearly out of her element. He knew the feeling from his own days as an immigrant with his mother in Miami. And he also knew that he wasn't going to make that appointment with Richard Gray. Only this was now by his own choice, not because of being delayed by the accident.

Chapter Two

When Amanda awoke in the hospital room, it was dark outside. It took her a minute to place where she was. Slowly, the memories came back to her. Bits and pieces: the noise of the streets, the blinking light at the crosswalk, the noise of the screeching brakes, the impact of the car as it hit her. For a while, she relived that moment, seeing the people staring at her sprawled on the ground. Groaning, she turned her head away from the memory and stared out the dirty window by her bed.

She could see the twinkling lights of New York City from the hospital window. It took her a moment to realize where she was; the white walls, the metal twin bed, the curtain that hung between her and the plain oak door, she took it all in. There was a large bouquet of flowers on the windowsill: pink and white roses. She frowned when she saw them and tried to count how many roses were in the tall glass vase with the pretty white bow around its neck. She stopped counting at twenty-four and left it as "a lot." But she couldn't begin to realize why there were "a lot" of flowers on a windowsill in a strange room that she imagined was inside a hospital.

Amanda shut her eyes and leaned back into the pillow. There was a dull ache in her left leg, and her head felt fuzzy. She couldn't move anything more than her eyes and even that hurt. Why was she here? she wondered as she tried to piece together the events that had led her to this hospital bed when, instead, she should be home, helping her *mamm* clean up the dishes from the evening meal.

The door opened, and she saw a nurse in a white uniform walk through it. She flipped on a light switch, and Amanda blinked as her eyes adjusted. The nurse was an older woman with graying hair that was curly around her forehead and ears. She wore wire-rimmed glasses and had rosy cheeks. When she looked up and saw Amanda looking at her, the nurse smiled. "Well, look who has decided to wake up!"

"Where am I?" Amanda asked, pulling the sheet and white blanket up to her chin. She tried to remember what had happened, but everything seemed a blur. One minute she had been crossing the street among a crowd of people, the next she was waking up in this strange room by herself. There were faint images that clouded her memory: bright lights, the man with the dark glasses, the loud noises, a police car, and all these Englischers. But she just couldn't seem to piece it together.

"NewYork-Presbyterian Hospital, my dear. You had quite a nasty accident," the nurse said, reaching for the chart that hung from the foot of the bed. "Let's check you out and see how you're doing, if it's OK with you?"

Amanda watched as the nurse checked her pulse. "What happened to me?"

"Just a few bumps and bruises, dear," the nurse said, smiling. She seemed pleasant enough, not like the other Englischers that Amanda had met on her journey. "And a broken leg. Nothing that a month in a cast won't fix."

"A broken leg?" She reached down to feel her leg. Sure enough, her left leg was in a cast, all the way up to her thigh. She groaned. What could be worse than a broken leg at the beginning of the summer? How would she be able to help her *daed* with the harvest? How would she be able to help her *mamm* with the garden? They were counting on her, she thought to herself. She'd have to find a way. And then it dawned on her. "How long have I been here?"

The nurse marked something down on her chart, her head bent over the clipboard. "Since yesterday before noon. But you're in good hands, dear." She clicked the top of her pen and slid it back into her pocket. "And you seem to have quite an admirer," she said, nodding toward the flowers.

"What about my parents?" Amanda asked in a panic, her eyes big and wide as she stared at the nurse.

They hadn't wanted her to go on the trip by herself. They had insisted that she travel with her older sister when they went out to Ohio, but just before the return journey, her sister had decided to stay. Amanda suspected that their cousin's friend, Jonas Wheeler, had something to do with that decision. Everyone had asked Amanda to stay, but she had insisted on leaving, knowing that her *daed* would need her help plowing the fields. Without any sons and only two daughters at home, her *daed* would need all the help he could muster.

Her parents had been expecting her to arrive home yesterday evening. She was to catch the connecting train at Penn Station in New York City headed for Lancaster, Pennsylvania, where her parents had arranged for a Mennonite neighbor to meet her and drive her home.

"They must be terribly worried about me!" she exclaimed, knowing full well that they would be panicking. Guilt racked her body, and she shook at the thought, trying not to imagine the worry that her parents were going through on account of her.

The nurse smiled again. She had a pretty smile that lit up her entire face. "Not to worry! I do believe that it has all been taken care of, Ms. Beiler." She patted Amanda's arm gently before hanging the chart back at the foot of the bed. The gesture calmed Amanda, and she felt her pulse slow down. The nurse began fiddling with the equipment behind the bed. "How do you feel otherwise?"

"It hurts, and so does my head," Amanda said, lifting a hand to her forehead. She was surprised to feel her hair against her cheek. Her prayer *kapp* was missing, and her hair hung loose in gentle waves over her shoulders. She blushed. She had never been in front of a stranger with her hair free. In her world, only a husband should see her loose hair. "It feels like I'm dreaming," she said to the nurse. Indeed, everything seemed foggy and strange, as if she were floating around the room.

The nurse laughed. "That's the pain medicine, dear. If you are starting to feel uncomfortable again, I'll get your next dose. You're actually due." She glanced at the watch on her wrist. "Plus, it'll help you sleep," she said and smiled. "I'll be back momentarily. You do need a good night's rest."

Sinking back into the pillow, Amanda turned her head to look out the window again. Outside, she could see the reflection of tall buildings, many with floors still lit up. The lights were fascinating to her. There were so many of them. How could so many people live in such a small place? she wondered. There were no trees, no grass, no cows. It was a strange place, and she certainly didn't like being so far away from home and her own people. Yet she was curious. She wished that she could see the city, listen to the people, and taste some of the different foods.

Throughout her life, she had rarely left the small town where she was born and raised. Occasionally, she had traveled with friends and her extended family to work at the market in Maryland. Those were long days, requiring that she'd leave the house by four in the morning and not return home until after nine in the evening. But she had enjoyed meeting the Englischers and answering their questions, even though most of their inquiries were rather silly. Unlike many of her friends who avoided the Englischers, Amanda hadn't minded being the center of their curiosity. And that had made her quite popular with the tourists and local people who shopped at the market.

Those days had been few and far between since her *daed* needed her help on the farm. Unlike other families, her parents had not been blessed with numerous children. So Amanda did her fair share of the work in the fields. She loved the smell of freshly tilled soil, lived for the days when they planted seed, and felt the true glory of God during the harvesttime. Her father used to brag that she did the work of two sons. But that had been a long time ago, she thought.

Her eyes fell upon the flowers. Roses, she thought. Her mother had several rosebushes at the farm. They were tall and bushy with clusters of vibrant red roses. The buds were small and delicate, unlike these roses that stood tall, with perfectly formed dainty cups, the petals peeling back just slightly to hint at the beauty inside them. Who on earth would have sent her flowers? And roses at that!

"Hey, you," a deep male voice exclaimed from the doorway.

Amanda turned her head around, startled by the familiarity of the voice. A man stood in the doorway, his broad shoulders accentuated by the fact that he wore a crisp, clean black suit. He wasn't particularly tall, but he seemed to fill the room with his presence. His white shirt was perfectly tailored, and he had on a thin black tie. Despite being indoors, he wore dark sunglasses that hid his eyes. His thick, curly brown hair hung over his forehead, giving him a tousled look that was charmingly handsome and playful. And his voice: it sounded like a song, the words flowing with an odd accent that she had never heard before.

"The nurse told me you were awake. That's good," he said. When he said the word *good*, it almost sounded like *gut*. But he had a singsong way of speaking that sounded very different. The man who stood there, his hand on the door handle, smiled at her as if she should know him. But she didn't.

"Who are you?" she whispered, pulling at the blankets until they were almost under her chin. With her hair undone and not being dressed properly, she was more than uncomfortable having a strange man approach her.

Usually, she didn't mind meeting strangers. On this trip to Ohio, she had met plenty of them. But for the most part, they had merely stared at her and her sister, Anna. That was quite the usual. Having grown up at the heart of the Amish tourist mecca in Pennsylvania, she was used to being stared at by strangers. Even going to the market involved dealing with the Englischers and their staring eyes, so full of questions that only the bravest managed to ask. While she normally didn't mind, Amanda hoped that this fellow wouldn't start with any of those intrusive questions. Her head was still feeling thick.

"May I?" he asked, gesturing toward the room.

Amanda hesitated a little, but after realizing that he was asking permission to enter the room, she nodded. This man seemed to know her, and he seemed to be concerned about her. She wondered if he was the doctor. He was dressed well enough, she thought. She watched as he walked into the room and softly shut the door behind himself. Then he approached her bed, and with another gesture toward the chair, he waited for her to give him permission to pull it closer and sit down beside her.

"Do I know you?" she asked, confused by his comfortable mannerism around her.

"Indirectly, yes," he said. "My name is Alejandro Diaz." He paused before adding, "It was my limousine driver who hit you yesterday."

A limousine? Amanda frowned, trying to remember. But she couldn't. Her head hurt, and everything seemed a bit fuzzy. She couldn't seem to make sense of what was happening around her. Clearly, he wasn't the doctor. "Why are you here, then?" she asked.

He raised a finger and tapped it in the air as if making a point. "That is a good question, yes." And then he smiled. His smile lit up his face and added to his charm. He reached up and took off his sunglasses, folding them carefully before sliding them into the breast pocket of his jacket. It was such a fluid movement that she was mesmerized.

She had never met any Englischer like this man. Usually the Englischers she interacted with were older men, accompanying their wives to Lancaster County to learn about the Amish and shop the handmade goods and fresh produce they brought to the market. They wore shorts and T-shirts with ratty-looking sneakers and baseball caps. The younger Englischer men who lived in the area were not interested in the Amish. They were much more interested in their cars and their music. This man was very different. He was no typical Englischer, that was for sure and certain.

With a deep breath, he sighed. "You see, I saw this beautiful damsel in distress, injured on the side of the road, *sí*? And when she spoke to me, I knew that she was far, far from home and all alone in this big, crazy city." He leaned back in the chair and crossed his leg over his knee. She noticed that he wore shiny black shoes with black socks. Not one smudge on them. "And I knew that I couldn't leave her alone to fend for herself."

Her mouth fell open, and she stared at him. He was a stranger. Yet he hadn't left her? "You've been here with me?"

"I've been here with you," he said, nodding his head once.

"The whole time?" she asked, amazed.

"The whole time," he repeated.

She shook her head. "I don't understand any of this, Mr. Diaz."

"Alejandro, please."

She frowned, chewing on her lower lip for a second. She had never had much of a reason to interact with Englischers, and certainly not Englischer men. Yet here she was talking to this complete stranger. There was something very disarming about him. Something very different. She realized that she felt relaxed and wondered if it was the pain medicine that the nurse had mentioned earlier. "Alejandro. That's a strange name."

"It's *cubano*."

"Cubano?"

He laughed. "*Cubano* as in Cuba." She liked the way that he said Cuba: *coo-bah*. But she still didn't know where it was. He must have realized that because he added, "It's near Florida. Certainly you've heard of that."

The color rose to her cheeks. "I know where Florida is, *ja*," she insisted.

He laughed again. But the sound was cheerful and light, not condescending. "*Ay*, Princesa, Cuba's a different country. It's an island. You have to get there by airplane or boat from Florida. But trust me, it's not a very nice country. Maybe to visit, but not to live there." His eyes shifted away as though remembering something from long ago. For a moment, he seemed as if he were transported somewhere else, to a previous life, and not an easy one. She wondered what could have happened in his past to make his eyes grow dark so quickly. But she wasn't about to ask him. She felt that it would be an intrusion; it would have been rude on her part. He sighed. "Certainly not as pleasant as Pennsylvania. Where is that little town you said you live in?"

"Lititz?" She wondered how he had known she was from Lititz. Had she told him? If so, she certainly didn't remember doing so. He sat in the chair by her bed, his chin resting on the back of his hand, watching her. The way his eyes sparkled as he waited for her to continue intrigued her. He was a complete stranger, yet she felt as though she knew him. There was something familiar about him in a comforting sort of way. "It's in Lancaster County," she replied. Then, a hint of a smile crossed her lips as she added, "Certainly you've heard of it."

When he laughed this time, he leaned backward in the chair and put his hands behind his neck. His face lit up, and he seemed to be enjoying their conversation. "Touché!" he said. "You are a worthy opponent, Ms. Beiler."

"Opponent?" she asked.

"In verbal sparring. One of my favorite pastimes."

Amanda narrowed her eyes and studied him. He was a handsome man, that was for sure and certain. Even by Amish standards, she could tell that his good looks would attract many women. Yet it was his personality that made her feel so comfortable. He seemed quite respectful and proper. His very presence commanded respect, which was something she was not familiar with when it came to any Englischer. Maybe these *cubanos* are different from regular Englischers, she thought.

"Alejandro," she said slowly. He lifted his eyes to look at her and waited for her to speak. "Could you tell me what happened? I cannot quite remember."

His expression changed as though a dark cloud were passing overhead. Sitting straight in the chair again, he sobered at her question. "That is the question, isn't it?" He tapped his fingers on the arm of the chair. He seemed to be studying her, trying to select his words carefully. But he never once broke his gaze, his blue eyes sparkling as he watched her. There was something mesmerizing about the way he stared at her. "I can't say that I know, Ms. Beiler, anything more than the streets were crowded and somehow you were in front of my limousine . . . the right place just at the wrong time."

"What is a limousine?" she asked. "Is it like a car?"

"*Sí,*" he said. "Only a longer one."

She frowned, her eyebrows arching on her forehead. "Why would anyone need a longer car?"

"Ms. Beiler—" he started.

"Please," she said softly. "It's just Amanda. Amish don't go by formalities like you Englischers."

"Ah, the Amish thing," he said. He was studying her again. "I searched on the Internet to learn more about the Amish thing." He smiled again. "And I realized that you were quite a long way from home, yes?"

"I was visiting family in Ohio." At the mention of Ohio, her heart jumped in her throat. The nurse had said that her family had been taken care of, but, as Amanda's head began to clear, she realized she hadn't asked how. "Oh!" she exclaimed. "My family! They must be very worried!"

The man seated before her held up his hands as if to calm her down. "I have contacted your family, Amanda. I've made certain to have my people keep them apprised of your situation. And I have arranged for transportation for your return to Lititz when the hospital releases you." She wanted to ask him how he had found her parents, but before she could speak, he stood up and reached down to gently touch her hand. "Now, no more questions tonight, Princesa. I will return in the morning." He squeezed her hand lightly. "Besides, you should rest some more. It's late at night, *sí*? The more you sleep, the sooner you will heal, Amanda. If you push yourself, you'll find yourself more weary than you would imagine."

He started to turn to the door, but Amanda called out, "Alejandro, if you don't mind, I have one question, please."

His hand was on the door handle as he turned to look over his shoulder at her. "*¿Sí?*"

"Why?" she asked, staring at him, her dark-brown doe eyes full of unanswered questions. With her hair hanging down her left shoulder in long, loose waves, she was a picture of beauty that he had never seen. Purity and beauty and innocence. The image struck him, and he blinked his eyes to see whether it was the product of his imagination or if she was for real. "Why?" she repeated softly. When she asked the question, he was taken aback. It was too simple, yet too difficult to answer.

He raised one eyebrow in a perfect arch. "Why what?"

"Does it really matter? Why do you care?" she said.

This time when he smiled, the corner of his mouth lifted and he reached into his pocket, pulling out his pair of sunglasses. It didn't make a difference that it was nighttime. He pushed them over the bridge of his nose, tossing a casual wink at her before his eyes disappeared behind the dark lenses. "You get some sleep, and I'll stop by in the morning, Princesa." And with that, he slipped through the door, smiling at the nurse who paused to let him pass, looking back at him with awe.

"So your special visitor was back again, I see," the nurse said as she walked in with two cups in her hands. She handed Amanda the smaller of the two. "Painkillers. You'll need them. Trust me."

"Who is that man?" Amanda asked, obediently taking the little cup, which held two blue pills. The other cup, larger in size, was filled with water.

The nurse shook her head. "I forgot that you wouldn't possibly know," she said. "That's Alejandro Diaz, otherwise known as Viper. I'm told he's one of the most popular music stars these days. The other nurses have been going crazy, fighting to take your case so that they could have a chance to meet him. Can't say that I know his music personally, but I sure do know that he's one of the most polite and gentlemanly celebrities that I've ever met." She smiled at Amanda. "He's certainly been concerned about you." The nurse waited until Amanda swallowed the medicine before she took both cups from her. "Now get some sleep, dear. It's going to be a long day for you tomorrow, and with any luck, the doctor will give you the green light to go home soon."

When the nurse left the room, Amanda turned her head to look out the window again. The lights were twinkling in the tall buildings, and she could hear the noise from the streets. New York City, she thought. She couldn't believe that she was lying in a hospital bed in Manhattan with a broken leg. What bad luck, she told herself. But to have been hit by a famous music star who was now visiting her! That certainly offered an interesting twist to the accident.

She had never heard of anyone named Viper. In fact, she had never heard rock music. She knew that other Amish youth liked to meet in school yards at night, listening to battery-operated music boxes or iPods, but she had never been interested in that. Her time was spent with her family, helping her *mamm* and *daed*. She liked to work in the fields, to tend to the cows, and to work the garden. She didn't mind the lengthy church services or the singings afterward. But she was perfectly content to be at home and to follow the Ordnung. Her *rumschpringe* was not anything worthy of talking about, she thought. Not like some other Amish youth who went to movies or dated Mennonites or even drove cars for a year or more before deciding whether to join through baptism. Taking one's vows was a very serious decision. It involved renouncing anything that had to do with the Englischers' way of life and deciding to abide by the Ordnung forever.

The medicine must have started to kick in as she began to feel drowsy. It was a sensation she was not used to, and she certainly was not comfortable with the feeling. New York City, the accident, this mysterious man . . . She let her mind wander more. She'd sort all this out in the morning, she thought. Figure out exactly what had happened and how to get home. But, for now, she wanted to sleep. Despite feeling uncomfortable because of the cast on her leg and the even more uncomfortable surroundings, she shut her eyes and allowed herself to drift into sleep.

Chapter Three

"What do you mean you're taking the girl back to Lee-tatz?"

The man's voice boomed, loud and clear, as he shouted at Alejandro. Several people glanced over their shoulders at the two men who were sitting at a large round table, enjoying lunch at an outdoor restaurant in Bryant Park. Both were dressed in suits, one in gray and the other in black. Clearly, they were businessmen and the lunch was not a social one. In fact, the men looked out of place among the other people in short-sleeved shirts and Bermuda shorts. After all, it was perfect early summer weather. No one could ask for a better day in New York City. Not too hot and not humid at all. The sun was shining in a sky gloriously blue.

Standing nearby were two larger men, their backs to Alejandro and his companion.

They seemed to be keeping an eye on the people who were milling about the entrance. The more people who gathered, the more curious others became, stopping to see what everyone was staring at inside the restaurant area. Wherever Alejandro went, a contagion followed him, an epidemic of interest from inquisitive bystanders. And he had become quite immune to it.

Good-naturedly, Alejandro laughed as he raised the glass of red wine to his lips. It was a cabernet, the perfect match for his meal. "It's Lititz," he corrected his companion before he tasted the wine. He swirled it gently in the glass. "Lititz, Pennsylvania."

"Lititz, *schmititz!*" the other man said with a disgruntled wave of his hand, looking away and shaking his head. He pushed a lock of graying hair back from his forehead that became stray again with the motion.

Alejandro kept his dark sunglasses on, shielding his eyes from the bright summer sun as well as hiding them from the photographs that were inevitably being taken by the gawking fans. After several years of high-pressure fame, he was used to it. There was absolutely no privacy in the world of the music industry. To have privacy meant that there was no fame. It came with the territory. Fame and privacy didn't mix. It was the trade-off for living the life.

"You should look it up, Mike," he finally said. "Lititz is a quaint little Amish farming town in Lancaster County, Pennsylvania."

Mike snapped his head back to glare at his companion. His eyes were sharp and narrow as he hissed, "Lancaster County?" The words rolled off his tongue as if they tasted bad. "Farmers don't buy no music and quaint don't make no money, my friend," he said, his voice dry and serious. He was an older man, short in stature, with thinning hair. In his youth, he had been considered a good-looking man. Now, the only thing good looking about him was the fact that he was seated before Alejandro. Indeed, Alejandro made everyone seem subpar, what with his powerful presence, magnetic charisma, and contagious charm. "Neither does taking this Amish girl back to that no-money-making town."

Money. It was always about the money with Mike. Alejandro took a deep breath, willing himself to remain calm. They had been working together for years, ever since Alejandro's second album had dropped five years ago. With Mike's help, Alejandro had crossed the chasm from a mediocre local hit to national superstar to today's brass ring of being an international sensation. During those years, Alejandro had learned how to work with Mike: give-and-take becoming the required modus operandi, with a lot of patience thrown into the mix. Slow and steady wins the race, he reminded himself.

"Fans aren't interested in a farming town!" Mike continued, emphasizing the word *farming*. The way Mike said it, it almost sounded like a dirty word. A place to be avoided, not embraced. "I don't think your sponsors would be too interested in this *farming* town, either! Or in this Amish girl, for that matter!"

A frown crossed Alejandro's face. He leaned forward and shifted his sunglasses so that his blue eyes peered over the top. "Have you been monitoring any of the social media?" Alejandro asked, lowering his voice so that they couldn't be overheard. Despite his hired team of security, Alejandro knew that there was no such thing as being safe from eavesdropping people. He had learned how to be discreet years ago. Leaning back in his chair, he glanced around at the people who were staring at them. He paused to smile and wave to one group, letting them take their photo, a photo that would certainly be posted on the social media networks within minutes, if not sooner.

"Of course I have!" Mike snapped. He looked insulted that Alejandro would even ask such a question. "I'm your manager! That's my job!" He pointed a finger at Alejandro and lowered his voice. "That, and keeping an eye on your image, Alex."

Alejandro returned his attention to his manager. "Then you know that this situation has now gone viral. And viral means people are talking, and what, my dear manager, does people talking mean?"

Mike made a huffing noise. It was the sound of defeat. Still, he shook his head defiantly. "You're preaching to the choir, Alex. I'm the one who always told you that if people are talking, that means music is selling." He picked up his fork and waved it at Alejandro. "We got your career launched on that philosophy, my friend. Let's not forget that it was at my urging."

Alejandro looked around at the crowd. It was getting deeper, and he knew he'd have to get his other security guards from the car in order to leave in any type of orderly fashion. "I stopped by the hospital this morning, Mike. The paparazzi are camped outside, just waiting for more photos. I saw tents, Mike. They are sleeping there, literally at the hospital's entrance!"

"So what?" Mike said, his expression showing a complete lack of interest. "They camp out at stores to meet you, they swamp box offices to buy your tickets, and your hotels are always surrounded by a mob screaming when you leave. What else is new? I fail to see the point, Alex."

He leaned forward. "She's Amish. That's the point."

Shaking his head, Mike frowned. "Why are you working that angle, Alex?" He sighed and rubbed his eyes. It was evident that the conversation was exhausting him.

"It's different," Alejandro said simply. "They like it."

"Alex," Mike sighed. "You should be visiting fans, the paying fans who support your lifestyle . . . not spending so much time with some farm girl who doesn't even listen to the radio and certainly doesn't buy music." He looked exasperated. "She probably doesn't even know what iTunes is!"

It was unusual that Alejandro had to explain things in such detail to Mike. Strange indeed, he thought. After all, one of the magical aspects of their relationship was their ability to understand each other. An ability that did not involve lengthy explanations or overcommunicating. Clearly, that was missing from this particular dialogue. "You don't get it!" Alejandro said sharply, exasperation apparent in his tone of voice.

After a late night at the clubs, Alejandro was tired and didn't feel like arguing with Mike. Being in New York City meant full days and nights. In the music business, impromptu appearances at the hottest clubs in town were mandatory: a causa sine qua non for maintaining one's popularity. Alejandro would show up, usually surrounded by a small entourage of friends and always with several bodyguards. It was the only way to control the crowds, something that was needed more often than not.

On this trip, he was joined by a few of his local friends. They made their rounds, sang some songs, and danced with the ladies before they were whisked off to another club where the same routine was followed. Some nights they visited as many as four clubs, and there were the private parties, too. The pictures would be posted on social media, and immediately there was a definite increase in the online sales of his songs. It was just the way the music industry worked.

Those types of evenings were typical and usually resulted in returning to the hotel suite close to sunrise. Alejandro had forced himself to get up early and down two cups of black coffee before visiting a local radio show for a thirty-minute interview with the DJs. It was more like banter, really: casual conversation back and forth. If it hadn't been so early, he would have actually called it fun.

Afterward, he had hurried to the hospital to visit Amanda. He spent an hour talking with her and even received an update from the doctors. The nurses had encouraged her to practice walking with crutches. Alejandro had insisted on helping her, walking by her side with his arm protectively encircling her waist. He had been too aware of the nurses who stole quick pictures with their cell phones. He didn't mind. He knew the photos would make their way to the Internet, and from there, they would be on the entertainment news programs and tabloids. It would just continue to fuel the fire. *Así es mi vida,* he thought. Such is my life.

"No," Mike snapped back. "*You* don't get it, Alex! The image we have created is being torn apart as we speak. You are missing prime-time real estate on the entertainment news channels. Viper cares about partying, about clubbing, about making a splash wherever he goes.

Viper doesn't care about . . . some little Amish girl lying in a hospital bed with a broken leg!"

"Woman," Alejandro corrected.

"Whatever." Mike waved his hand at Alejandro dismissively. "People talk about Viper because of his bad-boy image, not because he's a good little religious boy who is concerned about this Amish *woman*! Leave that image to the teenybopper wannabe stars with their screaming ten-year-old fan base!"

The bad-boy image, Alejandro thought. It always came down to that. He took a deep breath. He had hated those years, years of clubbing and fighting, surrounded by beautiful ladies who wore very little clothing and had even less intelligence—anything to hit the tabloids. Mike was right. Getting people to talk was indeed the reason why his career had skyrocketed. Alejandro was quite the master at making certain he was constantly in the news.

"Well, maybe it's time to move on to something new, Mike," Alejandro said. "The bad-boy image has too much competition these days." He lifted the wineglass to his lips and sipped at it, his eyes meeting Mike's over the rim of the glass. "And, to tell you the truth, it's starting to get boring, really!"

Hearing this, Mike froze, his hand in midair as he held his own drink. The word lingered in the air between them. "Boring?" He set the glass down on the table. "Did you actually just say 'boring'?" His eyes darted around the area, too aware that people were watching them, trying to read their lips and intensely listening in an attempt to grab some bits and pieces of the agitated conversation. Of course they are watching, he thought. I'm having lunch in Bryant Park with Viper, their idol. Women throw themselves at Viper. The tabloids follow him like his own shadow. The music charts cherish him. And award ceremonies keep honoring him. "Boring, you say? Well, you better get unbored quickly, my friend. That boring lifestyle is what keeps you living the life."

"Perhaps I'm tired of living the life," Alejandro replied, his voice emotionless. He stared into space, his eyes blank and his expression weary. He couldn't remember the last time he had taken time off for himself. Even when he was back in Miami, he spent his days at the studio working on new songs, and his nights making appearances at the best clubs. Appearances mattered, and there were no vacations in that work contract. "And, who knows, maybe it's tired of me!"

Mike drummed his fingers on the edge of the table, studying the man before him. They both knew all too well what *tired* meant in the industry. *Tired* wasn't a word that a manager wanted to hear. *Tired* wasn't a word the public would accept. *Tired* was, after all, the kiss of death to music careers. "So you think going to bumpkin land in *Schmititz*-ville is going to change that? Is that what you are saying, Alex?"

With a casual shrug, Alejandro replied, "I don't know. But I have a feeling about this. The way that everyone is reacting. It's quite amazing!" He leaned forward, tapping his finger on the table to emphasize his next point. "The media loves this. The story was all over the news for the past two days. And the fans? *¡Ay, mi madre!* They can't stop talking about it. I stopped counting the Retweets of my postings."

Mike stared at him in complete disbelief. "Retweets? You're basing your decision on Retweets? A whisper on social media?"

"I don't call half a million Retweets a whisper."

For a few moments, Mike stared at him. The silence between them was heavy and lingering. Both seemed engulfed in deep thoughts. Finally, Mike whispered, "He's actually serious!" Irritated, he slammed his napkin on the table. "I don't believe I'm hearing this from Viper."

"People like this caring side of me," Alejandro explained nonchalantly. "And maybe I like it, too."

Shaking his head, Mike took a deep breath. "Viper is not about caring, Alex. Viper is a womanizer. Viper is about desire and passion.

Love 'em and leave 'em. Do I actually have to remind you of this? Isn't it what we decided way back when?"

"That's not me." He paused. "Not anymore."

Mike clenched his teeth, trying to remain calm. After so many years of hard work in this demanding industry, leading to his success as one of the most sought-after agents in his profession, he had very little patience left for dealing with emotional considerations. Even with Alejandro, who had now become practically a friend as their relationship transcended the boundaries of the typical agent-client relationship. "You are who I say you are, Alex!" Taking a deep breath, he glanced around to make certain no one was listening. He leaned forward and pounded the table with his finger. "We've worked long and hard to get to this point, Alex. This is your time. Right here. Right now." Gesturing around the restaurant, and at the crowd of people standing on the other side of the planters that separated the diners from the park, he added, "This is what you always wanted. This is the peak!"

"I'm going to Lititz," Alejandro said flatly.

And, with that, Mike knew that the game was over. There would be no fighting Alejandro on this one. Once he had made up his mind, Alejandro Diaz did not change it. He was known for being impulsive and stubborn. Yet, for the most part, whatever he touched always seemed to turn to gold.

Mike frowned and reached for his cell phone. He pressed a few buttons and stared at the small screen. Finally, he looked up. "One week," Mike snapped, the irritation quite evident in his voice. "I can clear your schedule for one week. I can juggle your interviews and appearances. You're going to tick off a few people."

He shrugged. "Part of the image, *sí*?"

Mike leaned forward. "You have to get out to LA by the end of the month. You're scheduled to shoot your new video, and those entertainment talk shows are lined up to interview you before you head to Europe," he said as he slipped the cell phone back into his front pocket. "I can't hold them off forever, Alex. You need to strike while the iron's hot."

"One week? Seven days?"

"That's right. Just seven. Get this totally out of your system. Get unbored, and get unbored fast, Alex! We need you back on the bad-boy track. Can't have you turning Amish on me. Not after I've worked so hard to make you into Viper, with the sexiest sting in the world."

Alejandro laughed, the sparkle back in his blue eyes. He was looking forward to this impromptu adventure, to escaping the cities and the media. No one would find him in Lititz, Pennsylvania, that was for sure. For just a few days, he could relax, reflect, and revive himself. It had been years since he had been in the countryside, years since he had returned to his roots. To get away from the music and the media sounded like a little slice of heaven.

"I'll be back, Mike. And better than ever, you can count on it!"

Mike shook his head, still in disbelief over the turn that their conversation had taken. "You better! And before you disappear to Amish-land, make certain to get over to Richard Gray's office this afternoon." Holding up two of his right-hand fingers, he motioned to the waitress to bring two more glasses of wine. Then, turning back to Alejandro, he glared at him, but in a somewhat debonair way. "You don't know what kind of hoops I had to jump through to reschedule that appointment. The man is doing me a huge favor, and I hate to think of what it's going to cost me!"

"*Gracias*, Mike," Alejandro replied, flashing one of his famous smiles, the kind that melted the hearts of tens of thousands of women around the globe.

"Don't '*gracias*, Mike' me," he said scowling, but Alejandro could see that he, too, was loosening up. "You never should have blown off that appointment in the first place!" he reprimanded, shaking a finger at Alejandro, half-mocking but half-serious. "Of all the people to blow off, Richard Gray ain't the one!"

Laughing, Alejandro tried to turn the mood at the table back to a lighter tone. "I'll try not to hit anyone on the way to his office next time, I promise," he said.

"Not funny, Alex." Mike shook his head, but when faced with Alejandro's jovial expression and sparkling eyes, so similar to a naughty child after finagling his way out of trouble, even Mike had to relax. "But not a bad idea, after all." He lifted his drink and raised it into the air in a toasting gesture. "You can leave as Alejandro, but you better return as Viper, my friend."

Alejandro raised his own wineglass, acknowledging the toast. But as he lifted the glass to his lips, his eyes wandered as he stared into the distance, seeing nothing as his mind traveled far away. He hoped he could recapture the essence of Viper, if only he knew where and when he had lost it.

Chapter Four

"Good news, Amanda!" the nurse said as she walked into the room, a bouquet of fresh flowers in her arms. She set them down on the windowsill next to the roses. "Doctor says you can leave tomorrow."

Amanda immediately brightened at the news. "Tomorrow?" She couldn't wait to get home. Since she had awoken that morning, she had been staring out the window at the tall buildings on the other side of the cloudy glass. In the daylight, they were big and ugly, gray and dirty. She could barely see any blue sky. And the noise! Cars honking, sirens swirling. Now it was afternoon and the view hadn't gotten any prettier. She longed to hear horses gently trotting down the road and the metallic hum of their buggy wheels. She wanted to see peaceful green fields and colorful clothing lines waving in the breeze.

"That's right. Your friend has arranged for his car service to take you back to Lititz."

"My friend?" she asked.

"Alejandro," the nurse replied, smiling. She started to secure the blood pressure band around Amanda's arm. "How's the pain this morning?"

"In my leg? It hurts."

The nurse laughed. "I imagine so. That's what happens when you walk in front of cars, dear." Teasingly, the nurse looked at her and raised an eyebrow. "Now why would you have wanted to do that?"

Amanda frowned. She barely remembered the accident at all. In fact, her last truly vivid memory was riding up the escalator at Penn Station. The moving stairs had amazed her. She could have ridden them all day. "I don't really remember much after I was hit by the car. I just remember lots of people standing around, staring at me."

"Well, New York City sure has plenty of people," the nurse said, pumping the bulb of the blood pressure monitor. Amanda felt the blood pressure band tightening around her arm. When Amanda thought it couldn't squeeze any tighter, the nurse released the valve. It made a slight hissing noise as the pressure was released. Smiling, the nurse removed the cuff from Amanda's arm. "I'll make certain they get you some more pain medicine. It will help you sleep tonight," she said. "I'm afraid that leg is going to hurt a bit for a while."

Amanda didn't reply. She shut her eyes and leaned back into the pillows. "Who are those flowers from?" she asked.

The nurse glanced over at them. "The daisy bouquet? I hadn't looked." She walked over to the flowers and removed the card, turning to hand it to Amanda.

Amanda opened the card and read the typed words. The name didn't seem familiar, and she frowned. "I don't know who this person is . . ." She looked at the nurse. "Maybe they aren't for me."

The nurse glanced at the card. She caught her breath and handed it to Amanda. "The mayor of New York City sent them."

Absentmindedly, Amanda took the card and looked at it. The name still meant nothing to her. "Who is this mayor?"

The nurse laughed. "The mayor? He's the man in charge of this crazy place called New York City!"

"Why would he send flowers to me? I don't know him." Amanda shrugged, clearly not impressed and setting the card down on the blanket that covered her lap.

But from the nurse's reaction, it was clear that she was impressed. "That's quite an honor, my dear. His well wishes for a speedy recovery are quite unusual."

"How would he know about me? Why would he care?"

The nurse gave her a look as if to see whether Amanda was teasing. But when the nurse saw that the young Amish woman was serious, she took pity on her. "It's not every day that a famous star hits a young Amish tourist in the city, Amanda. To you, it's an accident. To the rest of the city, it's big news."

"'Big news.'" She repeated the words incredulously. She couldn't imagine that anything about her accident would be considered big news. Yet she knew that the Englischers had a different way of looking at the world. "I don't know anything about music stars," she sighed, turning her head to look back out the window. All she could see was the reflection of the buildings. It was an imposing sight, but it wasn't home. "But I sure do miss the stars in the sky over my *daed*'s farm."

"Now, now," the nurse said, changing the subject. "The doctor will be in first thing in the morning to speak with you. He'll have some specific instructions. Your friend has also contacted a nurse in Lancaster that will make a house call to check on you the day after you arrive."

"Oh my! That's not necessary," Amanda replied, alarmed at the extensive arrangements. "Truly. I just need to get back home to my parents. They need my help."

"I wouldn't be making too many plans for helping, Amanda. You need time to heal," the nurse said firmly but cheerfully.

"But my *daed* needs help with the harvest," she said, the concern in her voice matched by the concern in her eyes. "He can't do it alone."

The door opened, and Amanda looked over the nurse's head to see who it was. She wasn't surprised to see Alejandro standing there, more flowers in his hands and a smile on his face. *"Buenas tardes,* Princesa,*"* he said lightly. There was a tall man standing behind him, but he didn't enter the room. Amanda wondered who he was. "How are you doing this fine evening?"

"I can go home tomorrow," she said, her face glowing as she greeted him, the only person she knew in New York City.

"Sí, sí," he laughed. "I know that. I've made all of the arrangements." He handed the flowers to the nurse, who gave him a broad smile and took them willingly. With sparkling eyes, she set them on the table next to Amanda's bed. "I shall accompany you on the journey, if you permit me." He nodded to the nurse but continued talking to Amanda. "I must make certain that you arrive safely after this unfortunate accident."

She frowned but didn't respond to his inquiry. If she wanted to ask why he would want to drive out to Lititz, she didn't. It wasn't her business. She was also wondering why he was giving her so many flowers. His attention was almost embarrassing, but when he looked at her and smiled, his half-crooked smile that looked so mischievous in a playful way, she quickly forgave him.

"And I have a surprise for you this night," he said evenly. With a grand gesture, he swept his arm out before her. "You are in the greatest city in the world. I would like to honor you with a lovely dinner at a restaurant."

Both the nurse and Amanda stared at him. The nurse started to say something, but it was Amanda who blurted out, "I can't leave the hospital!"

"Ah," he said, waving a finger at her, a twinkle in his blue eyes. It was clear that he was enjoying this. "But I didn't say we were *leaving* the hospital." He winked at the nurse and smiled at Amanda before moving back toward the door. He rapped his knuckles twice on it, then stepped aside. As if on cue, the door opened and two men in tuxedos entered, one pushing a cart filled with covered silver trays. Both men wore white gloves and serious expressions. "Since I know you cannot leave the hospital tonight to dine at a restaurant, I have brought the restaurant to you, *mi* Princesa."

A blush covered Amanda's cheeks, and the nurse clapped her hands in delight. Embarrassed, Amanda looked away as the men set the cart aside by the window and began getting ready to serve her.

Alejandro laughed at her discomfort and went to her side. Gently, he took her hand in his. "*Ay*, Amanda, you must not be shy. It is my way of apologizing for all of this."

She shook her head and lowered her eyes. She didn't like the two strange men who were staring at her. "I don't know them," she whispered.

Alejandro motioned with his head, and the two men quickly left the room. The nurse followed, her eyes shining. She paused once to glance back over her shoulder, a smile on her face, before shutting the door as she left. Alejandro guessed that the social media would begin to catch wind of this romantic dinner for two within . . . minutes.

Once they were alone, Amanda seemed less tense. She chewed on her lower lip and watched as Alejandro made an exaggerated bow before presenting her with a silver tray. He set it on the raised hospital table and pushed it before her. Then, with a grin on his face, he lifted the silver dome and waited.

Nothing.

He looked at her, surprised that she didn't say anything. She was staring at him, not the food. He glanced down at the plate and saw everything that he had ordered for her. He looked back at her face, wondering if she hadn't seen the large lobster on the plate presented to her. "No?" he asked.

"What . . . What is this?"

He frowned. Could she not know what lobster was? Was it possible? He hadn't even considered that. "It's a lobster."

"It looks creepy." She paused. "Like a giant red bug."

"It's a lobster," he said again, enunciating the word in case she hadn't understood his accent.

"Oh, I heard you the first time," she replied gently. "But it still looks weird. People actually eat that?"

He hadn't read that Amish people had food restrictions. He had researched it when he had the idea to surprise her. He had never suspected that she wouldn't know what lobster was. "It's from the sea. It's delicious."

"Really? It's so . . . red." She poked at the shell covering the back of the lobster. "How on earth do you eat *that*?" She looked up at Alejandro, her eyes wide and curious. "I'll break all my teeth!"

This time when he laughed, he noticed that she started to smile. She didn't join him in laughing, but she certainly realized that there was a good joke in there somewhere. He was pleased that she was willing to play along with him. "Oh, Princesa, you have so much to learn!" He sat on the edge of the bed and tucked a white linen napkin around her neck. "Watch me. You will be amazed at how wonderful this is."

"I'll be amazed if you can figure it out," she said lightly. But she watched intensely as he gently tore apart the lobster and pulled the fluffy white meat from the shell. He dipped it in what appeared to be melted butter and held it out for her to eat. She hesitated, uncertain why he was holding the fork toward her as if he was going to feed her.

"Shut your eyes," he said softly.

His voice was so smooth and commanding, yet gentle at the same time. No one had ever spoken to her that way before. She felt her heart start to pound inside her chest, and then she felt dizzy. "I . . ."

He shook his head and tsk-tsked. "Do as I say," he said, his voice low and calm, but it was strong enough to warn her not to fight him. His blue eyes bore into hers, and the one side of his mouth lifted in a hint of a smile. "Trust me."

Hesitantly, she shut her eyes.

"Now, open your mouth," he instructed her.

Her blood seemed to race through her veins. It was his voice, so smooth and low, husky and musical. She realized that she had never been so taken with anyone in that way, and the feeling was frightening. He was in command, in complete control, and she knew that she would do what he said. With her eyes closed, she opened her mouth slightly and waited for what seemed like an eternity. But then she felt it. The soft warmth of the lobster was placed inside her mouth. She kept her eyes closed as she took the food from the fork, her hand slipping up to make certain the butter was not dripping on her chin. It was delicious. Absolutely divine, and her eyes flew open. They dazzled as she looked at him in complete amazement.

"That's *wunderbar*! I've never tasted anything like it!" she exclaimed.

He laughed at her, setting the fork down on the side of the plate and getting up from the bed. "I knew you'd like that." He stood at the bedside, looking pleased with himself. "You appreciate kindness, Amanda Beiler. That's quite unusual."

She wiped her mouth with the napkin and looked at him, her eyes wide and bright. "Is it?"

"From where I come from, *sí*." He turned back toward the cart and opened a green bottle of sparkling water. With a grand gesture, he poured the water into two glasses and put lemon wedges in each. The bubbles fizzed as he handed one glass to her. "Cheers," he said, tipping his glass against hers. "To going home, *sí*?"

She wasn't certain how to respond, so she sipped at the water. The bubbles tickled her nose. "Don't you miss your home?" she asked.

He walked over to the chair and sat down. "I'm not certain I even know where my home is, Amanda. I'm on the road so much. I have a condominium in Miami and another one in Los Angeles. When I travel, I'm usually at a hotel. I'm used to living out of a suitcase."

That didn't sound like a life she'd ever get used to, she thought. "What about your family?"

"My family?" he repeated, looking up at her with surprise on his face. "My mother lives in Miami. I bought her a house. She's happy."

"That's it?" She was taken aback by the flatness in his description of his family. She was also surprised to know that he had only one person who he considered family. "You have no other family? That's so sad." And she meant it.

He shrugged. "I have a daughter."

Something changed in her expression. "A daughter?" She hadn't thought to ask if he was married. "So she is in Miami with your wife?"

Alejandro paused. He seemed hesitant, as if considering how to answer her question. When he responded, she knew why.

"I'm not married, Amanda," he confessed, "and I don't know my daughter."

Her mouth dropped, but she quickly closed it and looked away. "Oh" was all that she could muster in response. Now she knew why Alejandro had hesitated. Clearly, he suspected her reaction to the truth. Even if Amanda disapproved of the divulgence, at least he chose honesty over lying to her.

"I wasn't raised like you, Amanda," he said quickly, as if defending himself. "Growing up in Cuba is very different than in America, and when we first came here . . ." He stopped. He tried to find the right words. "Well, we had little more than each other and our faith in God to take care of us." He waited until she looked up at him. "The streets of Miami are hard living, Amanda. I learned to survive, and that comes with a price. As does fame." He paused. "Please don't judge me."

"I would never!" she gasped. But then she quickly averted her eyes again. "I . . . I just wasn't expecting that."

"I'm not the same man I once was," he explained as he stood up and walked to the window. For a long while, he stared outside. It was a big world, and he didn't have time for a family. He certainly didn't have time for a child, and he hadn't even known the mother. But how to

explain that to a young Amish woman? "Things happen. I take care of
them the best that I can. I send money. That's all they want, actually."

"That's just so very sad," she repeated softly. His story tugged at
her heart, and she felt as though she could cry for him. To think that
people only wanted him for money?

He turned around and forced a smile on his face. "Enough of that.
Let's talk about happy things, and I want to see you enjoying that
delicious lobster. Do you need help getting more of the meat? The
claws can be tricky," he gushed, changing the subject and resuming his
vivacious, charming self. But she could still sense the sadness beneath
the surface. Despite his mischievous smiles and flashing eyes, there was
something deeper to this Alejandro Diaz, and she was starting to hope
that she'd get to discover it.

He helped her crack the lobster claws, making a big show of trying
to break through the shell. Her eyes flashed in astonishment, watching
his every move, and the more she gasped, the more he pretended that it
was difficult. When the shell finally split, she clapped her hands. "I've
never seen anything like that," she said breathlessly.

"You've had fish, *sí*?"

"Of course!" she said as if that was a silly question. "We go fishing
in the stream behind our property all the time in the warm weather."
She smiled as if remembering a specific day. "There's nothing like sitting
on the bank of the stream and enjoying the cool afternoon breeze."

"Well," he said, reaching for the small fork. "This is like a big fish.
Just with a hard shell on the outside." He showed her how to dig into
it with the tiny fork. "And it tastes better, *sí*?" When the big, fleshy
lump of meat popped out, some of the juices splattering onto her face,
she laughed and started to reach for the napkin. But it was Alejandro
who took it from her and dabbed gently at the moisture on her cheeks.

The color rose to her cheeks again, and she looked away. Clearly,
the attention that he was giving her made her uncomfortable, yet she
didn't know how to tell him to stop. She also didn't know if she really

wanted him to stop. He made her feel different from how any other Amish man had ever made her feel. She had attended singings for years and had even accepted rides home from several of the Amish young men. But she had never seriously courted anyone. There simply hadn't been time.

That had been part of the reason for the trip to Ohio, to get Anna and Amanda away from everything. Her parents had reasoned that the two girls needed a break, some time away from Lititz. The trip had been arranged over a six-month period of time during which Amanda had found herself increasingly despondent. She had never left her hometown before this trip. She didn't want to leave home, not for any amount of time. However, she was excited for a couple things: the train ride and the layover in the Big Apple. She wanted to experience everything that she could: the people, the food, the sights, the sounds, even the smells. Her sister, however, had refused to leave the train station. So much for her exploration of New York City!

If her parents had wanted Amanda to experience something different from Lititz, she hadn't. Not in Holmes County. Despite trying to appear supportive for her sister, Amanda quickly realized that they had simply relocated from one farm to another.

In truth, her cousin's farm in Ohio was no different from her *daed*'s farm in Pennsylvania. Amanda had put on a happy face, especially when Anna started to show new sparks of life in her eyes and a bounce in her step. Amanda suspected that the neighbor had something to do with it, but she kept her suspicions to herself. After all, Anna was older, and it was well past the time for her to settle down. If she waited much longer, she'd be labeled a *maedel*, and that would hurt her prospects for getting married to a nice young Amish man. Instead, she'd be a prime target for widowers who might already have children and would certainly have established ways about them.

"Penny for your thoughts." His deep, husky voice broke through her mental wanderings, and she looked at him.

"I was thinking about home," she replied, knowing that it wasn't entirely true.

"Ah," he said. "Home. Yes, let's talk about home." He moved back over to the chair and sat down. "I spoke with your parents and . . ."

"You spoke with my parents?" she interrupted. "How?"

He rubbed his chin with his finger. "How?"

"They are not like you with your cell phone that rings all the time," she said lightly. "We don't have a phone at our farm."

"I sent the police to your house," he said. "I spoke to them on an officer's cell phone." He paused, and Amanda shut her eyes for a minute, trying to imagine her parents' reaction to a police car pulling up their driveway and handing them a cell phone. "That was how they gave me your neighbor's telephone number."

"The Zooks?"

"*Sí*, the Zooks. They have a telephone, no?" He didn't wait for her to respond. "I've been speaking with your parents twice a day since you've been here, Princesa. I was sure that they were worried, and I wanted to make certain they knew that you were being cared for properly."

Her eyes grew wide, and she was speechless. For such a busy man, he had taken time out of his days to schedule calls with her parents? He had been updating them about her condition for three days now? And he was arranging for her trip back to Lititz? He hadn't told her any of this before today. In fact, he hadn't told her much of anything. Instead, his focus had always been on her and how she was faring. He had helped her with the crutches the day before when he stopped by in the morning. She had never thought to question him. People shared what they wanted to share, she told herself.

"Why are you doing so much, Alejandro?" she asked quietly.

He set his glass down on the cart and looked at her. She was watching him, her brown eyes so large and doe-like. Her hair was hanging over her shoulders, loose and wavy. He knew she was twenty years old from having reviewed her information with the doctor. Yet, there was a conflicting look about her. She was young and innocent looking, pure and natural. There was nothing worldly about this woman. Still, there was a sorrow about her that told him there was more to her than met the eye. "I know what it's like to be alone, Princesa. I have been in similar situations, and no one ever came to help me. I couldn't let that happen to you."

Her expression changed as if a cloud passed overhead. There was a look of sadness in that moment when she lowered her eyes and softly said, "I'm sorry."

Alejandro gave a curious laugh. "For what?"

"For any pain you have felt," she responded and lifted her eyes to meet his gaze. "Someone like you should never feel pain or sorrow."

He knew that she was also speaking from her own experience and not just about this accident with the broken leg. His jovial expression changed as he realized that there was something more to this young woman. Something deeper. And he was curious. What could have happened to her in the past that could make her, a young Amish woman, so aware of others' personal pain?

"Ay, mi madre," he said under his breath.

"What did you say?" she asked.

He shook his head. *"Nada.* Nothing." He tried to break his gaze from hers, but couldn't. There was just something so different about her, something he couldn't quite comprehend. He was used to women who were so worldly. By contrast, Amanda was simply pure. He found that he wanted to know her and protect her. She was worth the effort. *"Mañana* is a big day, *sí?"* he finally said, breaking the silence and forcing a smile. "I take you home at last."

"Oh, that just sounds so wonderful," she said, brightening a little. "Home." The word rolled off her tongue as if she had just tasted some sweet candy. And she smiled.

"Home," he repeated. The word seemed to echo in his head. He wondered about his own home. The word conjured nothing in his mind. It was empty, void, a blank space. It was an endless streaming of hotel suites and strange people. Even when he was home, he felt out of place. He wondered what it would be like to actually feel a longing for home.

Standing up, he moved over to the table and lifted a package from the corner.

She hadn't noticed it before, but now, as he walked toward her, she could see that it was a box with beautiful white wrapping and a big white-and-gold bow on it. She had never seen such an extravagantly wrapped box. Her eyes followed his movement as he paused, staring down at the box for just a moment, then turning around to approach her. He moved so smoothly across the floor, his body full of confidence and poise. Watching him gave her a small thrill, and she felt the color rush to her cheeks.

"I have a little something for you, Amanda," he said. She loved hearing him say her name: *Aman-tha*. He handed the package over to her, his blue eyes lit up with that mischievous smile on his face. "It is the perfect gift for saying good-bye to New York City and hello to Lititz."

Lowering her eyes, she whispered, "I can't accept a gift from you." Gifts were given between courting couples, not between strangers. The only gifts she had ever received had been cookbooks or sewing supplies for her birthdays, and those had been from her *mamm*.

He reached out, put his finger under her chin, and gently lifted it so that she was forced to stare at him. When their eyes met, he leaned forward and whispered in her ear, "You will like this gift. I promise." He pulled away and the package was mysteriously sitting on her lap. "Open it," he instructed, his voice soft but firm.

She wasn't certain how to go about opening the box but finally settled on tugging at the end of the bow. Several pulls later, the bow slid free, and she was able to lift the lid of the box. Setting it onto the side of the bed, she pushed through the layers of silky white tissue paper. Her hands then stopped as she stared inside the box. For a moment, she caught her breath and didn't know what to say. Never in her life had someone done something so thoughtful and kind for her.

"I . . ." She started trying to form words, but instead her eyes welled up with tears. She looked up and stared at Alejandro. "I'm speechless." She reached into the box and took out her white prayer *kapp*. It was cleaned, starched, and perfectly prepared as if she had done it herself. "How did you find this?"

He raised an eyebrow. "Did you see what else is in the box, Princesa?"

Her eyebrows knit together, and she looked back into the box. There, at the bottom nestled amid the tissue paper, was a pair of dark black sunglasses. This time, the tears fell from her eyes, but Amanda laughed at the same time. Her joy radiated on her face as she looked up at him and smiled. Then, wiping at her tears, she pulled out the sunglasses and slid them over her eyes. "My sunglasses!" She looked up at him, beaming. "And they are just like yours!"

He raised a hand as though to stop her in midsentence. "Almost like mine," he corrected. "They are for a woman, no? A bit more petite and ladylike."

"How do I look?" she asked, pretending to pose with the glasses on and moving her head from side to side.

"Magnificent!" He laughed at her, enjoying this playful side of Amanda. It amazed him that something so simple could bring her such joy. Not diamonds. Not fancy clothing or shoes. Just a $300 pair of Dolce & Gabbana sunglasses. He was touched that something so insignificant to him could mean so much to her. "I couldn't let you leave the city without those sunglasses you wanted so much. After all, you threw yourself in front of my driver in order to get them!"

Her mouth dropped open, and she was about to reply until she realized that he was just teasing her. Her eyes glimmered as she tried to hide a smile. Playing along with him, she raised an eyebrow, feigning seriousness. "How else could I have received such a wonderful gift?"

"The glasses?" he asked.

"No," she replied and reached down to knock her knuckles against her leg. "My cast!"

This time, when he laughed, it came from deep within him. A belly laugh. It had been ages since he had felt so jovial and alive. There was no pretense with this one, he thought, having enjoyed the playful banter with this surprisingly interesting young woman. "*Sí, sí,*" he said. "*¡Claro!* Your cast! That is the best gift of all!"

"I shall treasure it for always," she teased back. "And my glasses, too, of course."

"*Ay, mi madre,*" he said, laughter still in his voice. "You are something else, Princesa. Refreshing, no?" He leaned over and placed a friendly kiss on her forehead, ignoring the blush that covered her cheeks. "And tired, too, *sí?*" He started toward the door. "I will bid you good night as we have a big day tomorrow . . . getting you back home."

He knocked at the door, and the two men quickly reemerged to swoop away the remnants of the lobster dinner. Alejandro spoke to them in Spanish, and they nodded once before wheeling the cart back out of the room.

Before leaving, he stood at the opened door and turned to her. "Sleep tight, Princesa." With a quick wink, he disappeared through the doorway, and she was left alone.

Stilling her beating heart, Amanda slid the sunglasses back on her eyes and reached down to hold her prayer *kapp*. She had thought it was lost, gone forever. His gift had truly taken her aback. The tenderness and thought that he had put into it touched her.

Now that she was alone, she leaned back into her pillow and carefully held her *kapp* to her chest. Her mind raced through the events of the past hour, and she could barely imagine that something so magical had happened to her, Amanda Beiler. But she quickly reminded herself that he was not Amish and certainly not interested in the likes of a young Amish woman, no matter how much attention he bestowed upon her. Even still, when she finally drifted off to sleep, it was Alejandro Diaz's face that she saw in her dreams.

Chapter Five

The car ride seemed to drag on forever. From the back of the limousine, she felt small and quite out of place. It was too big and open and far too fancy. She wished that she could just blink her eyes and be home. She missed the farm buildings, the animals, the smells, and, above all, her parents. She missed the peace and tranquility of her familiar and quiet surroundings. She missed waving crops and blue skies, a landscape free from the crowdedness of big, bulky buildings and swarms of people. Staring people, she thought. She was tired of people staring at her, and her head was still reeling from when they had departed the hospital only thirty minutes ago.

Alejandro sat opposite her, his back to the driver and his cell phone pressed to his ear. He spoke in a language that she didn't understand, but the words flowed like rapid-fire music. She liked listening to the strange words, full of *s* sounds. The end of each sentence seemed to lift as if hooking into the next sentence. There was music to these words, music that she never noticed before she had met Alejandro. And she liked the way it sounded.

He pressed a button on his phone and glanced at her. Or, rather, she imagined that he glanced at her from behind his dark sunglasses that reflected her image. She could see herself in the reflection; her plain blue dress seemed too plain compared to the beautiful leather seats and sleekness of the limousine. "You are comfortable, *sí?*" he asked. "Would you care for some water or iced tea?"

Amanda shook her head. *"Nee,"* she said softly.

"Neah?" he repeated.

She smiled, despite her discomfort. "No, I meant."

"Ah." He nodded his head once. "In Spanish, no is the same as in English. I suppose in Deitsch, it's different, *sí?*"

"Ja," she said and smiled when he laughed at her. "Sometimes it's *nein*, too."

"Nein?"

She shrugged and turned her face toward the window. The scenery looked ugly and depressing. Cramped buildings. Gray sidewalks. Lots of people. There were so many stores with signs pushing sales and discounts. Garbage cans overflowed on street corners. The buildings were too tall. The streets were too crowded. And no one knew one another or seemed to care. She couldn't imagine living in such a big, dirty place, so far from nature and so disconnected from the earth.

"The city is ugly," she said, surprising herself and slightly ashamed when she heard the words come out of her mouth. But she meant it.

"Sí," he acknowledged. "This part is ugly."

"How can people live here?" She turned to look at him, surprised that he was staring at her.

He tilted his head, hesitating before he answered as though thinking about her question. "I suppose it's not so bad," he started. "There is a lot of life in New York City: theaters, museums, restaurants." She didn't look impressed. "People like culture, and cities tend to have a lot of it. Maybe it's not so ugly after all. Some of the buildings have beautiful architecture, no?"

"I suppose," she said, but he could tell that she didn't mean it. "Why did they steal my picture?" she asked, abruptly changing the subject.

He wasn't certain that he had heard her properly. "Steal your . . . ?"

"My picture. Those people stole my picture with their cameras. They didn't even ask," she said, the disapproval apparent in her voice.

"No, they didn't, did they?"

Earlier, when they had left the hospital, there had been a crowd of people outside, waiting as if someone had tipped them off that Viper was leaving with the young Amish woman. He had been pushing her wheelchair out the door to help her get into the limousine that was waiting to take them back to Pennsylvania. But the crowd was too much. Security had to come out to push people back. Alejandro had kept a serious face, his focus on helping Amanda to the car. Amanda, however, had ducked her head, shielding her face with her hands. She wasn't used to that much attention, and she certainly didn't like people taking her photograph.

Now Amanda looked at Alejandro, wondering how he could be so nonchalant about such crowds. "And you don't mind?"

Alejandro shrugged. "I'm used to it, I guess."

Her mouth fell open. Used to people stealing his picture? It was so invasive and bad mannered. The people had no qualms about shoving cameras in his face, and he was used to it? "That happens a lot to you?" To her surprise, he responded by laughing, a hearty and full laugh that confused her. She wasn't certain why. It was just a question, she thought. Not meant to invoke laughter. "Is that funny?" she asked.

"*Ay, Princesa,*" he said, reaching over for a bottle of chilled water from the ice bucket that was next to his seat. "It happens all the time to me."

"Why?" she asked.

He raised an eyebrow at her. "Good question," he responded. With one swift gesture, he uncapped his bottle of water and put the lid on the seat beside him. "Good question, indeed." But he didn't answer her.

"Don't you mind?"

He shook his head. "No."

His answer surprised her. She frowned. "No? Just no?"

He smiled at her. She liked the way he smiled. Only one side of his mouth curved up at the corner. It was such a mischievous smile and reminded her of her younger brother when he had been caught doing something naughty at the farm. That smile had gotten him out of a lot of trouble when he was little. Amanda missed that smile.

"Just no," Alejandro said nonchalantly, then looked down at his cell phone. How could he explain to her that every photograph that was taken of him created a new fan in his world? Good news, bad news: it didn't matter. When it came to fans, exposure was everything. Publicity was publicity. "Excuse me," he said politely before lifting his cell phone to his ear and engaging in a conversation in that strange language that she couldn't understand.

Sighing, she looked out the window at the passing buildings alongside the highway. They were in New Jersey now, and she thought it was also a very ugly place. The buildings were formless, and many of them had broken windows and spray-painting on their sides. She wondered why Englischers would find satisfaction in defacing the sides of their buildings.

"What do you find so interesting out there?" he asked.

She hadn't been aware that, his phone conversation now over, he had been watching her. In fact, she had been daydreaming and didn't realize that he had finished his phone call. "You get a lot of phone calls, *ja*?" He nodded but didn't speak. "Don't you find it annoying to be interrupted so much?"

"I hadn't thought of it that way," he replied truthfully.

"We don't have telephones," she said. "And I'm glad. I would not like to always be answering that thing." She frowned for a moment, deep in thought. Her eyes seemed to grow darker, and she looked up at him. "People steal your photos and also your time with the constant interruptions." She paused, staring at him and chewing on her lower lip. She was thinking, putting pieces of some unnecessary puzzle together in her head. "Is there any part of you that is left for you?"

And there it was.

Her words stunned him. What a question. He had never looked at it that way. *Is there any part of you that is left for you?* Would anyone care if he were gone, replaced by this fictitious brand image, an image created by paparazzi, the media, the fans, and his own manager? Every move he made was orchestrated. Every interview perfectly scripted. *Is there any part of you that is left for you?* Yet, once she had asked the question, he knew that was exactly how he had been feeling. In his world, Alejandro had disappeared, and the only thing left was Viper. Unfortunately, he suddenly realized, he was more Alejandro than they knew.

"You know," he said slowly, "you're right." He looked at the phone and pressed a button. "For the next three hours, it's off, and that's the way it will stay. Off!" With a great flourish, he tossed it onto the seat between them. "Just say no to technology!"

"I don't think you can last that long," she teased, her brown eyes shining. "You're always on it."

"Really?" he replied, a playful tone in his voice. Yet he knew that she was right. The gadgets ruled his life as much as the crazy schedule of interviews, meetings, concerts, and clubs. "Well, we shall see who wins, *sí?*"

For the next hour, they talked. He found that it was easy to talk to her. She had a very direct way about her, her answers to his questions honest and pure. There was nothing about Amanda Beiler that spoke of playing games: no half-truths, no dishonesty, no exaggerations. For

Alejandro, that was refreshing. He found that he could relax in her presence—be himself—and that, too, was refreshing. He was so used to people who wanted something from him that it was hard to know who was a true friend or who was just using him for money or fame. No one ever seemed to really care about what was going on inside his head. With Amanda, their dialogue seemed much more focused on real conversation, not peripheral topics that masked ulterior motives. She was refreshing, indeed.

When they crossed into Pennsylvania, Alejandro watched her staring out the car window. Her chocolate-brown eyes seemed to drink in the lush green trees and rolling hills. She smiled to herself, and he wondered what she was thinking. There was such a serene expression on her face; he suspected she was thinking about how glad she was to be returning home.

Home, he thought. As he let the word roll around inside his head, he could only think of the endless suites at fancy hotels with room service and housekeeping. He envisioned his bodyguards and staff of assistants, his entire entourage. When he thought of the word *home*, nothing popped into his mind. Nothing, he realized, that made him feel the way that Amanda looked as she stared out of the window.

The last part of the ride was quiet. He continued to watch her, his eyes drinking in her growing excitement as buildings disappeared, replaced with open farmland upon which horses and cows were grazing. As they neared her family's farm, they began passing horses pulling simple black boxlike buggies. Alejandro found himself enthralled with the musical rhythm of the horses' hooves against the macadam. When he looked over at Amanda, she looked like a smiling angel.

Nearly three hours after they had left New York City, they finally pulled off the road and turned down a narrow lane. Alejandro noticed that she sat up straight and seemed to become more energized. He was sure that her leg was bothering her, and he reminded himself to make certain she took her medicine when she was situated in her parents' house. From what little he had learned about her culture, he was fairly certain that her people accepted fate without question and that would most likely include accepting the pain without taking the medicine.

The limousine began to slow down. He looked out the window and caught his breath. The farm was immaculate. If he had imagined a small, dilapidated farm like he was familiar with, back in Cuba, he was more than pleasantly surprised. The large barn was painted a bright red with white-trimmed doors and windows. There were large yellow flowers alongside it that contrasted brilliantly against the red barn. The driveway curved around the barn and dipped down behind a small hill where the plain white farmhouse stood. There was a large garden on the side of the house with vegetables growing. And in the driveway was a small gray-topped buggy.

"This is home?" he asked, lifting his sunglasses off his face to peer at her.

"*Ja!*" she said, smiling. Her face glowed with excitement.

"Isn't quite what I was expecting," he said softly, sliding the glasses back on his nose.

The car stopped by the farmhouse, and Amanda sat up in the seat, anxious to get out and see her family. The driver parked the car and got out, walking around to the trunk for the wheelchair. Alejandro waited patiently, amused by Amanda's impatience. She was practically bouncing off the seat, her eyes scanning the farmhouse for any sign of her parents.

And then they saw them.

The door of the house opened, and an older couple emerged. The man wore simple black slacks and a white shirt, a straw hat on his head. He had a long white beard that hung down to the center of his chest. The woman wore a plain green dress with a black apron tied around her waist. She wore the same white prayer *kapp* on her head, covering her neatly combed hair, which was pulled back from her face. Amish,

Alejandro thought, highly curious and feeling a bit anxious in these new surroundings.

The driver opened the car door and bent down, reaching inside to help Alejandro get out of the car. Once outside, he stretched his back, then pulled gently on his beige jacket. His white pants were creased from having been in the car for so long, but he felt ready to meet her parents.

"*Ach vell* now," the father said as he approached, a smile on his face and his eyes shining. "That's some car you have there, young man!"

Alejandro reached out to shake the man's hand. "Alejandro Diaz, sir. We spoke on the phone."

"*Ja, ja,*" the man said. "That we did." He glanced down into the open door of the car. "My little girl somewhere in there, or is she lost in that fancy car?"

"I'm here, Daed," she said, peeking out as best she could.

"I have a wheelchair for her, sir. Might be easier to move around since the cast is up to her thigh."

"'Sir,' eh?" He pulled at his beard and stared at Alejandro. "That's a bit formal, don't you think? You can call me Elias, and this here is my wife, Lizzie." The woman at his side nodded her head but didn't speak. "We want to thank you for taking such good care of our Amanda. God has a way of providing in times of need, *ja*?"

Alejandro crossed his hands in front of him, his feet planted apart as he stood before this man. "Well, I felt a little responsible, to be truthful. It was my driver that hit her."

"That it was," Elias said, nodding his head. But he kept smiling. If Alejandro had expected the parents to be angry with him, he was pleased to be surprised. Again, he thought. That's twice in less than ten minutes. Elias rubbed his hands together and bent down, looking into the car again. "Let's see about getting her out of this fancy house on wheels, then."

It took a few minutes to get Amanda out of the limousine. Her leg felt heavy and awkward. When it was clear that she couldn't do it on her own, Alejandro gestured to her father to step back. *"¿Permiso?"* he asked but didn't wait for a response as he knelt on the floor of the limousine and lifted her into his arms. "Easy now," he murmured, his one arm under her legs and the other supporting her back. "Hold on to me, Princesa."

"Oh," she gasped, color flooding her cheeks. But she put her arms around his neck, avoiding the stunned gaze of her parents.

Carefully, Alejandro backed out of the limousine, and then even more carefully, he carried Amanda over to the waiting wheelchair. Gently, he set her down and started to stand up. But she was still clinging to his neck. He smiled to himself and reached up to touch her hands. "You can let go now," he whispered softly, his breath brushing against her ear.

Embarrassed, she looked away, her cheeks still crimson.

Her mother was quick to cover her legs with a small quilt that she had been holding in her arms. "You poor dear girl," her mother said, tucking the quilt around Amanda. "I never should have let you come home without your sister. Traveling alone through that big city? Terrible mistake! You must have been petrified!"

Recovering from her discomfort, Amanda turned toward her mother and reached for her hand. "Oh no, Mamm. Everyone was so kind and took such wonderful care of me! The nurses and doctors were very attentive." She glanced over at Alejandro, her eyes sparkling. "And Alejandro was there every day, talking to the doctors and making certain I was doing just fine. If it weren't for the pain and this lumpy thing on my leg that I'll be dragging around for a while, it was quite the grand adventure!"

Lizzie stood up straight, her hands planted on her hips and her mouth twisted in a grimace. She stared at her daughter with a look of complete disbelief. "A grand adventure, she says!" She repeated and looked at her husband. "Did you hear your *dochder*? A grand adventure!"

Elias laughed and put his hand on Amanda's shoulder. "*Ja vell,* let's have no more grand adventures, Amanda. You had your *mamm* worried half to death!"

"I knew you shouldn't travel by yourself," Lizzie complained.

Alejandro stood quietly, watching Amanda's parents fawn over her. He had his hands crossed in front of him, taking in the peaceful surrounding of the farm and feeling the love of Lizzie and Elias for their daughter. He could hear the cows in the field and horses in the barn. There were soft noises everywhere, reminders that he was no longer in the city but in a place where he might just be able to relax. No paparazzi, no fans, no phone calls, no interviews. Birds were chirping in the nearby trees, and he could hear the song of the cicadas traveling from a distant field.

Elias gently pushed the wheelchair toward the house, talking to Amanda in Deitsch. The words sounded musical, flowing together with lilts and dips. They were halfway to the house when Elias stopped as if he had forgotten something. He looked around and frowned. He glanced over his shoulder and saw Alejandro, still standing by the open car door, his hands crossed in front of him.

"You'll be coming inside, *ja*? Have some nice meadow tea and shoofly pie?" Elias said.

With a simple nod, Alejandro followed them into the house. He was still taking in this wonderfully strange environment. The smells, the colors, the sounds . . . everything was new and different to him. He was so used to airports and big cities that he hadn't been in the countryside for years. He was feeling himself relax, just being away from the craziness of his busy life.

The house was dark. Green shades were pulled halfway down the windows in the large kitchen. The walls were painted a softer color of green, but they were bare, all except a calendar that hung by the back door. The kitchen table had a simple green-and-white-checkered tablecloth on it with a basket of fruit set in the center. Everything was tidy and neat, clearly a well-cared-for home. It was a lot different from the farmhouses he remembered from his childhood in Cuba.

Standing in the doorway, he wasn't quite sure where to go. He waited for Elias to motion toward the sofa against the back wall. Obediently, Alejandro walked across the kitchen in six easy strides, pulling his pants up slightly before he sat. He took off his sunglasses and slid them into the pocket of his jacket.

"Alejandro, is it?" Elias asked.

"*Sí*, Alejandro. "

"Strange name, that. Almost sounds Amish!"

That image made him laugh. "I can assure you that it's not."

Amanda reached for her *daed*'s hand. "Alejandro is from Cuba." She said it the way that Alejandro said it: *coo-bah*. "It's a little island near Florida." She smiled at Alejandro. "Isn't that right?"

He was struck by her innocence. He knew that she was twenty years old, but she seemed so young and vivacious. He had caught glimpses of it when they were in New York City, but here at the farm, in her familiar surroundings, she was much more comfortable. Clearly, she was home.

"An island, you don't say?" Elias said, nodding his head in approval. "Can't say I know about this Cuba place."

"I live in Miami now," Alejandro offered. "That's in Florida."

"Ah! I know about Florida," Elias said proudly as he took the glass of tea from Lizzie and handed it to Alejandro. "So you are from this place Cuba, living in Miami, and were visiting in New York City. Now you are in Lititz, Pennsylvania. I'd say you are quite the traveling man."

Again, Alejandro laughed. "I'd say you're right. That's what I do. Travel."

"Travel, eh?" Elias sat down in the chair next to the sofa. He eyed Alejandro, a hint of suspicion in his face. "And do what when you are traveling?"

Amanda lifted her eyes and stared at Alejandro. She seemed to wait patiently for his answer. He was too aware of her stare, steady and curious. He didn't know how much she knew about his lifestyle, apart from what he had told her. From what he had gathered over the past few days and from what little research he had conducted, he imagined she didn't know very much about his world.

"I'm an entertainer," he finally said, speaking slowly and carefully. He wasn't certain what their reaction would be.

"What kind of entertainer?" Elias asked, direct and to the point.

Clearing his throat, Alejandro took a deep breath. Here it goes, he thought. "I'm a singer."

"They call him Viper," Amanda said softly.

"Viper?" Lizzie chimed in, her hand rising to cover her mouth, which formed a perfect O from her surprise at the word. "Oh my!"

"Well," Elias said. "Can't say I know much about entertaining people, but we do know about singing. At least in church," he teased.

"I'm sure that I like the name Alejandro better than Viper," Lizzie said under her breath, but not unkindly.

"It's my stage name," he offered. "What my fans call me."

Elias and Lizzie exchanged a glance. The unspoken language shared between them did not escape Alejandro's attention. It was a language that took years to develop and came from the heart. He had seen that silent language before, from his grandparents in Cuba. They could read each other's minds, it seemed. Whatever it was Elias and Lizzie had just said to each other without words, only they understood. Yet Alejandro waited for the next question, suspecting he knew what it would be.

It was Lizzie who cleared her throat and asked, "That means you sing for people? On stages?"

He nodded, too aware of their curiosity. "Yes, that's correct." He paused. "That's why I was in New York, meeting with a music producer."

Elias stared at Alejandro. "You headed back to New York, then?"

He raised an eyebrow and glanced out the window. "Los Angeles in a week, then Europe for a two-week tour. Thought I'd find a little hotel and stay here for a few days." He looked back at Elias. "It would be nice for a change. I'm tired of cities." And he meant it. He was tired of cities and people and paparazzi. Especially the paparazzi. He knew they'd never find him here. Viper didn't vacation in small Amish farming villages. Viper stayed in Paris or Rio, places with nightclubs and media on the prowl for a good story.

Elias glanced at Lizzie. Again, there was an unspoken communication between them. But whatever the communication was, they were both in agreement. *"Nee,"* Elias said. "You can stay here, Alejandro. You took care of our *dochder* and brought her home to us."

"It was my limousine that hit her," he reminded them, humbled by their willingness to forgive and forget so easily.

"Accidents happen and now she's fine, *ja?*"

Lizzie nodded. "We have the *grossdaadihaus*. It's empty and private. You are welcome to stay there."

"Grossdaadihaus?" he asked, repeating the strange word that Lizzie had said to him.

"Where my parents used to live. It's next door to this house," Elias said. "No one has lived there for a few years since they joined the Lord. Lizzie will straighten it up for you. But it's yours to stay in while you are here."

For a moment, he hesitated. He was used to hotels and servants. He was used to five-star dinners and hordes of people who clamored around him. He was used to sleeping late in the morning and staying out until the wee hours. But he had wanted a change, even if just for a few days. This was definitely not what he had expected, but he wondered if, perhaps, it might be just what he needed.

"I'd be honored, sir," Alejandro said, a serious look on his face. "I could use a change of pace, and this might be just what the doctor ordered."

"The doctor ordered?" Lizzie repeated. "Are you ill?"

"It's an expression," he said lightly. "It means that it would make me happy to be here."

Elias laughed. "Well, happy is a *wunderbar gut* thing, *ja*? And you can always help me in the dairy, if you want to get some farming under your belt and dirt under those fingernails."

"I can do that," Alejandro said. "Used to farm in Cuba when I was a boy. Would bring back some memories."

"We shall see what kind of farmer you are, then," Elias teased. He turned his attention to Amanda. "Now, as for you, young lady," he started. "I understand you will be in a cast for quite some time."

"*Ja*, four weeks."

Lizzie tsk-tsked and shook her head. "What were you doing? You should have stayed in Ohio with Anna."

"Your *mamm* fixed up the downstairs bedroom for you."

"Oh, Daed," she said softly. That was her parents' bedroom. "I don't want you to move upstairs. It's so hot in the summer!"

Her father held up his hand to stop her. "*Nee*, none of that. We'll move into your brother's room."

Alejandro frowned and looked around. "Brother?" He knew that Amanda had an older sister, but she hadn't mentioned a brother.

Lizzie lowered her eyes, and Amanda bit her lower lip. They waited for Elias to say something. It took him a minute to compose himself. "Our son died when he was twelve."

Immediately, Alejandro stared at the three of them. Grief was still apparent on their faces, and he could tell that it was a sensitive subject. "I'm so sorry."

"Been three years now," Elias said in a very matter-of-fact way. No one spoke for a few moments. The silence seemed heavy, and Alejandro sat there respectfully. And then the subject was dropped. "Well, best be getting to some of my chores," Elias said, slapping his hands on his knees before he stood up.

As Elias left the kitchen, Alejandro wasn't certain what to do. He felt out of place and was suddenly sorry that he had agreed to stay at the farmhouse. What would he do all day? Was he expected to help Elias? He stood up and carried his glass of tea over to the sink. "I suppose I should go speak with my driver. Let him know that I will be staying here."

Lizzie frowned and glanced toward the window. "You should have invited him in."

Alejandro appreciated her generosity, but he wasn't certain how, exactly, to explain the situation. "It's not like that, you see."

Lizzie questioned him with her eyes before asking the question: "Not like that?"

"He wouldn't come in."

"Where will he stay?" Lizzie asked, alarmed. "There is room for him here, too."

Alejandro smiled. "He'll stay at a motel and be nearby if I need him."

"That seems rather foolish when there are empty bedrooms." He knew it wasn't said as a criticism, just a mere statement.

Alejandro shrugged. No matter what he said, it wouldn't be understood. He knew that right away. Simply put, as a hired man, the driver would never stay with Alejandro. The driver wasn't paid to be his friend, just to be available and, if needed, to help protect Alejandro. But getting personal with each other was not an option. Alejandro suspected that it was not a philosophy that would be easily understood by Amish people; they seemed to be genuinely generous in spirit and in deeds. "If you'll excuse me," he said and slipped out through the door.

After exchanging a few words, the driver quietly took Alejandro's bag out of the trunk and carried it to the porch of the house. He set it down and waved at Alejandro. As the limousine pulled away from the house and disappeared around the corner of the barn, Alejandro felt a weight lift from his shoulders. Despite feeling alone and somewhat insecure in this very different environment, he also felt more alive and freer than ever. If only for a few days, he had escaped the limelight and could relax . . . It was the first time in years, he realized as he bent down to pick up his bag, that he was truly on his own.

Carrying the bag back into the house, he stood in the doorway and looked around the kitchen. The house was quiet, the only noise coming from the ticking of a clock that hung on the wall and the running water from the sink where Lizzie was working. Everything was neat and tidy, from the dark-green window shades that were pulled down to block direct sunlight to the vinyl floor. Amanda was on the sofa, staring out the window at the fields. He tilted his head, watching her. The sun was coming through the window, casting a warm glow on her face.

She was beautiful. He couldn't help but stare at her, noticing her high cheekbones and full lips. Her eyes were so large and full of life. Despite being so petite, she was clearly a strong young woman. He realized that over the past few days he had become quite fond of her zest for living. It was so different from what he was used to in his own world, where the women were focused on fashion and looks, vying for his attention but not necessarily for his affection. This one who sat before him on the sofa didn't even know he was in the room and, most likely, didn't even care.

He cleared his throat.

Lizzie looked up. "I didn't even hear you come back in," she said, smiling. She wiped her hands on the towel that hung over the counter. "Let me get you situated. It's nice that someone can use the empty *haus*." She hurried over to a door behind the sofa. "You'll be all right for a few minutes, *ja*?" she said to Amanda.

Alejandro followed Lizzie through the door. There was a larger room, empty with the exception of a bookshelf in the corner. It was dark and clearly not used very often. The shades were pulled completely down, covering the windows so that only a sliver of light filtered through the glass. Lizzie didn't seem to notice the darkness as she bustled along and opened another door.

When Alejandro stepped through the second door behind Lizzie, he caught his breath. It was a smaller house but equally as pristine. A kitchen with a sitting area looked as if it was completely ready and waiting for him. The light hanging over the kitchen table was polished and reflected the rest of the room. He had never seen a light like this. He glanced at it and frowned.

"*¿Qué es eso?*" he said, slipping into Spanish. When Lizzie looked at him, he apologized. "I'm sorry. I mean, what is this?"

She laughed, her eyes turning into half-moons. "It's a light. Since we don't use electricity, we use propane and kerosene lanterns." She moved over to the counter and pointed to a box on the wall. "The matches are kept here." She reached into the small metal box and pulled out a matchstick, then struck it against what looked like the back of a matchbox that was adhered to the wall. It hissed as it lit. She carried it back to the table, reached for a knob on the light, and lit the lantern. "See? Now you can see better." She waved her hand to extinguish the match.

"Fascinating," he said, and he meant it. The light was bright and noisy, with a steady whooshing sound that filled the room.

"The bedroom is behind the stairs," she said pointing toward the wooden staircase. "There are three bedrooms upstairs, but it will be cooler down here, *ja*?" She hurried over to the door behind the staircase and opened it. "Everything is fresh, but I haven't cleaned the windows this month," she said by way of apology.

Alejandro turned around, staring at the room. A beautiful handmade quilt covered the bed, the mixture of colors vivacious and welcoming, not the usual silk comforters that he slept under in his hotel suites. There were hooks on the wall with empty hangers, but no closet. He quickly understood that clothes were hung on the wall, not hidden away.

"You should be comfortable here," she said, backing out of the room. "Nice to have someone use it. Been empty since my own *daed* passed a few years back."

Alejandro raised an eyebrow. "And yet you clean it every week?"

"Of course," she said, looking at him as if he was kidding. "Doesn't take much time after all to keep it tidy and ready."

He wondered what the purpose was for keeping it tidy and neat if no one was to live there. But rather than ask, he settled on, "Who will live here?"

Lizzie averted her eyes but not before he saw the dark cloud that passed through them. "No one, I imagine." She paused, still looking away. It seemed that there was more that she wanted to say, something that was difficult for her. She struggled to find the right words and finally settled on, "Elias and I would have moved here when our son married and took over the farm. The girls will most likely move to their own husbands' farms when they marry. We'll eventually sell it to another young couple then." She said no more, and Alejandro realized that it was not a subject that she wished to continue discussing. "But now you can stay here. Anyone who has taken such wonderful care of our dear Amanda is a blessing and welcomed in our home!"

Thankful for the gracious out, he bowed slightly. "I cannot thank you enough for your hospitality."

She looked up and forced a smile. "You must be tired after so much travel. It's a long journey from New York City, *ja*?" She started to walk toward the door. "Rest up, and we'll have a light supper at six, after Elias is finished with the evening milking, if you'd care to join us."

Engulfed in silence, Alejandro stared after her when she disappeared through the door. A surreal feeling hung over him, and he wondered what, exactly, he was doing at this farm, by himself, and far from his people. He was used to having a small entourage of friends and associates surrounding him, guiding him, and abiding him. Now, alone, he was staying with people who neither knew him nor particularly cared about his music. It was truly a liberating experience.

With a sense of serenity, he realized that Lizzie was right. He was tired and could use a rest. He unbuttoned the top of his shirt and sat down on the edge of the bed. Sleep, he thought. Even if just for an hour. He lay back on the pillow and shut his eyes, realizing that he hadn't had a break in his life for over five years that permitted him the luxury of a late afternoon nap. He fell asleep with a smile on his face and peace in his heart.

Chapter Six

Alejandro had awoken shortly after five in the evening. He stretched as he walked around the small house, noticing every detail from the half-drawn green shades to the woven rug under the rocking chair. It was so different from what he was used to. His world seemed so far removed. Gone were the marble counters and tile floors. Missing were the leather sofas and silk draperies. Instead, he felt as though he had returned to his roots, a plain and simple time that reminded him of his childhood.

He sat down in the rocking chair and reached for his cell phone. Reluctantly, he flipped it open and checked his messages. Too many phone calls, he thought. He ignored them and switched over to his e-mail. Over two hundred messages. He glanced through the list and responded to a few of the electronic correspondence from Mike before tucking his phone back into his pocket. He knew that he'd regret not responding to the messages later. E-mail had a way of breeding more e-mail. But, he rationalized, he was on vacation and didn't want to get bogged down with electronic communications.

Electronic communications, he thought as he stared at his silenced cell phone. When had his life taken such a turn? When had he begun to live through 140 characters in Twitter messages and Facebook statuses?

Gone were the days of living life and enjoying the moment. Instead, he answered to Likes and Retweets. His life was managed by technology and by whatever the world decided was all right to pass along through these social networks.

He rubbed his forehead. When had his inner self disappeared? He felt lost and alone in a world of a million followers and fans, people he would never meet and whose snapshots were their only identities when they commented on his own postings. Some of the fans even went too far, creating their own fantasy world about him, posting lies or accusations. That was part of being a celebrity, dealing with the crazies, and he had learned that there were plenty of them out there. Sometimes he felt as if he had created another planet. His own planet, where he now lived, surrounded by his fans and followers.

America, he thought with a sigh, and shut his eyes.

The sun was beginning to sink in the sky. Despite the fact that it was still bright outside, he knew that the day was ending. He had two choices: stay in the peaceful solitude of the house or venture outside. While there was a certain appeal to being alone, something that was unusual at best, he found that he wanted to explore the world that Amanda Beiler had introduced to him. How often would he be able to truly be himself, without flashbulbs and photographers chasing him? Venturing outside held a higher appeal than sitting in the empty kitchen, pontificating on the ills of the world of music. So he stood up and headed toward the side door, then proceeded down a walkway and toward the driveway.

He paused at the end of the ramp and shut his eyes. For a long moment, he breathed deeply, feeling his lungs fully expand. The fresh air calmed him, quickly erasing the past weeks—no, months—of hard work and travel.

Instead of taking the driveway, he wandered over to the barn to see if he could help Elias with the evening milking. The dairy barn was dark and shadowy. The black-and-white Holstein cows were standing in the long aisles, eating hay and waiting for their turns to be milked. When Alejandro finally found Elias, he was carrying an empty bucket back to the cows.

"Need some help?" Alejandro asked.

"*Nein,*" Elias said, smiling as he waved a hand. "Just about finished." He set the bucket down by a cow and laid a hand on her rump. "But I'll be thankful for some help in the morning, then."

It was a long process for a single man to manage the herd. Every twelve hours, Elias explained, he had to milk the cows. Some farmers liked to milk them every ten hours in order to get extra milk, but Elias shook his head. "That's not for me. You would have to get up in the middle of the night to milk them some times, and other times get them in the barn in the middle of the day! Can't plan much with such a crazy schedule."

When the two men walked into the kitchen, there was a pleasant aroma that filled the air. Alejandro couldn't remember the last time he had come home to a home-cooked meal. Most of his meals were either brought in or eaten out. He felt the tug of a memory from his childhood back in Cuba with his grandparents, aunts, uncles, and cousins on Saturday afternoons. They would have fiestas with dancing and outdoor cooking. There was always music and laughter that was served along with the food. Of course, that was before they had immigrated to America.

Elias hung his hat from a peg on the wall and took off his dirty boots, setting them neatly by the side of the screen door. The table was set, and the food was placed upon it. Amanda sat in the wheelchair at the table so that her leg could rest in an elevated position. Her father assumed his position at the head of the table, and Lizzie sat on a chair to his left. He noticed that both of her parents sat in chairs with wheels on them. He quickly learned why. If they needed anything from the refrigerator or counter, they would just roll over to it. He almost burst out laughing the first time he saw Elias do just that.

Alejandro was seated across from Amanda on a hard bench. He noticed that she tried to not look at him. He felt out of place in her parents' kitchen. He knew that she felt that way about him, too. Every so often, she'd glance at him and smile before quickly looking away. After all, she had become used to seeing him in charge at the hospital with the staff fawning over him. It felt awkward seeing him at their family table, seated on a hard bench, bending his head when it was time for the meal's silent blessing.

At first, Elias and Lizzie asked Amanda about her stay at the hospital. She told them about the nurses and the flowers and the people who had stopped into her room to visit. "People I never met before," she added. "They just came in to sit, talk, and make certain I was comfortable."

"That was right *gut* of them," Lizzie said, nodding her head as she reached for the basket of fresh bread. Taking a piece, she set it alongside her plate and passed the basket over to Alejandro.

"And the food," Amanda praised, her eyes glowing. "Alejandro was kind enough to have some special meals brought in for me."

"Is that so?" Lizzie asked, her voice songlike as she spoke the words. "It's only right that we thank you with some of our own home cooking over the next few days, then!"

"Mayhaps some homemade ice cream, too?" Amanda asked hopefully.

Lizzie and Elias laughed. "You and your ice cream," Elias said. He looked over at Alejandro and quickly explained to let him in on the joke. "Our daughter was born with a sweet tooth. I think she'd do just about anything for ice cream!"

Alejandro watched the exchange between parents and daughter. It was a scene that he had never experienced. Without having known his own father, there had never been a casual family meal with laughter, inside jokes, and storytelling. Once they had arrived in Miami, his mother had worked two jobs when he was younger and he had to fend for himself for many years. Family dinners were nonexistent during those hard times. Alejandro had made his own meals, living off cooked pasta and the generosity of sympathetic neighbors. When he was older, he had discovered the streets: a way to make money while his mother worked. That was when his life had changed.

His thoughts were interrupted when Elias turned his attention away from Amanda. "So, Alejandro," Elias started. "You said you are a singer, *ja*? What kind of singing do you do?" Elias asked as he bit into a sweet roll.

"It's called rap but mixed with a touch of hip-hop," Alejandro replied, knowing full well that they would not be familiar with that type of singing. "The words are like poetry to music," he explained.

"Poetry?"

He nodded. "Fast-paced poetry."

"And you make a living from that?" Elias said, his eyes large and full of disbelief.

Alejandro laughed. *"Sí,"* he said. "I make a living from that."

Elias shook his head. He seemed to be deep in thought for a moment as he digested what Alejandro had just said. "Don't seem right," he muttered. "You just sing words. Doesn't make anything, and sure don't put food on anyone's plate, ain't so?"

"Well," Alejandro replied good-naturedly, pointing to his plate, "it puts food on mine."

Both parents laughed at the joke, and even Amanda joined in.

"Well, speaking of food," Lizzie said, turning her gaze to Amanda. "Tomorrow we'll be canning beef for the winter. Daed will be picking up the meat in the morning, no?" She looked at Elias for confirmation.

"Ja, nine o'clock. After milking." He nodded. He reached for the pickled cabbage and dished some onto his plate before handing it to his wife. "Mayhaps you want to ride along with me," he said by way of asking Alejandro to accompany him.

Alejandro took the bowl of boiled potatoes that Amanda passed to him. His hand brushed against her fingers, and he glanced at her, noticing that she quickly looked away. If her father hadn't been staring at him, he would have smiled at the innocent expression on her face. Luckily, Elias hadn't seen it. "That sounds like a fine plan, Elias," Alejandro said quickly. "Although I'm not so sure about canning beef. Never heard of such a thing."

"Never heard of canned beef?" Elias said, his eyebrows raised and a smile breaking onto his face. "How can that be?" He shook his head. "You Englische live a strange life, with that! No canned beef? Singing for a living? What's next?"

"Maybe you can help with the canning, too," Amanda said softly, turning her attention to Alejandro.

Her father waved his hand dismissively but with a twinkle in his eye. "*Pssh*, don't bother him with that. That's women's work!"

"Elias!"

Sensing tension, and uncertain if it was real or in jest, Alejandro jumped into the conversation. "I'd be glad to help. I sure don't mind working in a kitchen. I helped my own mother for years when I was living at home."

"Women's work, indeed," Lizzie muttered as she used her fork to crush her boiled potatoes. She reached for the container holding her homemade butter and spread it on top of her potatoes. "As if you have never helped me in the kitchen."

"Help you eat the food," Elias said, winking at Amanda. "But not making it."

This time, it was Amanda's turn to tease when she added, "And if you did, no one would eat the food, that's for sure and certain!"

The sun was still high in the sky after the meal had ended. The family bowed their heads in silent prayer when everyone was finished. Then Lizzie stood up to clear the table. "Amanda," she said. "You may retire to the porch, if you've a mind. Cool breeze might help you sleep tonight."

"I should help clean up," Amanda offered.

"*Nein*, not tonight, daughter."

Alejandro took that as his cue to help Amanda. He stood up and offered her his arm. "Here," he said. "Lean on me." He felt her hand on his warm skin as she stood up. Her touch was soft and gentle, her hand surprisingly cool given the warm temperature in the kitchen. He also hadn't noticed how petite she was when she stood next to him. Gently, he helped her toward the front porch as she used the crutches that her mother had handed to her.

The early evening sky was slowly changing from a brilliant turquoise to purples and oranges and reds. Amanda sat in the rocking chair, her leg propped on an overturned wooden crate with a pillow underneath her heel. Lizzie had brought that out for her after Alejandro had helped her to the chair.

"This is a good place," Alejandro said, leaning against the wall of the house. "I like it here."

"It's not always like this," she said, staring at the green field of growing corn. There was a gentle breeze that caused the corn to ripple. It looked like a wave. "When my sister is here, it's more noisy, I suppose."

He couldn't imagine that. Everything was so peaceful and quiet. Even the playful banter between husband and wife was light and cheerful. Certainly Amanda couldn't comprehend what true noise was. After all, it wasn't everyone who stood on a stage, hot lights beating down from the ceiling while ten thousand fans screamed at the top of their lungs and the band played as loud as they could. "Concerts are noisy," he offered. "You can't imagine the noise! In fact," he laughed, "everything about my life is noisy . . . the music, the fans, the concerts."

"But you like it, *ja*?"

He shrugged. Did he like it? That was the question he had been asking himself these days. "It's what I do" was the only answer he could think of. "Usually it's fine," he added. "But sometimes it is tiring living on the road and never being home. It's tiring having no privacy and following a tight schedule of meetings and interviews and photo shoots. In my world, I'm always moving. There is no downtime."

"Oh, I wouldn't know about that," she said lightly and with a casual shrug of her shoulders. "I'm just a farm girl. We have plenty of that."

The way she said those words, *just a farm girl*, struck him. He stared at her for a moment, wondering what that meant to her. If being a "farm girl" meant living this life that he saw around him, it wasn't such a bad living at all. Quiet, peaceful, and surrounded by the love of a family. Three things he had never truly experienced.

From the distance, the sound of an approaching horse could be heard. The noise started softly but increased as it neared. Lifting his head so that he could hear it better, Alejandro shut his eyes and listened to the sound. Music. When it was just down the lane from the farmhouse, it began to decrease. At the moment when he could no longer hear it, he opened his eyes, surprised to see Amanda staring at him.

Quiet, peacefulness, family. If he never had those things growing up, he certainly didn't have them now. Instead, his life was in a constant motion, and while he wasn't always certain of the direction in which he was going, he always knew where he was headed. His life was everything that hers was not. But it was a good life, a storybook life of rags to riches with no end in sight.

"*Sí,*" he finally admitted. "I like it."

"What do you like about it?" Her voice was soft and her eyelids drooped as she looked down at the ground, avoiding his eyes.

What did he like about it? He didn't know how to answer that. It wasn't something he often thought about. "Well," he began, trying to think as he spoke. "I used to like the attention, and I certainly like the money."

"Money?" she interrupted, her eyes flying to meet his.

"Is that so strange, Princesa?"

With a simple shrug of her shoulders, she looked away. There was a disappointed expression on her face. "Money is just that: money. It's not family. It's not happiness. It's not love."

"True," he admitted.

She shook her head. "In fact, isn't money at the root of many Englische problems?"

"Money is good to have and bad not to have, sí?" he said lightly.

"Mayhaps, but it sure seems to me that you sacrifice an awful lot of life in order to get that money," she stated.

She was right. He knew it. Yet he felt compelled to explain to her that having money was not all bad. "But it enabled me to bring my mother's family over from Cuba. It enables me to let my mother live a better life." He squatted down next to where she sat. "But it's not all about the money." He touched her knee gently. "It's about creating something that touches other people. That's what I like about it."

For a long moment, she remained silent. Her eyes watched his hand, which lingered near her leg. She seemed to be digesting what he said, and finally she nodded her head. "I can understand that," she said, emphasizing the word *that*. "I love gardening and being creative with how I plan the layout. Other people like flower gardens. My *mamm* loves to bake pies. Each is creative in her or his own way, I imagine. And that makes us feel good because it touches other people."

"There you go," he said.

"And your music touches people, then?"

In his mind, he saw the thousands of screaming fans, crowded around the edge of the stage, the crowd stretching back farther than he could see. He saw the young girls standing outside of his hotels and chasing his limousines. He thought of the thousands of e-mails that he received every day. "Yes," he said. "I believe it does."

"Then it's good that you do that, Alejandro Diaz," she relented with a smile. "And it's even better that you like it. I sure would not like the thought of you doing something you hated."

Her words struck him like a jolt. No one ever seemed to care about what he wanted. Instead, he was always told where to go, what to do, how to behave, even what to wear. He had image consultants, makeup artists, choreographers, voice coaches, managers, and an entire entourage of staff when he was on the road. Yet not one of them ever seemed interested in his thoughts about their decisions. They dictated; he followed. On a few occasions, he might refuse, but it often came at a high price. After all, their sole interest in his success was what they could gain from it themselves.

"You are quiet now," she said softly.

He glanced around the farm. "You are lucky," he replied.

"That's what you were thinking?" she asked.

"No," he said, moving his head so that he faced her and not the fields. "But that's what I'm thinking now."

She smiled at him and, as her eyes sparkled, he reached over for her hand and lifted it to his lips. Gently, he pressed them against her soft skin, never taking his eyes from hers. He watched as the color flooded her cheeks, and he lowered her hand.

"You blush?"

She looked away, but her cheeks were still crimson.

"I embarrassed you?"

She shook her head. *"Nee."* Avoiding his eyes, she changed the subject. "It's been a long day and if you intend to help Daed tomorrow, you should be retiring soon, *ja?*"

With a careless lift of his shoulders, he shrugged. "I am not tired. The sun has barely set in the sky."

"You'll be tired tomorrow," she said, a light tone returning to her voice. "You'll see."

He stood up and reached down for her hand, the same hand that he had held and kissed just a few seconds before. She hesitated to take it before realizing that he was merely offering his hand to help her stand. Grateful, she accepted his gesture and let him guide her to her feet. It was still very cumbersome with the cast on her leg. She was too aware of how awkward she looked, probably as awkward as she felt.

"In that case, Princesa," he said gently. "I shall assist you inside so that I may retire to my own quarters. I have e-mails to check on my phone, no?"

"*Ach,*" she scoffed as she released his hand. "That silly thing?"

He laughed at her. "That silly thing is what keeps my career going, *sí?*"

She shook her head as she started to move toward the door, the crutches helping to stabilize her. "Such a small device to take up so much of your time," she remarked. "Seems like communicating in person would be much more effective."

Reaching out, he held the door open so that she could move inside. "That's one way of looking at it, but not very realistic in my world," he tossed back at her playfully.

"Well," she added, glancing up at him as she slightly crouched to move under his arm. "Like I said, I'm just a farm girl. Wouldn't know much about that. Good night, Alejandro." And with that, she disappeared inside, leaving him standing on the porch, a smile on his face at her ability to warm his heart.

Chapter Seven

It was five in the morning when Elias knocked at the bedroom door. The noise was sharp and loud, jolting Alejandro from his sleep. He jumped up and shouted, *"¿Quién es?"* His eyes were wide-open and trying to adjust to the darkness that engulfed him. He had been sleeping, a deep sleep that he hadn't reached in the past weeks. Startled from the abrupt awakening, he reached out for the nightstand, looking for something that wasn't there. Then, feeling his cell phone, he grabbed it and flipped it open to see the time: 5:05 a.m.

"Time for milking, *ja?*" Elias called out from the other side of the door. It sounded as though he were chuckling.

Milking? It took Alejandro a moment to place himself. He wasn't in a hotel. He wasn't in Miami. There was no one with him, not this morning. There was no fancy breakfast waiting in the outer room with people to serve him. No, he realized, he was in Lititz, Pennsylvania, and being awoken at a time of the day when he normally was just going to bed. And by an Amish man, of all people! For a moment, he wondered if he was still dreaming.

"Five minutes," Alejandro finally called out, trying to shake the sleep from his head.

Despite it being June, the morning air was cool when he exited the house. He was wearing slacks and a shirt, opened slightly at the collar. The sun wasn't even cresting in the sky, but there was a faint light that wrapped around him. The radiance of morning. Everything felt mildly fresh and new, the breaking of dawn as he had never seen it. Birds were singing their morning songs, and a few rabbits were nibbling at the grass by the back fields.

When he walked into the barn, he was overwhelmed by the smell. Cows. Manure. And lots of both. It was a pungent odor, somewhat familiar but offensive to his nose. *"Ay, mi madre,"* he said quietly. What had he gotten himself into?

"Guder mariye," Amanda called out cheerfully to him. She was using her crutches, trying to carry a full bucket of warm water. Unlike Alejandro, she looked as if she was wide-awake and ready for the day, wearing a faded work dress, a blue bandana over her hair, and an old, clunky boot on her one foot. "Not used to getting up so early, *ja?*"

He tried to smile but was too tired. "Getting up early, going to bed late. Same thing, I suppose." He saw her struggling with the bucket and frowned. He ran his fingers through his hair, a loose curl draping over his forehead, and walked toward her. "Let me help you, Amanda." He took the bucket from her and followed behind her. She moved slowly down the aisle between the barn wall and the cows. "Why are you out here anyway, Princesa? The point of my staying to help was so that you wouldn't have to."

She glanced at him and laughed, her dark eyes twinkling. "Was that the point?"

It was too early for laughter and teasing. First thing in the morning, his brain wasn't that quick. He needed some coffee to help him wake up. Actually lots of it. Despite having slept so well, he felt tense. He wasn't certain whether it was the fact that he was up so early or because Amanda was up, too. "You should be resting," he scolded her. "This is too much for you."

She shook her head. "If I can help just a little, I'll feel better. No use in sitting around when there is work to do," she argued gently. She ignored his scowl and tried to move past him. When he touched her arm, she looked up at him and added, "Besides, my *daed* needs me."

He frowned. "No good, Amanda." But he let her be, knowing that she was old enough to make her own decisions, even if they were not necessarily the right ones. Who was he to tell her what to do? he thought.

For the next two hours, he helped Elias with milking the cows. Amanda did what she could, using her crutches: carrying empty buckets to the men and trying to bring the full ones back to the containment system, which would keep the milk at the right temperature until it was picked up later in the week. She never complained and seemed quite content to be helping, even if she couldn't do too much. Alejandro kept an eye on her, noticing that she looked pale and worn-out by the time they were almost finished with the milking.

"Farming never quite leaves you," Elias said, clapping Alejandro on the back. Clearly, he was impressed that Alejandro had been able to roll up his sleeves and start milking the cows. "You are a *gut Schaffmann!*"

Alejandro rubbed his eyes. He still needed that coffee. "*Schaffmann?*"

"Worker," Amanda chimed in. "He's calling you a *gut* worker! It's a compliment."

"*Ja*, worker." Elias laughed. "Whoever taught you how to milk cows in that island place did a mighty fine job. You did a *gut* morning of work this day, son!"

Son. The word resonated in his head. He had never known his own father. His mother wouldn't speak about his father, not once. After they had left Cuba for America, there was no one else to ask. His grandparents were dead, and his uncles had never known his father. On the few occasions when Alejandro had tried to bring up the subject with his mother, she had shut down, not unlike the Beilers yesterday when the subject of their son had been mentioned. He had seen the pain in Elias's and Lizzie's eyes, and he suddenly realized that whatever had happened between his own father and mother must have caused the same amount of pain.

When they had finally finished and returned to the main house, the kitchen smelled of fried eggs and bacon. Alejandro breathed in deeply, loving the wonderful aroma of fresh farm food. He was starving after the light supper from the previous evening and for having been awakened so early. Hard work made a man hungry, and he hoped that there was coffee waiting for them, too. He was not disappointed.

After breakfast, Elias walked with Alejandro out to the horse barn. In silence, Elias quickly curried the horse before he started the process of hitching the bay to the black buggy. Alejandro watched, amazed, as Elias slipped the harness saddle over the back of the horse, resting it just behind the withers. He stretched the girth around the horse's barrel and tightened it to ensure that it was secure. He explained to Alejandro that the girth needed to be tight so that the harness wouldn't slip sideways while supporting the shafts of the carriage.

The horse stood patiently, immune to the familiar touch of the expert hands that placed the leather pieces onto its back. Elias continually ran his hand down the horse's flanks, talking softly to it as he worked. When he moved toward the tail, he gently patted the muscled croup twice, a kind and calming gesture showing how much he cared for his horse. Carefully, he attached the black crupper, a V-shaped piece of stuffed leather, latching it around the tail and buckling it at the dock. He explained that this would prevent the harness from sliding forward. Then, in one quick motion, he slipped the breast collar, a wide piece of padded leather in dire need of some leather polish, over the horse's head. The horse lifted its head but didn't fuss beyond that simple gesture.

Crossing the leather tugs over the back of the horse, Elias gestured toward the buggy. "Could use your help here, son," he said. Together, they pulled the buggy toward the horse, carefully guiding it so that the shafts would slide into their holders, one side at a time. Then, after clipping the holdback straps to the breeching, a clever yet simple apparatus that would prevent the buggy's kick plate from hitting the horse's hocks when driving downhill or suddenly stopping, Elias uncrossed the tugs and secured them to the swiveling base. It hadn't taken more than five minutes to get the horse and buggy ready for the journey to town, where they were headed to pick up the meat.

"Sent the cow to the butcher just two days ago," Elias said as he held the reins in his hands, steering the horse down the lane and onto the main road. "Shop should be open by now, I reckon."

The front window of the buggy was open, and Alejandro watched the horse's hindquarters as it trotted down the road. The noise was musical in rhythm, and for a while he got lost in the beat. The early morning air was cool and felt refreshing on his face. If he had thought it would be warm and stuffy inside the buggy, he was pleasantly surprised to find otherwise. But he was also surprised to feel something tickling his face. The faster the horse trotted, the more he felt something brushing against his skin. He lifted his hand and touched his cheeks.

"Ah, the horsehair," Elias laughed. "Should have warned you earlier. I curried her right *gut* this morning, but there's always horsehair floating around."

Alejandro saw it now. Hair from the horse was floating back through the open window. He was glad the horse's coat was bay instead of white; otherwise, his dark clothing would definitely show the hair.

"Well, hello there," Elias called out as they reached the village, and he slowed the horse down in the driveway of another Amish farm. An older Amish man was walking from the house to a shop at the back of the property near the barn. "Come for my meat, Jeremiah."

The man eyed the Englischer seated next to Elias with suspicion. "Who you got there, Elias?"

With the buggy stopped, Elias slid open the buggy's door and jumped down. "Alejandro Diaz is staying with us for a few days. He helped Amanda in that New York town."

At the mention of Amanda, the man softened his harsh expression. "How is your *dochder*?"

"*Gut, gut,*" Elias responded. "*Danke* for asking."

As Alejandro approached, the older man stared at him. "Bit fancy dressed for helping with butchering, ain't so?"

Alejandro reached out to shake the man's hand. "Pleasure to meet you, sir."

Raising one eyebrow, the man hesitated before taking Alejandro's hand. "Jeremiah Smucker," he finally said, introducing himself. Then, formalities over, he turned back to Elias. "Got your meat all ready. You tell Lizzie that I made sure to grind some extra special, just the way she likes it."

Alejandro waited by the buggy while the two men disappeared into the shop. Minutes later, they came out carrying two large boxes. One of the boxes was open, and he glanced inside at the large plastic bag brimming with various cuts of meat. After they had put it into the back of the buggy, they disappeared and shortly returned with two more boxes.

"That should hold you over for the winter, *ja*?" Jeremiah said lightly. "Especially since I heard that one *dochder* might be staying in Ohio. Something about a special new friend, ain't so?"

Elias laughed and turned to Alejandro. "Mayhaps we don't have fancy phones like you Englischers, but our Amish gossip spreads just as fast without 'em."

When they returned to the farm, Alejandro helped Elias carry the boxes of meat into the canning room located off the kitchen in the farmhouse. The house was quiet. Neither Amanda nor Lizzie was in the kitchen. Alejandro realized that it was the perfect time to steal away for a few minutes and catch up on his own thoughts.

For a long time, he walked along the fields and breathed in the fresh air. At the edge of the cornfield, he stopped and watched the birds flying overhead, dipping down and disappearing among the growing stalks. In the distance, he could hear the sound of an approaching horse and buggy rattling down the road. Shutting his eyes, he listened to the noise, catching the rhythm in his mind until it disappeared. Taking a deep breath, he felt his lungs opening up, free from smoke and city fumes. A man could get used to this, he thought. No pressure, no deadlines, no commitments.

Unlike New York City, Los Angeles, or Miami, there was no loud background noise. No cars. No beeping. No voices. Just the gentle song of the birds and the whisper of the crops, stalks gently brushing against one another in the summer breeze. He shut his eyes and listened to the sounds of nature. They soothed him, and he realized that he was relaxing for the first time in months . . . perhaps years. Yes, no matter what Mike had thought, the small farming town of Lititz was exactly what he needed to recharge his batteries.

He was surprised to see a car in the driveway when he returned from his walk. He knocked at the door to the main house before opening it, and slipping inside, it took a minute for his eyes to adjust. Lizzie was standing with another woman by the sofa where Amanda was lying. Alejandro took off his sunglasses and waited for any indication that he should enter. The other woman was dressed in regular clothing and was checking Amanda's blood pressure and heart rate.

"Looks good," the woman said, standing up straight. "But I don't want to hear about you doing chores, young lady. You need your rest."

Alejandro cleared his throat. "Those very same words were spoken by me this morning." The three women looked up and stared at him. He took five strides and reached out his hand. "Alejandro Diaz," he said. "I believe we spoke on the phone a few days ago."

"Of course," the woman said, smiling at him. She glanced down at Amanda. "The patient is doing quite fine. But I heard that she has been helping with the morning milking. She really needs to stay put. If someone will push the wheelchair, she can go outside. I don't even mind if she goes visiting other places. But she needs to be still and relax or that leg will not heal properly." The nurse started packing up her things, putting the blood pressure monitor back into her bag. "And keep that leg elevated as much as you can."

Lizzie shook her finger at Amanda. "Did you hear that, now?"

"Yes, Mamm," she said, sneaking a quick look at Alejandro. "But I don't like it."

He was caught off guard by the expression on her face. It was so peaceful and serene, such a joy to behold that he wondered if he had ever experienced anything even remotely similar. While the visiting nurse and Lizzie stepped away to privately discuss Amanda's condition, Alejandro knelt down before her. He glanced over his shoulder to make certain that no one was watching, then he reached for her hand. He noticed that she caught her breath and almost pulled her hand away, but her own gaze darted over his shoulder to make certain her mother wasn't watching.

"You need to listen to these people," he said softly. "You have no idea how long it can take to heal, Princesa."

"Do you have an idea?"

"Sí." He nodded, ignoring the sassiness of her tone. "I broke my arm two years ago." She raised her eyebrows, an unspoken question. "I was in a fight," he admitted and flushed at the disapproving look on her face. "I pushed it and did too much. It took much longer than it should have to heal." He waited until she looked at him. "You can't afford to push it."

She chewed on her lip and lowered her eyes, watching as his thumb caressed the back of her hand. She liked the feeling of her hand in his and realized at that moment that she was tripping down a dangerous path. Her heart fluttered. Dangerous indeed, she thought.

"My *daed* doesn't have a son anymore, Alejandro," she whispered, as if apologizing. Lifting her eyes, she stared into his. "He needs my help."

"I understand that," he replied, nodding at her. "But that doesn't mean you have to be the one helping. We can arrange for help. This accident is my responsibility. I will see that your father has help. I will take care of you and your family."

She frowned and withdrew her hand. "Is that why you are here? You feel that you are responsible?"

"No, that's not it at all," he started to say. He took her hand back in his and squeezed it. It was soft and warm, the skin silky smooth. For a moment, he didn't say anything. Instead, he stared into her face. The frown disappeared, and he was, once again, struck by how beautiful this young woman was. "There are a lot of things I would like to say to you, Amanda, but this isn't the time." He leaned down and kissed the back of her hand, noticing that the color rose to her cheeks. He chuckled softly, peeking over his shoulder at Lizzie. He was pleased to see that she was still engaged in a discussion with the nurse. "Later, *sí*? Maybe tomorrow. But for now, I'm going to take a ride into town for a little bit. I have some phone calls to make, and I want to see your Lititz." He stood up and straightened his pants. Then he pointed to her. "Stay put, *sí*?"

"Ja," she replied, the color still painting her cheeks. But her eyes shone, the adoration more than apparent.

He had called the driver earlier, asking to be picked up at eleven o'clock by the roadside. He didn't want the family to see the limousine in the driveway and felt it was better this way. For the first hour, the driver meandered through the back roads, driving slowly so that Alejandro could take in everything in sight. The farms were beautiful, dotting the landscape. Each one was more appealing than the next. Some had clothing lines filled with colorful dresses, black pants, and white shirts drying in the sunshine. The fields were lush and green with black-and-white cows grazing side by side, their tails swishing at the flies that bothered them. Truly, he thought, I have found a small slice of heaven.

When the driver finally took him into town, Alejandro noticed that people stopped and stared when the limousine passed. Unlike the big cities, it was clear that limousines were quite a rarity in this community. He glanced at his phone, which he had been charging from the unused cigarette lighter. He hadn't checked any messages or e-mails, and he hesitated to browse through the social media. But curiosity got the best of him, and he pressed the "On" button.

Sure enough, there were pictures of him taking Amanda out of the hospital, flooding the various social media websites throughout the Internet. The entertainment channel was in a frenzy, asking for any information about the young woman in the wheelchair. There was even a photograph of Alejandro helping her into the limousine. He paused when he saw it. She was looking over his shoulder, her dark eyes staring directly into the camera lens. With her tanned skin and dark hair, she was hauntingly beautiful, despite her look of innocence. Yet, at the same time, there was something fierce about her expression. It was the look of strength and determination. Sighing, he pressed the "Off" button and tossed his phone aside. He didn't want to get distracted by the news. Let them have their field day and ask their questions. He wasn't taking the bait. Not this time.

"See if you can find a clothing store, my friend," Alejandro called out to the driver. "I could use some casual clothes, I think." If he had six more days at the farm, he didn't need to ruin his fancy Gucci clothes and Armani shoes. He could get some more simple clothing and, perhaps, blend in a bit more. "And see if you can find another car to drive while I'm here," he added. "Something that doesn't stand out so much, sí?"

It was almost three in the afternoon when Alejandro returned to the farm. They had driven into Lancaster to find a mall, and to Alejandro's surprise and slight displeasure, several people had noticed him, crowding him at the mall. While Alejandro had been willing to take a few photographs with his fans, he was worried about what might happen next. Teenagers were unpredictable and viral. The wrong words could set off a firestorm. Luckily, the driver had accompanied him inside the mall and managed to whisk Alejandro away before there was a mob scene. It was clear that, even in Lancaster, Pennsylvania, Viper could not remain anonymous.

He let himself into the *grossdaadihaus* and changed his clothes. With simple black trousers and a plain white shirt, Alejandro felt better. Gone were the linen shirt and jacket. He wore a sleeveless T-shirt underneath the shirt, just in case it got too hot working in the barn. And boots. Real boots. Not the fancy Italian leather shoes that he was so used to wearing around the city. There was no mirror in the house for him to see how he looked, but he knew that he would definitely blend in better.

When he walked into the Beilers' kitchen, Amanda was sitting at the table, her wheelchair pushed in so that she could help her mother with the beef canning. There were newspapers spread on the table and empty glass jars waiting for her to shove the beef mixture into each container. Her sleeves were rolled back and her apron smudged with stains. She looked up at Alejandro and quickly looked away, trying to hide her laughter. Lizzie heard the noise and turned around. When she saw Alejandro, she smiled.

"All you need are suspenders and a straw hat," she said. "You might even pass for Amish."

"Hardly," Amanda giggled.

"Amanda!" Her mother frowned at her. "Manners," she whispered.

He held his arms out and looked down, turning slowly. "What's so funny?"

"Even trying to be plain, you still look fancy," Amanda said good-naturedly. She looked at him again, meeting his eyes. Her own were twinkling with mischief. "You would never fit in here, Alejandro."

"Can't blame a fellow for trying now, can you?" he replied with a wink.

"Now, now, let's leave our guest alone," Lizzie said, scowling at Amanda. "Remember that he's the one who brought you home from that terrible city. I think a little more respect is in order, *ja*?" But when Lizzie turned back to the sink, Amanda stuck her tongue out at him. The playful gesture caught him off guard, and he started to laugh. Lizzie looked at him over her shoulder. Turning, she put her hands on her hips and gave him a fierce look, despite a smile on her face. "Not you too, now!"

Amanda gestured to him, trying to remain serious. "Mayhaps you'd rather help with the canning?"

He surveyed the room. There were lots of large silver bowls and clear jars on the table and counter. Lizzie was mixing spices with chopped beef, her strong arm moving the large wooden spoon to stir the mixture. "I suppose I can help if you tell me what to do," he said.

Lizzie didn't waste any time and immediately motioned toward the filled jars on the counter. "*Gut* then! Start by taking those into the canning room. Clear some space for more." She watched while he did as instructed, carefully cradling eight jars in his arms, and headed for the outer room. "And bring back some more wide-mouthed canning jars from the pantry, *ja*?"

For the next hour, he helped pack the raw meat into the jars, laughing with Amanda, who teased him that he didn't pack them tight enough. She showed him how to do it properly, pushing the meat down and sprinkling some salt on top before wiping the jar clean with a damp rag and twisting on a special canning lid. When they were finished with that task, Alejandro carried those jars into the outer room and returned with more empty ones.

"I love Mamm's meatballs," she confided in him as they began rolling meatballs and dropping them into the empty jars. She glanced at what he was doing and shook her head. "That one is too big," she pointed out.

"*¿Sí?*" he asked, raising one eyebrow at her in question.

"Just pinch off a little bit and reroll it. Otherwise, it won't cook evenly," she explained. She reached over and showed him how, her fingers brushing against his. He glanced at her and smiled, that half smile that curled up just one side of his mouth. Blushing, she tossed the extra meat into the bowl and looked away. "Like that, *ja?*"

"I see," he said, his voice teasing.

Boldly, she turned her head back and stared at him. There was something daring in her eyes. "Do you?" she said, her voice barely louder than a whisper. He raised an eyebrow at her tone and was glad that her *mamm* hadn't heard. "I wonder about that, Alejandro."

He couldn't help himself. She was clearly flirting with him and *flirting* was what Viper did best. "What do you want me to see, Amanda?" he asked, his voice low and soft.

She blinked her eyes and met his gaze, refusing to falter as he stared back at her. "You don't belong in that world of yours," she boldly ventured. "Mayhaps that Viper does, but Alejandro doesn't." She lifted an eyebrow and tilted her head. "And I think you are more Alejandro than Viper, after all."

Once again, her words stunned him. She was right. After years of playing the role, it was catching up to him. He was tired of acting, tired of being someone else. He was living a lie, and it was exhausting him. Viper would not have brought Amanda back to the farm. No, he would have sent her back to Lititz in a car service that would have been arranged by his people. Viper would not be milking cows at five in the morning. Instead, he'd be getting home from the clubs at that hour. And certainly Viper would not be canning beef with a young Amish woman, even if she were as remarkably beautiful as Amanda. More likely, he'd be trying to coax her into spending the night with him at a nearby motel.

He stood up and walked over to the sink to wash his hands. His heart was pounding inside his chest as he realized how profound and truthful her words really were. How could she, a simple farm girl by her own admission, have such a clear eye in assessing him? How could she cut through to the core of what his inner feelings were? Her ability to see through him unnerved him. She had hit it right on the nail, and that was an understatement.

"I think you have this under control, *sí*? I'll go out to the barn. See what Elias is doing and if I can be of any help," he managed. He couldn't help but hear the catch in his own throat.

Amanda stared at the door, long after he had disappeared. She retreated into her thoughts, trying to imagine what his life was like performing onstage in big cities. She didn't know much about that world, but she could dream. While she had never listened to music, not like other Amish youth on *rumschpringe*, she had heard music in the background at youth groups when they were gathered at volleyball games or for singings. Indeed, there was always a young person who had an iPod or a battery-operated music box, playing it to try to impress a girl. But personally, Amanda had ignored it. Music was worldly and something she didn't really care to learn about. So she knew very little about the world of a famous rap star. Yet now, she could only dream.

She wondered why he was so interested in staying at the farm. Certainly he had a lot of obligations, important meetings with important people. But he seemed relaxed and at ease at her parents' farm. The change in him was obvious, even to her. Even after such a short time.

Back in the city, he had always seemed to be too aware of his own behavior, too concise with his movements and words. His life appeared . . . orchestrated. He had seemed to relax a little as they had gotten to know each other, but nothing like he was now. He seemed lighthearted and carefree, as if the weight of the world had been lifted off his shoulders. She liked this new side of Alejandro, she realized.

She liked that he wasn't so stiff, so obsessed with that little gadget he checked every few minutes. She liked that he was so easygoing and quick to laugh, even though he had just shuffled off rather quickly. But most of all, she liked those few moments when he would talk just to her, sometimes touching her hand or her knee. She wasn't used to being touched and certainly not by a man. Among the Amish, that was inappropriate. But when Alejandro did it, she felt pleasant chills course through her veins. Yes, she liked his attention most of all.

Smiling, she turned her thoughts back to the meatballs, rolling the fresh ground meat between her hands, Alejandro's gentle touch on her skin still somehow lingering in her memory.

Chapter Eight

The next day followed the same routine. Alejandro awoke at five and helped with the morning milking. It was easier to get up that second day, and he didn't seem to mind greeting the dawn before the sun rose. Indeed, he stood for a moment on the porch and stared at the bluish-gray skies. It was breaking dawn, and he found it inspiring to watch it happen. Usually he was heading back to bed at this hour, not starting his day.

The barn was quiet when he walked inside. The cows were already lined up and ready for their milking. Elias glanced up, greeting Alejandro with a simple head nod before returning to work. Looking around, Alejandro was relieved to not find Amanda also at work in the barn. Clearly, the visiting nurse had helped her realize that she needed to take it easy for a while. He just hoped that she kept listening and laying low.

During breakfast, Amanda seemed quiet and withdrawn. From time to time, she glanced at him but quickly looked away if he caught her gaze. He wondered about her shyness this morning, finding it charming after all that they had been through. They had spent a lot of time together in the past week, he realized. More time than he had spent with any single person in quite a long while. The people he usually met came and went quickly, mostly because of his own crazy schedule, but also because he just wasn't interested in expanding his trusted circle of close friends. With Amanda, he realized, he felt different. She didn't expect anything from him, and that was something he found refreshing.

After breakfast, Alejandro volunteered to help Elias in the fields. He was relieved when Elias smiled and thanked him. "Sure could use the help," he had said.

Alejandro noticed that Amanda sighed at her father's words and looked away.

For the rest of the morning, Elias and Alejandro worked at cutting the hay, the disk mower being pulled behind the team of four mules. Elias told him that the hay had to be left to dry in the sun for a few days before it would be baled. To bale it sooner was to risk having the barn catch fire because damp, smoldering hay was a fire hazard to any farm.

"Does that happen frequently?" Alejandro asked, wiping the sweat from his brow. He wondered when was the last time that he had worked so hard, and realized that he couldn't remember. He didn't count his endless concerts or interviews, despite the fact that it was, indeed, hard work. It was just not the same as laboring in the fields. He decided that it had been close to twenty years.

"*Ja,*" Elias said. "Young farmers just starting out often bale it too soon. They learn from experience. You hear about a barn or two burning each year."

"What happens then?"

Elias shrugged casually. "We build them a new barn!"

"We?"

"The other farmers and the surrounding community." Elias took off his straw hat and waved it back and forth to cool down his burning cheeks. "We take care of each other here."

That surprised Alejandro. In his world, someone's loss was another performer's gain. It was rare to have true friends among the circuit.

There were alliances, true. But, for the most part, it was every man for himself. Even the female performers were known to be cutthroat. These days, Alejandro was fortunate to be at the top of the food chain, which meant less need to battle others but always harboring a lingering concern about watching his back.

"Sure is *gut* to have some help," Elias said, rubbing his brow and sliding his battered hat back onto his sweaty head. "A strong man in the fields is a blessing." He smiled at Alejandro and clapped him on the back. "Company ain't so bad, either!" It was clear that a friendship was rapidly forming between the two men: one for want of a father figure, and the other for want of a lost son.

"Who normally assists you?" Alejandro asked. Clearly, Elias owned a large farm, larger than one man could possibly handle by himself. From what little he knew about the Amish, they tended to have many children. Yet, it was clear that Elias and Lizzie had only conceived the three, and with the son having passed away, that left little help for Elias.

"The girls help," he replied, leaning over to pick up a large rock that was half-buried in the soil. He tossed it as far away as he could. Looking back at Alejandro, he smiled, but there was a definite sadness to his expression. "My Amanda sure does work hard. As *gut* as any son, I reckon."

But she's not a son, Alejandro thought. "She's a lovely young lady," he said casually.

"*Ja,*" Elias agreed. "That she is. Make a *wunderbar gut* wife to an Amish man one day." He gave a slight shake of his head. "If only . . ."

Alejandro raised an eyebrow. "If only what?"

"*Ach vell*, she has these ideas," Elias said. "That she has to stay here to help us." He paused, then added, "Help me, I reckon. Ever since Aaron . . ."

Elias didn't finish the sentence. Alejandro respected his silence, feeling his pain. Several birds flew overhead, swooping down to collect some seeds from the cut timothy grass. A gentle breeze blew over the hill, and Alejandro shut his eyes, enjoying this newly found feeling of becoming so in tune with nature, even if only for a few seconds while Elias collected his thoughts.

Finally, Elias took a deep breath. "*Vell*, she seems much more lively these days, ever since that trip to Ohio. Must have done her some good to get away." He started to walk toward the mules, grabbing the reins and leading them down the hill toward the farm. "Reckon the other one won't be coming home at all."

"Anna?" Alejandro inquired.

"*Ja*, Anna," Elias said. "Reckon she found herself a young man out there who captured her fancy. As long as he's a good Christian and follows the Plain way, I won't be having no objections." He smiled at Alejandro. "That's just the way it works. The young need to live their own lives, *ja*?"

Back in the barnyard, Alejandro helped Elias unhitch the mules and put away the equipment. Both men remained deep in thought. Alejandro couldn't stop thinking about what Elias had said about Amanda. Without a son and with Anna possibly staying in Ohio, Elias needed Amanda's help to run the farm. That meant a limited opportunity for her to have a social life that might introduce her to young men for courting. He didn't know the culture well enough to understand their approach to dating, but he did know that she didn't seem interested in any men. No, he corrected himself. *Not any Amish men.*

It dawned on him why she had been quiet that morning, and he felt his own heart quicken. Indeed, he knew that she had grown too familiar with "Alejandro" and not enough with "Viper." He sighed, suddenly realizing that, despite his own tender feelings for the young woman, hers may have taken a turn in a direction that needed to be changed. Unlike Amanda, he knew that Viper could walk away without looking back. But it was Alejandro who didn't want to leave a broken heart behind.

***

Amanda was sitting on the porch when Alejandro returned from a late afternoon walk through the fields. Her leg was propped up on a chair while she folded laundry that had just been pulled off the clothesline stretching from the corner of the house to the near side of the barn. For a moment, he paused and watched her. Her head was bent down, a blue handkerchief covering her hair. She seemed to be humming while she worked, a slow and soft tune that kept her distracted. There was a radiance about Amanda, a softness in her expression. If he had thought she was a pretty girl before, he saw how truly beautiful she was at this moment.

Woman, he corrected himself.

It was hard to realize that she was, indeed, an attractive woman. She was so different from the women who infiltrated his world. He leaned against the barn as he continued to watch Amanda. There was no comparison. She was pure and honest, beautiful on the inside as well as on the outside. He had learned that much about her in the short time that he had known her.

In his world, sophisticated women wore $1,500 dresses and $700 shoes in order to attract his attention. With fancy makeup and professionally coiffed hairstyles, these women wanted one and only one thing: to claim Alejandro as their own. But it wasn't Alejandro, he reminded himself. It was Viper. The image of Viper caused women to do things that they were not raised to do. Too often, Alejandro had succumbed to their pretty faces and fashionable looks, taking them to big-profile clubs and parties, only to later end up in his hotel room. In the past, he hadn't thought much about it. However, at this moment, he realized that he wasn't proud of his past. Not now as he watched Amanda, sweet Amanda, sitting on a porch in the shade folding laundry with a soft tune on her lips.

"You scared me!" she said as he approached her.

He leaned against the porch railing, still watching her. Suspecting that the shine in her eyes was more than just friendship, Alejandro had to remind himself to pull back. But as he watched her, it was more difficult than he could have imagined. There was something so striking about Amanda, so endearing.

"Did I?" he asked, his voice soft.

She laughed. "Were you out walking, then?"

"*Sí.*"

"It's beautiful, *ja*?" she asked, looking around at the fields. The sky was blue and the field green with grasses waving in the gentle breeze. The contrast in colors was glorious, and she smiled. "Now you can see for yourself why I think the city is so ugly."

He didn't respond right away, and after a few long seconds, she turned to look at him. The breeze caught a stray piece of hair and brushed it against her cheek. Her dark-brown eyes narrowed, just momentarily, as she met his gaze.

"Beautiful, *sí*," he said, his voice low and his eyes still holding hers.

She looked away.

"How is your leg today?" he asked, changing the subject as he sat down on the porch stairs.

"It was hard to sleep last night," she admitted. "But it doesn't hurt so much anymore. How long did the doctor say until the cast comes off?"

Alejandro glanced at the fields. The corn was growing, lifting its soft green blanket toward the sun. He wondered when it would be ready to be harvested. Surely Elias would need Amanda's help. "Four more weeks," he responded. "It wasn't a bad break. We were lucky."

"We?"

He looked at her. "You," he corrected. "You were lucky."

"I was lucky," she repeated, her voice barely a whisper.

Raising one eyebrow, he tilted his head as he stared at her. Her eyes broke free from his gaze, and she looked at the cows wandering through the fields. Her skin was a golden brown, flawless in complexion and tone. With high cheekbones and a full mouth, she was truly a natural beauty. "I was lucky, too," he said, his voice husky and low. She turned to look at him, a question in her expression. "It brought me here, no?"

"But you will leave for more exciting adventures," she said matter-of-factly. "For you, that's what this is, Alejandro. An adventure. For us, it's our way of life."

He took a deep breath and nodded. "*Sí, sí,*" he admitted. "But I'm glad to have this . . . adventure, as you call it."

She bit her lower lip, assessing him for a moment as if to gauge whether he was serious or just mocking her. "I wonder if I'd feel the same about experiencing your way of life."

At this, he laughed. He couldn't imagine Amanda on the road, living the life of a pop star. "If I were a betting man, I'd say that *that* would be highly unlikely."

"Why?" she demanded, an unexpected edge to her voice.

"*Ay,* Princesa. My life is everything that you are not."

"Really?" she said, a hint of sarcasm in her voice.

"Really!" he teased back. Sobering, he watched her reaction. When she didn't look away, he realized that she was waiting for him to go on. He sighed and rubbed his temples. "It's a hard life, Princesa. Constantly traveling. Constantly living out of a suitcase. Constantly wondering who to trust. The days and nights are switched. There are concerts and crowds and photographers everywhere. There is no such thing as privacy. You sell a piece of your soul when you become famous."

"That's a horrible thing to say!" she gasped.

But it's true, he thought. "The public owns you, Princesa. They love you. They hate you. They want to be you. They want to destroy you."

She stared at him, the color draining from her face. "Then why? Why do it?"

He shrugged. "It's the price you pay to do what you love to do."

"What's to love about it?" she demanded.

He smiled wistfully. "There is good, too. Music is the universal language. It changes lives. I love traveling, meeting new people. Before concerts, there are VIPs to meet. After concerts, there are parties to attend."

"VIPs? Parties?"

He shut his eyes for a minute, visualizing the large rooms with a bar in one corner and a DJ in another. Usually tall cocktail tables covered with white linens surrounded the perimeter of the room, the center space reserved for a dance floor. Meandering through the crowds, well-dressed servers wearing white gloves carried a never-ending stream of food to offer the guests. Oh, the food! Appetizers of shrimp and lobster and caviar. And the alcohol: champagne, vodka, cocktails, and wine. Alejandro usually didn't partake, sipping on his bottled water while the people clamored around, eager for a few minutes of his attention before the show was scheduled to begin. He had always vowed that he wasn't going to become one of those singers who partied before shows and delivered less than 100 percent onstage.

"VIPs: very important people. Sometimes, for political reasons, I have to meet with certain people such as mayors, congressmen, businessmen, promoters. Other times, people pay a lot of money to spend a few minutes with me."

This time, she laughed. "People pay money to meet you?" It sounded ridiculous when she said it or, rather, the way she said it.

He smiled at her innocence. "*Sí*, just to meet me. To shake my hand and have a photo taken with me." He paused, wondering how far to push the subject. Without giving it too much thought, he plunged ahead. "There are even women who cajole their way backstage to meet me."

The tone of his voice seemed to sober Amanda, and she stopped laughing. Clearly, she understood something was amiss with that last statement. "Women? Why?"

He cleared his throat. "Most of the time, Amanda, they want to spend the night with me."

The fact that he said it so casually must have startled her. She blinked for a few seconds as if trying to understand what he'd said. When she finally made sense of his words, the color drained from her face and her back stiffened. He had thought that the truth would get her attention. There were extreme differences between their lifestyles, and he needed to ensure that she understood that. No, he told himself. We both needed to understand that.

"That's disgusting," she said, breaking the silence.

Again, he shrugged. "I suppose."

His casual response stopped her, and she stared at him for a long moment. She was thinking and replaying what he had just told her. He knew what was coming and quickly tried to decide on his response.

"And do you?"

Bingo, he thought. He was as good as a mind reader. "Sí," he admitted. "Sometimes." Now she would know who he truly was, he thought. What his life was truly like. And she would no longer be so curious.

"Why?"

That one word took him by surprise. Why, she had asked. He wished that he knew the answer. He wanted to tell her that it was because he was lonely or because he was a man with needs. He wanted to tell her that he was attracted to those women. But that wasn't the truth. What was the truth?

"Because I can," he finally admitted.

She took a quick, short breath. For a moment, she looked away, avoiding his eyes, but he could tell that his words resonated in her head. *Because I can.* The meaning behind those three simple words left her visibly stunned, and he knew that she didn't want to imagine him being the type of person who lived that type of life. But when she finally did, she would know the extent of their cultural differences.

She lifted her chin and moved her eyes back to meet his gaze. "Would you sleep with me, if I were one of those women backstage?"

This time, it was his turn to be stunned. His mouth dropped open for a moment. Had she really just asked him that question? His thoughts of being a mind reader and sensing the predictability of people were shattered. He hadn't seen that question coming at all. "I . . ." he started but stopped. He wasn't certain how to respond to that. After all, he hadn't thought of her in that way. And he certainly hadn't expected her to even think in those terms. Let alone mention them! Yet she was staring at him expectantly, waiting for his answer. "I'm not answering that."

"Would you or wouldn't you, Alejandro?" she asked flatly, demanding an answer.

He rubbed at his upper lip and glanced away from her. He tried to imagine her backstage, tried to imagine her dressed like those women with short skirts and high stilettos. He couldn't envision her with long, flowing hair and makeup. It was just not something he could see. But she was still silent, her eyes on his face.

"No," he finally said.

"No?" She seemed disappointed.

"No."

"Why not?"

He rubbed his hand over his face. "*¡Ay, mi madre,* Princesa!* What are you doing to me?"

She frowned and appeared determined to elicit an answer from him. "I want to know why not. That's a fair question."

"No," he said sharply. "It's really not a fair question."

She remained silent, waiting for his response, her eyes narrow and piercing as she stared at him.

"Because I respect you!" he snapped.

He regretted the words the moment he said them. It sounded awful. He knew that. It was the truth. He knew that, too. And now it was out there, and he suddenly wished that Elias or Lizzie would emerge to interrupt their conversation. He had no idea where this was going and felt beyond awkward, sitting with this young Amish woman and discussing sex.

"I see," she said softly, her lips pressed tightly together in disapproval. Folding her hands on her lap, she took a deep breath. "So you spend the night with women you don't respect but won't spend the night with women who you do respect!" Put that way, it sounded as bad as he felt. Lifting her chin and squaring her shoulders, she said, "I'm glad that I'm one of those women who you wouldn't spend the night with. I'd hate to be treated so casually, like a discarded horseshoe! But I will tell you this, Alejandro Diaz. You should respect all women. Maybe then you wouldn't be so lonely on the road and spending your nights with strange women who you don't love."

He shook his head. "*Ay,* Princesa,*"* he mumbled.

"Maybe you could learn *that* from this . . . adventure, Alejandro," she said sharply.

"I think this conversation is finished," he said, standing up quickly, his knees creaking from having knelt for so long. He was sore from all of the work that he had done this morning. He didn't know why he was suddenly so irritated, and even worse, he wasn't certain if he was annoyed with her or with himself. Maybe, he wondered, she was right and that was what upset him. He was lonely, and he was tired of false friends and faceless lovers. He glanced at the fields one last time. "Do you need help with your laundry?"

He could tell that she was still upset about their conversation by the way she looked at him. He couldn't read her expression. Was she angry or disappointed? Either way, it was good for her to recognize how different they were. Him, too. Despite the fact that he was too aware of her natural beauty and intelligent wit, the truth was that he was leaving in a few days and his life on the road was the polar opposite to hers on an Amish farm. She needed to be reminded of that.

"Nee," she said and looked away.

"Amanda," he said quietly, waiting until she dragged her eyes back to stare at him. Her dark eyes seemed to bore into his soul, and he knew. She wasn't angry or disappointed. Instead, she was hurt. "You wouldn't like my world."

"Mayhaps not," she admitted. "Viper's world sounds most horrible, a world without love and respect. And it doesn't sound like the world for Alejandro, not the Alejandro that I know. But it doesn't seem like I need to worry about experiencing that world. It's not something that will happen, is it?" She bent her head down as she focused on folding the clothing as well as ignoring him.

There was nothing more he could say to her. She needed time to reflect on what he had shared with her and to realize that he was right. He sighed and turned around to walk away, realizing that he wasn't all too sure if he liked his own world, his planet, especially after he had seen it through her eyes.

Chapter Nine

Amanda leaned on the crutches as she stood at the edge of the garden. It needed weeding, that was for sure and certain. The sun was just over the treetops, the sky changing into a deep, rich blue that was almost matching the color of her dress. Carefully, she used the crutches for support, holding them halfway as she sat down on the ground, the cast sticking out from under her dress. She didn't care if anyone got angry with her. She was tired of sitting around the house. She wanted to help around the farm and, if nothing else, an hour of weeding would make her feel better.

The garden was coming along nicely. It seemed as if she had only planted it the other week, but she knew it was actually almost six weeks ago when she and Daed had plowed through the ground, fertilized it with some composted manure, and planted the rows of tomatoes, beans, beets, corn, and peppers. At the far end of the garden, she had even planted some watermelons and pumpkins. Her *daed* must have staked the tomatoes and beans while she was away in Ohio, for which she was grateful. Already, there were small green tomatoes just hinting at the possibility of turning red. Within a few weeks, they would have juicy red beefsteak tomatoes for dinner, that was for sure and certain.

And soon after that, they would be canning tomato sauce for the winter months.

But, for today, it was the weeds that needed tending.

When she had been younger, she had asked her *mamm* why God created weeds. It had seemed like it was already an awful lot of work to maintain a garden that was free from pesky weeds trying to strangle the good plants that would provide the family with vegetables to eat. Her *mamm* had smiled at her and explained, "It's God's way of making certain we appreciate what we have. The harder we have to work for something, the better it often is. This is the same with us people, Dochder. We have to weed our hearts and minds from ugly and ungodly thoughts in order to be welcomed in his garden, ain't so?"

It had been a good lesson to learn, Amanda realized, especially at such a young age. Life on a farm was fraught with hard work that reaped greater rewards. She had learned that early in life and had come to appreciate her *mamm*'s wisdom. It was the things in life that required hard work that meant the most to her. Ever since then, Amanda loved working in the garden. The feel of the dirt on her fingers, the smell of fresh growing vegetables, the sound of the quietness surrounding her . . . all of it made her happy.

Today, however, she was weeding more than the garden. It was the weeds in her mind that needed removing. She needed to be outside, close to nature and close to God. She knew that she was in great danger and the more she fought it, the closer it came.

She couldn't help herself. It was her fondness for Alejandro that was growing in her head and in her heart. A weed, she told herself, although her heart told her otherwise. She had never spent so much time with a young man. And from what she knew of the Amish men and the courting ritual, she might not know her own husband half as well as she already knew Alejandro.

With an Amish courting couple, it would be a buggy ride here, a walk there, maybe a dinner with the parents later in the courtship. No hugs, no hand-holding. Just companionship. Suddenly, that little bit of knowledge about the other person would lead to a marriage, a marriage that would span a lifetime filled with years to get to know each other.

No, Amanda couldn't deny her attraction to Alejandro. He was movie-star handsome, and his accent was charming. He had a sense of humor and was more than caring. Yet, she also sensed a darker side to him, the Viper side that was everything Alejandro was not. It was almost as though he was battling himself, suppressing the one side while fighting the other. She could tell that it didn't make him happy. How could it? Such inner conflict was certainly what had led him to stay at the farm for the week.

And, of course, he was an Englischer. Despite her attraction to him, she was smart enough to know that nothing could ever come of it. He was the epitome of worldliness, while she was the image of being plain. Those two worlds could never coexist.

As she pulled some of the weeds, her heart felt heavy. Even though he had confided in her about the ugliness in his world, she couldn't fight the attraction, the desire to help him be happy. He deserved it, she told herself. Under the Viper exterior, he was still Alejandro. Gentle, sweet, caring Alejandro.

By the time that she had cleared the outer row of the garden of its weeds, the sun was almost at its peak in the sky. It was warmer out, and she was sweating under the sun's heat. Looking back over what she had weeded, she felt disappointed. It had taken her a long time to clear that row, for she could only reach into the garden about eighteen inches. But there was still a lot more that needed to be cleared.

"There you are, Princesa," Alejandro called out as he walked around the side of the barn. He laughed as he approached her. "What on earth are you doing?"

At the sound of his voice, she looked up. "Weeding," she said simply. For a moment, she frowned. She could never understand why he always wore his sunglasses. They hid his eyes, and then she couldn't

Sarah Price

tell what he was truly thinking. Since their discussion the previous day, she had felt awkward around him, pleased that he respected her but confused about his other confession. "Why are you laughing?"

Casually, he squatted down beside her and knocked gently at her cast. When he looked at her, the sun reflected off the dark lenses, making his face seem ever more jovial and bright. Clearly, he had moved on from that discussion and was feeling at ease with her. That confused her, too. "You look silly with your leg jutting out so," he teased.

"I look silly?" she asked, color flooding to her cheeks. For a quick second, she saw herself reflected in his lenses. She did look silly with her blue dress and misshaped leg. Her hair was messy, stray wisps stuck against her sweaty skin on the back of her neck. She wasn't wearing her prayer *kapp*, just a thin scarf to cover her head. She was so common, so plain. It was no wonder that he was laughing at her. And now, she was blushing. She could feel the heat on her skin and tried to stand up. But it was almost impossible without the crutches, and they were tossed on the ground at the other end of the garden.

Alejandro jumped to his feet as he tried to steady her. As his hands touched her arms, she pulled backward and before she knew it, she toppled over and he fell to the ground beside her. Quickly, she sat up and pulled at the bottom of her dress to make certain her legs weren't too exposed as Alejandro got to his knees. He started laughing again, the sound ringing in the wind.

Running his fingers through his hair, he shook his head. "Oh, Princesa," he murmured, a smile still on his face. He reached out to touch her arm again, and this time she didn't struggle. Instead, she let him help her to stand. Catching her balance, she fell against him, and instinctively he wrapped his arm around her waist to make certain she didn't fall again. "You are something else." He paused. *"Dulce,"* he whispered into her ear.

"I don't know what that means, but I do know that you can let me go now," she said flatly, convincing herself that she meant it. Deep down, she really didn't. She liked feeling the pressure of his arm around her waist. She liked smelling his woody cologne. She liked simply being near him. But to say such things . . . *nee* . . . to even think such things was most un-Amish and definitely *verboden*, forbidden by the Ordnung.

She wasn't certain if he read her mind or not, but he hesitated, just long enough to whisper in a teasing tone, "I can, *sí?*" His breath was warm on her neck, and she felt her skin jump, like tiny shock waves.

"*Ja!*" she said forcefully, trying to avoid looking at him.

Chuckling to himself, he released her from his grasp. But the movement was too sudden, and she wobbled backward. "*Nee,*" he murmured. "I think not." Pulling her back into his arms, he stared down into her face and hesitated for a moment. His eyes seemed to search hers, but it was hard to tell since his were hidden behind sunglasses. Then, smiling once again, he said, "I think, instead, you should lean on me, and we will get those crutches together."

Giving in, she let him continue holding her waist as she hopped beside him. She knew that her cheeks were still brilliant red and that she was beyond embarrassed. Yet, at the same time, she felt more alive than she ever had before. He had laughed at her, whispered in her ear, and held her in a manner that made warmth spread throughout her veins. She had never experienced anything or anyone like Alejandro Diaz before in her life.

He was a gentleman, holding her gently, and when they stood before the crutches, he leaned down to get them for her. For a moment, he focused on helping her gain her balance, his expression serious until he was satisfied that she wasn't going to fall again.

"I'm fine," she said softly. Then, before she forgot her manners, she quickly added, "*Danke,* Alejandro.*"

"Your *mamm* sent me to find you," he explained, obviously aware of her discomfort. "It's time for dinner, she asked me to tell you."

Trying to act calm and collected, she nodded her head in acknowledgment before using her crutches to walk back toward the house. She could still hear him chuckling to himself as he walked behind her. She wished that she could glance over her shoulder at him, to see the expression on his face, and to let him know that she didn't find this funny. But, instead, she felt that warmth inside her veins rise again as she remembered him holding her, her chest pressed just enough against his to feel his heart beating beneath the soft fabric of his fancy Englische shirt.

"My word," Lizzie said when Amanda came in through the door. "What happened to you?" She hurried over to Amanda and began brushing the grass off her dress. "Amanda!"

"I fell," Amanda offered, her explanation curt and simple. She set her crutches against the table as she sat down on the bench. When she noticed her mother staring at her, she sighed and provided more details. "I was weeding the garden, and Alejandro helped me get up."

"Are you all right, then?" Lizzie fussed.

"*Ja, ja,*" Amanda said, forcing a smile that she didn't feel like sharing. She was still thinking about his arms around her. She had felt so warm and safe in his hold, even if only for those brief few seconds. It made her long for more time alone with him. "I just have to learn my limits, I reckon."

Alejandro and Elias walked into the kitchen, talking between themselves about plans for the afternoon. Amanda felt her heart jump as she saw the glow in her father's eyes. Clearly, he was enjoying having some male companionship around the farm. And from the looks of it, she realized, Alejandro was feeling just as relaxed around her *daed*.

"Might take a ride over to the Edwardses' farm later," Elias said after they had prayed. He picked up his fork and started to eat.

"You mean that Jake Edwards?" Lizzie said as she passed around the bowls of steaming potatoes and vegetables. She frowned. "Whatever for?"

"Thought Alejandro might like seeing some of his horses," Elias said, winking at Amanda. "I'd offer to take you along but . . ."

"But what?" she said, perking up.

"Not so sure with your leg and all," her *daed* said.

She slumped on the bench and scowled as she picked at her food.

Lizzie frowned. "That's an awful long ride just to see some horses."

Elias looked at Alejandro, ignoring Lizzie's comment. "This Edwards fellow moved here a few years back. Inherited his grandfather's farm. Breeds the most gorgeous Standardbred horses you've ever seen."

"We don't need any horses," Amanda said wryly.

"He was an Englischer," Elias added, ignoring Amanda's comment. "Married a young Amish woman, and they both joined the church later."

Alejandro raised an eyebrow. "Really? People do that?"

Lizzie looked up and, for the briefest moment, stared at him. Amanda noticed the look on her mother's face and saw her expression change. She was glad that no one else was looking at her mother for certainly they would have read her mind as easily as she had. "Not very often," Lizzie finally said, a serious tone in her voice. Her eyes flickered toward Amanda, and she held her daughter's gaze.

"Can't imagine just anyone could do that," Alejandro said, unaware of the unspoken conversation between Amanda and Lizzie. "It would be hard to leave the convenience of the world, *sí*? As peaceful as it is here, I can't envision many people being capable of doing it."

Lizzie lowered her eyes and picked at her food. She didn't seem to follow the conversation anymore. Amanda was too aware of her *mamm*'s silence, but after a few minutes, she shrugged it off. If her *mamm* was worried about Alejandro wanting to convert to being Amish, she was a long way off track. He was too much a product of the Englische world to give it up, that was for sure and certain.

Yet she envied him. Unlike most folks, he had the opportunity to straddle both worlds. Not many people could travel the world, entertaining millions of adoring fans, then disappear to the quaint peace and quiet of Lititz, Pennsylvania. She wondered what it would be like to experience *his* world, even if just for a few days. Her curiosity was piqued, and her mind wandered as the afternoon passed. She tried to imagine what life would be like in big cities, living in hotels and having people fawn all over her.

She was stretched out on the sofa in the kitchen, a basketful of thread at her side as she crocheted a blanket in various colors of blue. She hated the scratchy feeling of the blanket against her skin and kept pushing it onto the sofa. If she couldn't help around the house or outside in the garden anymore that day, she could at least keep busy with the crocheting.

"It's awful warm for crocheting that blanket, ain't so?" Lizzie asked with a look of concern as she sat down in the chair next to the sofa. "Mayhaps you should crochet something lighter, like a table runner or place mats."

Amanda shrugged. "Need to finish this one, Mamm. Might as well do it now while I have time." But she kept miscounting her stitches and having to pull out some of the rows. Frustrated, she shoved the ball of yarn and crochet hook aside, then leaned her head back on the sofa.

She needed to get out of the house, wanted to walk around or go somewhere. She was tired of not being able to move freely and at her own will. She wondered why her *daed* hadn't asked her to ride along to the Edwardses' farm, to see the horses and visit with his wife, Sylvia. Clearly, he was bonding with Alejandro, viewing him as a surrogate son. A wave of guilt flooded through her, and she reached for her crutches.

"Going to go lie down a bit, Mamm," she said.

She shut the door to the downstairs bedroom and sat on the edge of the bed. Her mind floated back to the conversation she'd had with Alejandro the evening before, and she flushed as she remembered how bold she had allowed herself to be. How could she have asked him that question? she wondered. And why did his answer bother her so much?

Covering her face with her hands, she tried to erase the memory. *Because I respect you,* he had said. That said so much about who he was as a man as well as whom he truly wanted to be. She had suspected that he was troubled, struggling with inner demons. Now she knew for a fact that he was staying at their farm for more than just a few days of relaxation. Indeed, it was a respite with the intention of searching for himself. Unfortunately, the more he searched for himself, the more she felt as if she was losing herself. Yes, she realized, she was losing herself to him.

Even when he had held her earlier, she had felt lost. She imagined it was the same feeling someone would have if she were drowning. Yes, that was how she felt, as if water surrounded her, embracing her and calming her in the very moment when she knew that, unless she could break free, she would be lost forever. Would she give in to the final hold of the depths of the sea or would she struggle to return to the only world she had ever known?

It was close to evening chores time when she heard the buggy wheels rattle down the driveway. Her heart began to flutter, and she quickly moved over to the dresser, picking up the small hand mirror in order to fix her hair and pinch her cheeks. Then, grabbing her crutches, she hobbled into the kitchen and, as quick as she could, she sat down on the sofa. Leaning back, she tried to look as if she had been sitting there for a while.

Her *mamm* was coming down the stairs when the men walked into the kitchen. She paused at the bottom step as they entered the room, laughing and smiling. Clearly, they had enjoyed themselves on their excursion to the Edwardses' horse farm.

"How were the horses?" Amanda asked, sitting up straight as Alejandro entered the room.

"Ay, Princesa,*"* he gushed, rushing over to her. *"¡Qué lindos!"* She frowned at him, and he laughed, kneeling before her. "Beautiful, just incredibly beautiful." He winked at her and playfully mouthed, *"Como*

tú." She didn't have to understand Spanish to know what he said. Immediately, she blushed and looked away, clearly thankful that her parents hadn't witnessed that tender moment. Her reaction delighted him. "I wish you could have gone. The young colts were running in the field."

Elias nodded, turning his attention to Lizzie. "Becoming quite a breeder, that Jake Edwards. He is training some *wunderbar gut* horses. Says he already has quite a waiting list for next year's foals."

"Expensive, too, no?" Alejandro added, twisting on his knee so that he was looking at Elias.

With a simple shrug of his shoulders, Elias agreed. "For sure, but a *gut* horse is worth it, *ja*? And cheaper than an automobile."

"I don't have to scoop up after my cars," Alejandro replied lightly, and they both laughed. He stood up and walked over toward the door that led to the section of the house where he was staying. "Now, if you will excuse me," he said. "I must check my messages."

Amanda stared after him, her heart pounding inside her chest. To him, it was teasing. She knew that, by now. But she felt different about his words and flirtations. That drowning feeling overcame her once again, and she tried to will herself to calm down. But she couldn't. Her heart fluttered, and her face felt flushed. She knew that the water was over her head, and for the first time, she realized that she was giving in to the feeling, allowing herself to fall even deeper into the dark, watery abyss that surrounded her.

Chapter Ten

Later that evening, as the sun set behind the fields, casting a bright mixture of colors against the blue sky, the crickets chirped from the growing grasses and the birds sang from the branches of the trees. The air had cooled, but there was still a layer of humidity. Still, it was pleasant enough that Alejandro asked to take Amanda for a walk down the driveway.

Elias was quick to grant permission, saying it would be right *gut* for her to get the exercise. Only Amanda noticed the look of concern that crossed her mother's face. But Amanda ignored it, eager to escape the house and more than happy to have an excuse to spend more time alone with Alejandro, this amazing *Englische* man who had captured her thoughts all afternoon. Perhaps even more than her thoughts, she started to wonder.

As always, Alejandro was the perfect gentleman. He walked next to her, matching her slow pace, for she was still adapting to using her crutches. He guided her as she carefully walked down the dirt lane that cut through the back of the farm.

Now the sky was changing colors. The more the sun set, the more the horizon darkened, the reds and oranges blending into grays, blues, and deep purples. A cool breeze blew from the northwest and rippled across the growing crops of corn.

As they walked—Alejandro, with his hands behind his back, and Amanda, focusing on avoiding holes in the lane—he asked her questions about growing up Amish in Lancaster County. Unlike the questions most Englischers asked on the few occasions she encountered them, during her recent summer trip to and from Ohio or at the market, his questions did not seem condescending. Instead, he seemed genuinely interested in learning about the culture and the religion.

"No electricity at all?" he asked.

She shrugged her shoulders. "Obviously, diesel-fuel-powered energy in the dairy for keeping the milk fresh."

He gave her a sideways glance. "But why, Princesa?"

The explanation was involved, too involved, and sometimes she didn't understand it herself. So she hesitated, trying to find a way to explain the rationale behind that decision. "Hmm," she said, still thinking. She could feel him watching her, those blue eyes drinking her in, and she felt the color flood to her cheeks. Lowering her eyes, she cleared her throat before speaking. "It's a connection, Alejandro. A connection with the outside world that isolates people. Without electricity, we have to work together, help each other with chores, and spend time together. It keeps us closer to each other and, by extension, to God."

From the way his expression changed, she could tell that he was contemplating her words, and when he nodded his head, she knew that he understood.

"It's like in Cuba," he said. "We grew up poor and didn't have much. So we spent time together and that helped create the ties of family."

Oh, how she wanted to know more. She wished she could see his memories and feel his experiences. It sounded so romantic: life on an island, surrounded by crystal blue water and festive music. She wanted to know what it was like moving to a new country and learning a new language.

"Tell me," she said. "Tell me how you feel about your life then, Alejandro."

Lifting one eyebrow and tilting his head, he smiled, but just slightly. She knew that most people didn't ask about his upbringing. In fact, she sensed that, in his world of music and travel and fans, he didn't have many people who cared about his past . . . only his future.

"You want to know about Cuba?" he asked.

Nodding her head, she met his gaze and felt the warmth of his appreciation for her interest in his culture, especially when so many people were curious about her own.

So he talked. He told her about growing up, first in Cuba, then about his days as a young Cuban teenager in Miami. His father drank a lot and spent most of their money on himself. Alejandro declared, however, that despite those flaws, he was a decent man. There was always food on the table, even if it wasn't good food. When his mother finally had enough of the drinking, she found a way to leave and bring her son to America.

He told her about living in Miami and how the streets became an extension of his home. "I learned to fight early," he said. "Survival of the fittest."

She didn't want to admit that she didn't know what that meant. Amish people never fought, unless they were small children, and even then, the consequences were so severe that it usually only happened once in their lifetime.

"My mother, *sí*? She worked several jobs and . . ." He paused, thinking. His eyes misted over, and she knew that he was remembering his youth. "Let's just leave it that there are things I did to survive that would not have impressed you."

"I wouldn't judge you! I told you that before," she gushed. In truth, what did her opinion matter? The final judge for each individual was God. "God forgives those who confess their sins," she added softly.

The lane didn't seem long enough as they came to its end, the continuation simply consisting of two ruts in the dirt where her *daed* regularly drove the mules and field equipment.

"Santa Barbara got me through some rough times," he said, his voice breaking the silence.

Amanda looked at him. "Santa Barbara?"

He reached into the front of his shirt and pulled out a gold medallion that was hanging from a thin chain. He kissed it once before showing it to her. "Santa Barbara," he said by way of introduction.

A frown crossed Amanda's face, and she refused to touch it, despite him leaning over for her to see it better. "What is that?"

"It's a medallion of Santa Barbara," he said as if she should know what he was talking about. But from the look on her face, he quickly assessed that she was not familiar with patron saints. "You don't know?"

"Is that part of your religion?"

"*Sí.*" He nodded, tucking the medallion back inside his shirt. "She protects us."

"God protects us," Amanda said quickly in response.

"*Sí,* God protects us," Alejandro agreed. "But he, too, can use some help from time to time, *sí?*"

Amanda looked away from him. She wasn't certain how to respond. After all, she had never heard of saints before, so she didn't want to insult his beliefs. Obviously, they both believed in God and Jesus Christ. Was it sinful to believe in something more? Did that dilute his love for God? Could it dilute God's love for him?

"I'd like to think that he has everything under control," she finally said.

"Hey," he replied, dropping his voice so that it was low. He stood in front of her and reached out to take her chin in his hand, gently forcing her to look him in the eyes. "There are many religions in the world, *sí*? Maybe there is more than one way to worship God."

"You aren't supposed to worship anyone above God," she said, meeting his gaze straight on.

He clasped her hand in his and smiled at her. "Not above God . . . I promise that to you." He leaned down to kiss her fingers before, still holding her hand, he looked around at the fields with the sun setting behind the house. "How can you doubt the magnificence of God when you see such an amazing sight as that?" he asked, gesturing toward the sky. "How many colors do you see, Amanda?"

She was taken aback because he rarely used her name. Since the first time they had met, she had been Princesa. But she liked it when he did use her name. Especially now, for his voice was husky and thick. She liked the way it rolled off his tongue. His accent made it sound beautiful, and she repeated it in her mind as if to hear it again and again: *Aman-tha.*

He looked at her, wondering why she wasn't answering. But she wasn't staring at the sky. Instead, her eyes were on him. For a moment, he met her gaze, and there were no words to express the unspoken emotion shared between them. He was struck by the feeling that flooded through him and squeezed her hand gently. It didn't surprise him that she squeezed his in return. But he turned his head back to stare at the sky. "I see every color in God's brushstroke. Red, blue, purple," he said.

"Yellow and orange," she whispered.

"Ah, *sí*, yellow and orange." He nodded. "Those colors are there, too."

A silence fell between them. He was lost in the moment, trying to understand what he was feeling. There was a beauty at the Beiler farm that he had not seen for many years, not since his early childhood in

Cuba. There was something magical about living off the land. It was pure and it was honest. And he missed it.

"Sing me a song."

Her voice was so soft that he wasn't certain he had heard her properly. *"¿Qué?"* he asked, asking her to repeat what she had said.

"I should like to hear a song from you," she whispered, avoiding his gaze for fear he might laugh at her.

But he didn't.

Instead, he began to sing in a low, soft, slow voice.

> *Arrorró, mi niña, arrorró, mi amor,*
> *arrorró, pedazo de mi corazón.*
> *Esta niña linda, que nació de día,*
> *quiere que lo lleve a la dulcería.*
> *Esta niña linda, que nació de noche,*
> *quiere que lo lleve a pasear en coche.*
> *Duérmete, mi niña, duérmete, mi amor,*
> *duérmete, pedazo de mi corazón.*

When he stopped singing, the last syllable seemed to float through the air, the melody lingering between them. He watched her as she stared at the sky. She hadn't moved while he was singing, listening to the words while her eyes took in the different colors of the sunset. Yet now that the song was over, he could see that there were tears in her eyes.

"You cry?" he asked, leaning over once again. "Why the tears?"

"Your voice," she said. She turned her head to look at him, her eyes large and full of emotion. "Oh, Alejandro, you sing like an angel!"

This time, it was Alejandro who felt the color rise to his cheeks. Over the years, he had heard many things about how he looked, how he danced, and especially about how he sang. But no one had ever been so moved by a song. And such a simple song, at that. "You humble me, Amanda."

"Tell me about that song," she whispered. "It sounds beautiful."

"It is beautiful," he said, reaching out to brush the tears from her face with his thumb. He couldn't help but stare at her, moved by her emotions from his song. "Beautiful. Like you are . . . on the inside and out."

She caught her breath. "Oh." *Beautiful,* he had said. The word echoed in her head, and she flushed. *Beautiful.* It was a word she heard in reference to sunsets and growing crops, not people. Indeed, no one had ever told her that she was beautiful. She had never even considered such a possibility. Lowering her eyes, she felt her heart quicken and her blood race. *He thinks I'm beautiful.*

"It is a lullaby," he said quickly, stopping her from protesting against his compliment and trying to shift the mood back to one of congeniality. He sensed that his compliment had thrown her off track, and immediately he regretted having said it. "My mother used to sing that to me when I was a child. She would tuck me in at night, and I would be upset about her leaving the room. It was just the two of us, *sí*? I didn't like to be separated from her at night." He paused. "I felt that I couldn't protect her if I wasn't with her. So she would sing me that song."

"What does it mean?"

He took a deep breath. Turning his back to her, he stared across the fields. His mother, he thought. No, he hadn't been able to protect her, not then. But at least now he was able to take care of her needs. He paid for everything: her apartment in Miami, her food, her clothing, her housekeeper. It was a man's job to protect and provide for his family. That was how he had been raised. Yet, when was the last time he had seen her? He felt a tug at his heart. He could still hear her voice as she sang the song to him in Spanish. Now he quickly translated it and sang it again, only, this time, in English.

Hush, my child, hush, my love,
hush, piece of my heart.
This pretty child who was born at daytime
wants me to take her to the candy shop.
This pretty child who was born at night
wants me to take her out for a ride in a car.
Sleep, my child, sleep, my love,
sleep, piece of my heart.

He glanced over his shoulder at her. She was moved. He could tell that much simply by how she was looking at him. There was a distance between them, and briefly he contemplated taking the three steps to embrace her. But he knew from the look on her face that doing so would be a bad idea. He knew from the pounding inside his own chest that doing so would be disastrous.

So, instead, he cleared his throat. "I suppose we should start heading back."

"Alejandro," she said softly.

"¿Sí, Princesa?"

"Danke," she responded.

"For?"

She looked at the sky. "For helping me see the sunset through new eyes." When she turned back to meet his gaze, he was struck by the depth of emotion in her eyes. He felt something stir inside him, and he took a deep breath. When she smiled, he realized that she was glowing. Such beauty, he thought and took a step backward.

"Anything for you, Princesa," he said and realized that he meant it. He took his place beside her as they walked back to the house, a comfortable silence falling between them.

Chapter Eleven

The temperature gauge outside the kitchen window was at nearly ninety degrees, and the humidity was thick. It had been a temperate summer so far, but the heat had rolled in overnight and everything felt thick and muggy.

"What do you think about making some ice cream later on this afternoon?" Lizzie offered as she started clearing the dinner dishes from the table. Instead of a large, hot meal, she had served cold cuts and applesauce, coleslaw and chowchow, anything that didn't require cooking on such a hot day.

Amanda looked up from where she sat at the table, one hand pressed against her cheek. Despite the heat and the beads of sweat that dotted her forehead, she gave her *mamm* a big grin. "Oh *ja*! *Wunderbar gut* idea!"

Lizzie laughed. "Somehow, I knew *you'd* say that!"

Alejandro leaned against the open door, the breeze from outside cooling him. It was hot outside, but it was even hotter inside the house. Despite the fact that the windows were open, the room was stifling hot. The thought of ice cream sounded good to him, but he had never had it homemade. "How do you make ice cream?"

"Freeze a cow," Elias said as he struggled to put his boots back on.

Amanda burst out laughing, and even Lizzie had to smile at the incredulous look on Alejandro's face. "You'll see," Amanda said, trying to stop laughing.

Standing up, Elias grinned at Alejandro. "You Englische. So gullible." He chuckled. Walking to the door, he placed his right hand on Alejandro's shoulder. "I'm headed out to the field to check the fence line. You're welcome to join me or hang with the womenfolk."

"Fence it is," Alejandro said, glancing over at Amanda and winking at her. "Had enough canning to last me a lifetime the other day. Easier to work outside in the fields."

"Shh," Elias said. "Don't let them figure that one out or they'll be out in the fields and we'll be stuck in the kitchen."

"Now, Elias!" Lizzie scolded. "You go on and check that fence, if you must. No need to tease so!"

Amanda stared at the door, long after the two men left. She wished that she could join them outside, but it would be too hard to walk the fields with her crutches. Yet she longed to be alone with Alejandro, even if only for a few minutes. Her heart felt heavy, and she sighed, knowing that it was only a matter of time before he left for good. He had his own world to return to, whereas she knew that she was already in hers.

"Don't be getting too attached," Lizzie said, breaking the silence.

Amanda looked up, surprised to find her *mamm* staring at her. "I don't know what you mean," Amanda replied, a little too quick in her response to sound truly unaware of her *mamm*'s meaning.

Wiping her hands on a towel, Lizzie moved over to the table. "I can see that look on your face, Amanda. Won't do you no good to get fancy ideas," she offered gently. "He won't stay, and you can't leave."

Amanda grimaced at her *mamm*'s words. "You are imagining things, Mamm."

"I am, *ja?*" She reached out and touched Amanda's hand. "He's an Englischer, Amanda. And from what I can see, a very different one at that. You, however, are Amish."

"And from what I can see, very different at that," Amanda added defiantly.

"*Ja,* different, but still Amish." Her voice remained stern. "Your *daed* might be missing Aaron and seeing something in Alejandro that just ain't there, too. I fear you both are in for some heartache." She stood up. "Sooner he leaves, the better. Was a mistake having him stay here," she added as she turned back to her work, the conversation clearly over.

It didn't matter. Amanda had nothing to add. She knew her *mamm* was right, but she didn't want to admit it. They had been so grateful for everything that he had done that no one thought of the impact Alejandro's presence would have on the family. But the damage was done, and Amanda's heart felt heavy.

It was three hours later when Elias and Alejandro returned from working in the field. They were laughing as they walked up the porch steps. Amanda had moved over to the sofa and looked up as she heard them approach. Despite it being midafternoon, it was still hot inside the house. She lifted her hand to her head, touching her hair to make certain it was still under her prayer *kapp*. Her *mamm* was at the stove, standing in front of a big silver pot and hadn't noticed the subtle move.

"Looks like rain," Elias said as he removed his hat and placed it on the peg on the entrance wall. "Will give us a break from the heat, that's for sure and certain."

Lizzie nodded but didn't say anything. She was cutting curds to make cheese and needed to concentrate. "Rain is *gut,*" she finally said.

Then, looking up, she addressed Elias as she motioned to the stove. "Need to pour that into the mold, Elias. Would you mind?"

But it was Alejandro who hurried to help her. "Let me," he said. When he saw her hesitate, he smiled. "I would like to help," he added. Amanda wondered if he sensed her *mamm*'s apprehension, the slight shift in her comfort level with his presence in their lives. If so, he was doing a good job of breaking through her guarded shield.

Elias sank down into the chair next to Amanda as Alejandro followed Lizzie into the canning room where she would pour the curd into the cheesecloth and put it into the cheese mold for pressing. Elias removed his boots and leaned back, shutting his eyes. For a moment, he stayed like that, relaxed and quiet.

"You want the *Budget* to read, Daed?" Amanda asked, leaning over to pick up the paper and hand it over to him.

"Nee," he said, opening his eyes. "But *danke.*"

He glanced around the room. Through the windows he could see dark clouds rolling across the sky, blocking the sun, and the room had suddenly gotten darker. "Best be lighting the lanterns, *ja*?" He stood up and hurried over to the lantern over the kitchen table. On the wall by the refrigerator were a strike pad and a metal box. He reached inside for a match and struck it against the pad, using the flame to light the kerosene lantern. With a soft poof, followed by a gentle hiss, the room became suddenly awash in a bright glow.

Lizzie and Alejandro returned to the kitchen. She noticed the lantern was on and quickly turned to peer out of the window. "You're right about that rain, Elias. Best be making that ice cream before it starts!"

She hurried to the counter where a large bowl with a custard mixture was cooling. She had started preparing it earlier, knowing that Amanda would want to show Alejandro how they turned it into ice cream. "Alejandro," she said, "if you open the refrigerator door, I have a big plastic bag with ice all ready."

He did as he was told while she poured salt into a measuring cup. "Now, pour this over the ice."

"*¿Sí?*" he asked, taking the salt and opening the plastic bag. "Salt over ice?"

Lizzie didn't respond, as she was focused on pouring the custard mixture into smaller Ziploc bags. Amanda watched from the sofa for a few moments before she swung the cast down and reached for her crutches. She was tired of feeling helpless, and the next part was always her favorite. Lizzie took the larger bag of salted ice from Alejandro and opened it in order to put the four smaller bags inside. Then she shut it and handed the bag to Alejandro.

"Shake," she said.

"Shake?"

Amanda laughed at his expression. "Shake. You know how to do that, *ja?*"

He lifted an eyebrow at her sassiness and smirked. "I've been known to shake some in my day," he quipped. "But only onstage." He began to shake the bag from side to side, his eyes still holding her gaze. "Good?"

"*Nee!*" She leaned against the counter and reached out. "Let me show you how the Amish shake," she teased back, ignoring the tense look on her *mamm*'s face. Instead, Amanda took the bag and began rolling it back and forth in her hands so that the custard moved consistently against the cold ice. "Like this."

"*Ay, mi madre,*" he exclaimed, looking at both mother and daughter. "That's not shaking! That's rolling!"

Again, they laughed, and Lizzie took a deep breath. "Less chatter and more shaking, or rolling, or whatever you call it, if you want some cold ice cream after supper," she replied, leveling her gaze at Amanda, an unspoken warning in her eyes.

Elias waved his hand as if dismissing Lizzie's words. "It's *gut* to hear laughter in the house, Lizzie. Been too long," he mumbled, shutting his eyes as he rested his head against the back of the chair. "But a little less noise is just as *gut*, I reckon. Might take myself a nap before evening chores," he added.

By the time the rain rolled in, the plastic bags of custard had turned into a soft batch of vanilla ice cream. A cool breeze blew into the kitchen from the windows, and then the sound of rain pelting against the house immediately created a peaceful change in the room. It was going to be a lazy afternoon with little chance of going outside, Amanda realized.

Alejandro excused himself, explaining that he wanted to check some messages and send some e-mails before his cell phone ran out of battery. As he disappeared through the door that connected the two houses, Amanda found herself resenting her broken leg that made it so hard to move around and escape the ever-increasing watchful eye of her *mamm*.

An hour later, she found her chance. The rain had stopped, and Elias was still napping. Lizzie had looked out the window and sighed. "I hate to do it, but I need to run to market," she said, lowering the plain white curtain back in place. She glanced over at Elias. "Hate to wake him; he's been working so hard."

"I'll tell him if he wakes," Amanda offered.

"Won't be gone but for an hour . . . if that," Lizzie said, scurrying to collect her purse and hurry out the door.

Amanda listened for the horse and buggy to rattle down the driveway toward the road before she reached for her crutches. Her *daed* was still snoring, and she knew that, should he wake up, he wouldn't think twice about her not being there. Carefully, she walked toward the door that divided the two houses, and after a quick glance over her shoulder to make certain her *daed* was still sleeping, she quickly passed through and shut the door behind her.

There was a passage between the two houses, and she paused at the door, knocking once. Her heart raced inside her chest. She wasn't certain what she was going to say when he opened the door. She was acting on an impulse. It was a new feeling for her, and she wasn't sure about how to deal with it.

There was no answer.

She knocked again and reached for the doorknob. When he didn't answer, she opened the door and peeked inside. It was dark, but she could still see since the sun was starting to peek through the storm clouds that had rolled in earlier. He was standing in the kitchen, his back to her, and dancing. She shuffled inside the door and shut it behind her, her eyes transfixed on Alejandro. He hadn't responded to her knock at the door because he wore earbuds attached to his phone.

She had never seen anyone dance with such fluid movements, such grace and sensuality. The way he moved, his hips rolling from side to side, caused a blush to rise to her cheeks. What was it about Alejandro that made her so quick to feel embarrassed and yet, at the same time, totally unable to walk away?

"¡Ay, Princesa!" he exclaimed when he turned around and saw her watching him. He lifted his hand to his ears and removed the earbuds. "I didn't know you were there!"

"Obviously," she said softly.

There was a moment of awkward silence. Neither one knew what to say.

"You want to listen?" he finally offered, crossing the room until he stood before her. "It's one of my songs."

She lit up. "Really?"

Gently, he placed each earbud in her ears. He fumbled with the device in his hand, and suddenly her head was filled with music, fast-paced and heart-stopping music. The beat of the music pounded against her ears, and she jumped backward, as if trying to escape the noise. Alejandro quickly clicked a button on the side of the device, decreasing the volume, and she relaxed, lifting her eyes to stare at him as she heard the music, softer now.

And then she heard it.

His voice.

He was singing, his words fast and in rhythm with the music. Most of the words she could not make out, and she wasn't certain whether he was singing in English or Spanish. But she did know that she felt the passion of his words inside her chest. Shutting her eyes, she listened to the words and the music, feeling her body sway in unison with the beat. When the song ended, she opened her eyes.

"Oh, Alejandro," she breathed, her words barely audible.

"You like?"

"I think I do, *ja*," she whispered as she took the earbuds out.

He laughed. "You think?" He accepted the earbuds from her and held them in his hands. "That's a first. Most people either love it or hate it."

"I've never heard anything like that," she said quickly. "And how you dance . . ."

"*¿Sí?*"

She stumbled over her words. "I don't think I could ever dance like that."

"Probably not, with a cast on your leg," he said. He hesitated, setting the earbuds and iPod onto the top of the table, and then he approached her. "*¿Permiso?*" he asked as he reached out his arms for her. "May I?" he repeated in English.

She didn't answer but looked down at his hands. He placed one hand on her hip, and then he gently pulled her closer. His stomach brushed lightly against hers, and he held her there. With his other hand, he touched her free hand and let his fingers entwine with hers.

"Like this," he said, moving his feet slowly, careful to hold her upright until she gained her balance.

"Oh," she whispered, uncertain of her movements and feeling awkward with her cast. It made any kind of graceful sidestep impossible. "I'm not good at this," she said, trying to pull away. She could smell his cologne, feel the tightness of his muscles, and sense the danger in his touch. She had to get away from him.

"No, no," he said, his voice low, as he tightened his grip on her. "You just are not used to it." He began to hum softly and moved his body in time with the tune. "Just follow my lead," he murmured, lowering his chin so that his mouth was beside her ear. "Slowly," he said. "Slow."

"Alejandro," she said, wishing that she knew what to say. His arms held her so close, and she felt her own heart pound inside her chest. She had never been so close to a man before, and despite her own willpower, she liked it. "I . . . I . . ."

"*¿Sí, Princesa?*" he responded, his voice barely audible. She didn't have to look to know that his eyes were shut. He was listening to music that only he heard. He seemed to fold her body against his, the pressure from his chest and hips tight against hers. "*¿Qué quieres?*" he murmured.

"I really should go back before my *mamm* returns," she blurted out, hating the words as soon as she uttered them.

Gently, he released her. For a moment, there was a guilty look on his face. "I'm sorry, Amanda," he said. "I forgot, for a moment."

In that instant, she knew. She knew that it was time for him to return to his world. For all of the energy and life that he instilled in the farm, and in her, he was too much of the other world and needed to return. Whether he knew it, she was well aware that he missed it. Even if there was an attraction between them, and that she could not deny, she was also well aware that nothing would come of it. Nothing but more heartache.

She reached for her crutches and shuffled back to the door. "Supper will be ready in a short while," she said, refusing to look at him. "Mamm went to market, and when she returns, we'll sit for supper." She didn't wait for a response before she slipped through the door; fighting the tears that started to flood her eyes, she hurried back to the other side of the house.

Chapter Twelve

On Saturday evening, Elias had invited Alejandro to attend the church service on the following morning. "You might like it, being that you're into singing and all," Elias said.

"I might just take you up on that," Alejandro had replied, glancing across the dinner table at Amanda.

"It's long," she had warned him, her voice a soft whisper. "Three hours."

"Not too long for thanking the good Lord," Lizzie had reprimanded.

Amanda had rolled her eyes, but only so Alejandro could see.

Now, he stood in the doorway, watching Amanda as she paced in the grass just off the farthest edge of the porch. Over her dark-blue dress she wore a white organdy bib and apron. On her head, instead of her usual white one, she wore a black, heart-shaped prayer *kapp*. Her face was scrubbed clean and shone in the early morning sun. The length of the dress did not hide her cast completely, and she leaned on the crutches as she waited for everyone.

She presented a pretty picture, and he enjoyed watching her, especially since she sang to herself, completely unaware that she was being observed. He listened to the tune and tried to see the music in his head. It flowed slowly but with an interesting beat. Her voice was light and airy, each note ever so sweet to his ears.

"What do you sing, Princesa?" he asked as he approached her.

When she turned around, startled by his presence, she didn't speak. Instead, she stared at him as if seeing a stranger. He suspected that she was taken aback by his perfectly tailored suit jacket and crisply pressed shirt, a reminder that he was not Amish, but an outsider given the honor of accompanying her family to worship.

"Princesa?" he asked, reminding her to answer him.

"I'm sorry." She shook her head as if clearing away her thoughts. "What did you ask me, now?"

He laughed and crossed over the porch to her side. "The song. What were you singing?"

"Oh!" she exclaimed, color flooding her cheeks when she realized that he had been watching her. "It's one of our hymns."

"Elias mentioned that you sing. I'm interested to hear your hymns."

Amanda laughed, her eyes sparkling. *"Ja,"* she said. "We all sing a lot."

"I grew up in the Catholic church. They sing, too." He leaned forward and added, "A lot."

"I'll be interested to hear how the two services compare," she replied, a teasing tone in her voice.

At that moment, Lizzie emerged from inside, shutting the door behind her. It was close to eight o'clock, and the church service started at nine. Elias had told him that they liked to get there by eight thirty in order to greet their friends and welcome the other members. Amanda was quick to add that most of the young people arrived closer to nine. Alejandro suspected that when Anna was home, Amanda would drive with her after her parents, enjoying the unusual treat of having extra time at home alone and delaying the three-hour church service.

Elias and Alejandro helped Amanda into the back of the buggy. Her leg felt uncomfortable. She had to sit sideways in the back. Alejandro sat next to her, his own legs pulled up toward his chest so that he didn't touch her cast for fear of hurting her. As the buggy lurched forward, he swayed over and his arm brushed against Amanda's. She blushed and turned her head to look out the back of the buggy window.

The ride was silent, except for the humming of the wheels and the horse's hooves hitting the macadam in a rhythmic melody. Alejandro shut his eyes and listened. It was music indeed. The beat sank into his memory, and he found himself forming words to go along with it.

She reached out and touched his arm. When he opened his eyes and looked at her, she frowned as if to ask him what he was doing. But she didn't have to ask the question. He knew. Smiling, he leaned over and whispered, "I'm making a song from the beat of the horse's hooves."

"A song?" she whispered back.

He didn't have time to answer as her *daed* pulled into another farm, the lane already littered with other buggies. Men were congregating around, talking, and catching up on the latest news. Alejandro stared out the back window, feeling a little more than foolish for having said that he would attend. Clearly, he was an outsider. Despite having known that feeling for much of his life, he suddenly felt trepidation about being among so many Amish people.

"Don't worry," she whispered and placed her hand on his. The gesture startled him, and he stared down at her hand. Then he looked up and met her gaze. Her dark eyes seemed to dance at him as she smiled. "They don't bite," she said quietly.

He caressed her hand with his thumb and squeezed gently. There was something so charming about her tenderness and caring for his feelings. He wasn't used to such true empathy. In his world, the women cared only for themselves and what they could get out of him. They wanted to advance their careers in modeling or dancing, or just in hitting the tabloids by attending an event, clinging to his arm. Once he tried to get to know most of them, they were shallow and empty shells of people, devoid of true intelligence or spirit. They were quite unlike Amanda, who lived for ice cream and hummed while she waited for people.

He leaned over, his lips almost brushing her ear, and whispered, *"Danke."* When she blushed, he couldn't hide his mischievous smile. "I don't bite, either." He winked at her.

As soon as Amanda emerged from the buggy, she was lost in a sea of people. Women clamored around her, helping her into the farmhouse where the church service would be held. At the door, she glanced over her shoulder and searched through the Amish men for Alejandro. He was easy to spot as he didn't wear a hat and his suit was different. Their eyes met, and he waved his hand, just enough so that she would know he was going to be fine among the Amish men.

"Come meet some of the community," Elias said, clapping his hand on Alejandro's shoulder. "They'll be curious to know about you, now!"

The men were lingering in the barn, most of them having unhitched their horses and tying them up near hay bags that the host family had provided. If Alejandro felt out of place, it wasn't noticeable. Immediately, he began talking with two men whom Elias had introduced to him, laughing with their jokes and stories. When he glanced around at the other men, it was clear that this was community time, a day to unwind and share with one another after a long week of working in the fields, farms, and shops.

"So I hear you have a knack for running over young Amish girls in the city," one of the older men teased.

"Dat's gut! Keeps our young folk from wanting to leave the farm, that's for sure and certain," the other man joined in.

Alejandro smiled and shook his head. "I assure you that it was a once-in-a-lifetime event," he said. "Wasn't intended, and certainly was a blessing that she wasn't hurt worse."

Elias placed his hand on Alejandro's shoulder. "Took *wunderbar gut* care of our Amanda, and that is a blessing, too."

The first man, Jonas Yoder, tugged at his graying beard. "Funny accent, that," he said, peering at Alejandro.

"I'm from Cuba."

Several other men seemed to be listening but were reluctant to join the two men who stood near Elias and Alejandro. Jonas frowned. "Cuba, you say? Not familiar with that town."

Alejandro laughed. "It's a country, not a town." He noticed that the men were watching him, waiting for more details. "It's an island south of Florida."

"I take it you're not a farmer, then," Jonas said, obviously curious about Alejandro's background. It wasn't often that strangers came to church, especially ones who wore fancy suits and spoke with thick accents from another country.

Elias chimed in and explained, "He's a singer." Several eyebrows were raised, and a few men nodded their heads. "Performs in different countries, he says."

"*Ja vell,*" Jonas said. "You'll hear singing today. Might not understand it if you don't speak German, though."

It wasn't until a few minutes before nine that the men began to move toward the house. Alejandro stayed near Elias, following his lead in order to stay as inconspicuous as possible. Clearly, that was impossible. He stuck out among Elias's neighbors, and he noticed that the women were not nearly as warm and welcoming as the Beilers. Most of them eyed him suspiciously as did most of the younger men and children.

Inside the house, he noticed that the women were standing in the kitchen, forming a semicircle. Several younger ones had just arrived and moved through the circle, shaking hands and kissing the other women on the lips in greeting. Once they stood at the end of the circle, Alejandro noticed that several men moved away from the group of

Amish men and moved toward the women, shaking hands and greeting each one individually.

Once those men were finished, they walked into the large gathering room, which was really three rooms with dividing walls that had been opened, and sat in chairs that were situated in the middle of the room. There were two rows of six chairs in the center, facing each other. Several men sat in those two rows. Behind the chairs were rows of hard benches. After the first men sat, the older women walked into the room and sat on the benches to the rear of the room. The men then walked into the room and sat on the other side. Once they were situated, the young unmarried women sat behind the older ones. Only then did the unmarried men enter and sit on the benches behind the other men.

Alejandro watched the progression and orderliness with amazement. He had followed Elias into the room and had sat down behind the chairs. Elias had whispered to him that the men sitting in the chairs were the leaders of the church district as well as the man who owned the farm where the service was being held.

The room was silent, no noise, not even from the small *kinner*. Without warning, the men simultaneously reached up and took off their hats in perfect unison, sliding them under the bench where they sat. Some of the men in the back of the room were able to reach up and hang theirs on hooks that were nailed into the walls. More silence.

And then the singing began.

Alejandro listened to the music, so pure and natural. The words flowed smoothly. One man would sing a word, dragging it out for almost thirty seconds in a specific melody that only the Amish knew. When he was finished with the word, the rest of the congregation would pick up and sing, each word stretched out in the appropriate melody, the unison of their voices breathtakingly beautiful. Elias joined the men, clutching a chunky book in his hand. When Alejandro looked at the book, he saw that it was written in High German, the words almost impossible to read. Yet the Amish not only could read it and understand it but also sing it.

Alejandro felt at a disadvantage since he could only listen to it.

Still, the music emanating from the gathering touched his soul. He found himself shutting his eyes, listening to the sound. It was haunting and ancient, reminiscent of years of suffering and perseverance. He didn't have to know the words to understand that much. He knew the history of the Amish from having researched it back in New York City. He understood that they had suffered as much at the hands of the Catholic Church as his own people had suffered at the hands of the government. Like the Anabaptists, his own mother had fled the country, taking Alejandro to the safety of America so that they, too, could live their lives in the manner they wanted, without fear of persecution.

Were they really so different after all? he wondered.

When he opened his eyes, he saw that she was watching him. Her mouth was moving, but her voice was lost in the sea of others, singing. She didn't have to look at the book in her hands to know the words. She held his gaze, and he felt something move within him. For the longest time, he couldn't tear his eyes from hers. The music, the people, the feeling of spirituality. He had never felt so close to God as he did at that moment, seated on a hard bench, listening to hymns in a language whose words he did not understand but whose meaning he could truly sense, and staring at a young woman he knew he could never have.

Amanda could not help but stare back. She was mesmerized by his expression, so full of grace and peace. She knew that he came from a different world. Just looking at him was a reminder. The way he dressed, the way he walked, the way he held his head up so high and shoulders back so straight. He was so confident, a true man of the world. Yet as she had watched him, she realized something: despite his worldly lifestyle, he was also a child of God.

When he sat on the bench, with his eyes shut, she could tell that he was listening to the sounds of the voices singing together in unison of the glory of God and the frailty of humankind. The path to heaven might be narrow, she thought, as the song said, but she also wondered if Alejandro had been correct. Just as there was more than one way to worship God, perhaps there was more than just one path that led to heaven. It was a moment of clarity for her, and she realized that Alejandro had helped her to comprehend it.

After the service, Alejandro helped the men set up the room for the noon meal. The men lifted the benches into holders so that each was quickly and easily transformed into a long communal table. Then he placed himself beside Elias while the congregation bowed their heads in silent blessing.

Amanda stood near the kitchen, knowing that she would be exempt from her normal job of helping to serve the food. With her leg in a cast, she certainly couldn't maneuver between the three long tables. Instead, she leaned against the wall near an open window, the breeze helping to cool her down as the day was becoming quite warm. She took advantage of the organized chaos of the post-service fellowship meal to collect her thoughts.

She couldn't help herself from watching him. Wherever he was, her eyes were drawn to him. He was magical, the special way he blended in despite being an outsider. He seemed to ignore the fact that others considered him as such. It was a role he had played many times before in his life. He was comfortable in even the most uncomfortable situations. His movements were smooth and calculated. He never seemed to take a misstep or stumble. Unlike the younger Amish men, Alejandro wasn't awkward, insecure, or unsure of himself. Instead, he was always calm and confident, even when surrounded by a group of strangers, and Amish men at that.

He sat next to Elias, speaking with the menfolk around them. He ignored the fact that some of the men were initially uncomfortable having an Englischer in their midst. His charm and humor quickly won them over, and she could see that the ice was slowly melting. Without his dark sunglasses covering his eyes, it was obvious that he radiated poise and positive energy. There was a new glow about Alejandro since he had come with her to the farm. He was experiencing an aspect of life that she understood had been missing from his own for quite some time. Without the cell phones, the crowds, and the commitments, Alejandro was allowed to be himself. And he was clearly enjoying it.

"Glad to be home, then, *ja*?"

Amanda turned to the young woman in the green dress, one of her friends, who stood at her side. "Oh *ja*," she said. "Ohio was nice, Katie, but was I ever so glad to come home!"

"Was sorry to hear about your accident," Katie said.

With a shrug of her shoulders, Amanda smiled. "God has plans for us that we sometimes can't explain."

"I wonder that," Katie replied. Her friend's eyes scanned the tables of men eating. "Is it true that he's a famous singer?"

It took Amanda a moment to comprehend what Katie was asking. Famous singer? "Alejandro?"

Katie's eyes shifted back to Amanda, and she made a face. "Who else, goose?"

"I reckon; not that I know his songs," Amanda said.

"What's it like?" Katie asked, her voice lowered and her eyes sparkling. "Having *him* stay at your farm?"

Amanda laughed. "Like a person staying at the farm." She frowned at her friend, despite still smiling. "What are you getting at, Katie Miller?"

"He's a handsome Englischer." Her friend pursed her lips and stared down her nose at Amanda. "Mayhaps your sister Anna's not the only one who found a beau on this trip, ain't so?"

The directness of Katie's comment startled Amanda. How could her friend even suggest something like that? "Katie Miller! He's an Englischer!"

"Plenty of Amish women have left for Englische men," Katie said lightly. "I just hope you aren't one of them," she added with a giggle. With that, Katie hurried away to make her rounds with the pitchers of water to refill the glasses of the people who were at the first seating for the noon meal.

With her mouth hanging open, Amanda stared after her friend. She hoped that other people weren't thinking the same thing. It was true that Amanda wasn't courting anyone in the community. But she hadn't had a lot of time, especially after her brother, Aaron, had died. She had needed the time to grieve, and then, after the grief subsided, if such a thing were truly possible, she had thrown herself into helping her *daed* on the farm. No one had pushed her, at least not until recently when her parents suggested that both daughters visit relatives in Ohio.

Yet despite her own self-denial, Amanda knew that she had to fight harder to hide her feelings toward Alejandro. Was how she felt becoming so transparent? She knew that nothing would come of her friendship with Alejandro. Their worlds were simply too different. She wasn't about to leave the Amish community, and he was too involved in his world—his own planet, as he sometimes referred to it, to consider joining hers.

Lowering her eyes, she turned away and, using her crutches, hurried over as best she could to the kitchen sink to help wash the dishes, hoping that work would move her mind toward a different direction.

Chapter Thirteen

At first, the movement was subtle. There was a casual turn of some heads as they strolled through the town of Intercourse, Alejandro walking patiently next to Amanda, who was moving slowly on her crutches. He caught these looks from the corner of his eye. Then he saw the whispering and a few people stopping in the midst of what they were doing. People were noticing them. No, he corrected himself. *Noticing me.*

Earlier that morning, he knew that it was time to return to Miami. The next few months would be busy, an endless stream of appointments in Los Angeles before his winter concerts on the West Coast and the holidays. Before he knew it, January would roll around and it would be time to prepare for his upcoming South American and European tours. Knowing this, he had wanted one last drive through the backroads, a final chance to observe the peace and quiet before he returned to his life as Viper, a life filled with meetings, travel, interviews, and concerts.

To his surprise, Amanda had asked if she could come along. Before her *mamm* could object, Amanda had even suggested that they could stop at the store on the way back to pick up some groceries for the house. Besides, she argued, she was perfectly able to use her crutches now and Alejandro could help her into and out of the car.

"That might not be such a good idea, Amanda," Alejandro had said slowly, not wanting to hurt her feelings.

"Why? I'm quite mobile with the crutches, and I'm tired of being housebound," she said defiantly. "We could get some ice cream in the center of town. It's so hot, anyway." She rubbed at the back of her neck. "Vanilla ice cream from Lapp's farm? What could possibly be better?"

Elias and Lizzie had exchanged a glance, another one of those looks that could only pass between couples who've shared many years of married life. Alejandro saw it and knew enough to step back and let them figure out how to respond. While he didn't mind Amanda's company, he wasn't certain it was the greatest idea. Only ten days had passed since the accident and, despite their friendliness, Alejandro wasn't quite certain how they felt about Amanda being alone with him. He had noticed, however, that they tended to cater to her few requests. She wasn't demanding and she was rarely unreasonable, a quality he had noticed about her in the hospital and one of her traits that he truly admired.

To his surprise, Elias finally nodded his head. "I'll agree, but on one condition," he said. "Only if you take the horse and buggy. No need for calling that fancy car."

"I could use some fresh fruit and flaxseed from the store," Lizzie surrendered reluctantly.

Alejandro's jaw dropped. "The buggy?"

Elias clapped him on the back as he headed toward the door. "Welcome to the Plain ways," he said with a big smile across his face. "Let's go harness the mare. Might do you some good to stop relying on all that worldly technology."

An hour later, Alejandro had helped Amanda into the buggy. Feeling cramped and out of his element, he sat next to her in the buggy, watching as she took ahold of the reins. "You sure you know how to do this?" he asked suspiciously as she slapped the reins on the horse's back and the buggy lurched forward on the driveway.

She laughed at him. "Don't be silly. I've been driving horses since I was a young girl." She glanced at him from the corner of her eye. "Mayhaps I'll even let you drive a bit, *ja?*"

"Nee," he had replied teasingly. "You can be in control this time, *sí?*"

But now, as she hobbled on her crutches toward the village where she wanted to stop at a fabric store before purchasing her ice cream, he felt the start of a murmur in the crowd behind them. He could sense it without seeing it. There were just a few younger people in the summer crowds, but he knew it took only a few to start the wave of interest. Cell phones would begin ringing, texts would circulate, and suddenly . . .

It was half an hour later when the crowd began to thicken. If the movement was subtle in the beginning, now it was becoming much too obvious. Alejandro tensed and closed in around Amanda. "We need to leave," he murmured in her ear.

"I thought we were going to get some ice cream," she said, turning to look at him. Clearly, she was unaware of the energy that followed them. Unlike him, her inexperience with the public made her immune to what was happening. "What's wrong, Alejandro?"

"It's time to go," he said firmly and put his arm around her back, guiding her as best he could since she was using the crutches. "Where is the buggy?" he asked, looking around. He had lost his sense of direction in the village of small shops.

"Look, that's him!"

Alejandro took a deep breath and braced himself. And so it begins, he thought, waiting for the inevitable. Several young girls came running over, pushing themselves between him and Amanda. Before he knew it, there were more people gathering, and despite trying to be polite, he felt his pulse race. He could see Amanda struggling to keep her balance with the crutches as the crowd pushed her back, separating them from each other. Amanda frowned, looking up at him, her eyes large and frightened as more people wedged themselves between the two of them.

"Excuse me," he said, his voice stern and loud as he tried to make his way toward her. But the crowd was too large. And then, he saw it. Someone shoved Amanda, and she fell against a large man, who, when he whirled around, knocked her to the ground. Immediately, Alejandro pushed people aside, not caring if he was too rough. He had to get to her, to help her, before she was hurt, or worse, crushed.

"Amanda! *¿Estás bien?*" he asked, his voice thick with concern, when he finally reached her.

When she looked up at him, he saw that her face was washed of all color; she pleaded with her eyes for him to get them out of the crowd. He frowned, cursing himself for not having foreseen such a scenario. He had thought he'd be anonymous in Intercourse, Pennsylvania, where God and country music were tied as the number-one hits. But fame, while a blessing, was also a curse. There was no anonymity for the famous. Hadn't he preached that to her, earlier that very week?

Without a moment's hesitation, he scooped her into his arms. As he turned in the direction where he thought the buggy was parked, he felt her press her face against his chest and cling to his neck, hiding her face from the people and the cameras. He also felt something wet against his skin. She was crying. Not caring that he left the crutches on the ground, Alejandro carried her through the people. His face was strained, and he didn't smile for the cameras.

And the cameras were out. Cell phones were lifted, snapping photos of "Viper" carrying the young Amish woman in his arms. He knew that, within minutes, the photos would be littering the social media websites. Not good, he told himself.

When he found the buggy, he struggled to open the door. She was still in his arms, and he couldn't balance holding her with opening the buggy door. He was surprised when he felt a hand on his shoulder and a man stepped forward to help him. He was an older man but clearly not a tourist. "Let me help you get her in. My son picked up her crutches and put them in the back," the man said.

"*Gracias,*" Alejandro said as they helped Amanda slide into the buggy. Quickly, he shut the door and turned around to face the crowd. His expression showed his displeasure, but he managed to control his temper, refusing to address them. He had learned many years ago that one slip of the tongue became a sound bite that would circle the world many times over before he even realized what he had said. Straightening his jacket, he excused himself as he pushed through the people and hurried to the other side of the buggy. He remembered to untie the horse before getting inside and taking the reins.

"Keep down, Princesa," he commanded.

"You don't know how to drive horses!" she said, her voice cracking and tears in her eyes.

"Thanks for pointing that out," he replied sharply and pulled back on the reins, clicking his tongue. He didn't care if anyone was behind the buggy. He needed to get Amanda away from the crowd and back to the safety of her home. Once clear of the hitching post, he slapped the reins on the horse's back and steered the buggy through the parking lot and away from the people.

He turned on the main road and hurried to the first street where he could turn. He needed to get as far away from the main street as possible. He quickly navigated the side streets, getting farther and farther away from the center of town. At one point, she laid her hand on his arm and pointed to the left, indicating that he should turn there.

When they were far enough away that they were fairly certain no one had followed them, Alejandro exhaled heavily. In fact, he realized that he had been holding his breath for a while. "That was close," he said. He glanced at her. "Too close."

"What happened?"

She was staring at him, and he took the moment to see the panic in her face. In her world, she had never experienced the crush of a flash mob. He had and, despite years of dealing with it, was still not used to the feeling of powerlessness that came with being crushed by adoring fans. It was at that moment that he realized the danger that faced her. Worse, he realized it was all because of his selfish motives. He had wanted to escape, but instead, he had brought the enemy to her doorstep.

"You wanted to experience my world," he said, his voice breathless and husky. "I think you just got your first taste."

"What were they doing? What did they want?" she whispered.

"Amanda, you can't be seen with me," he said gently. "I told you that there is a dark side to fame. You just saw it." He exhaled. "I have to leave. They won't let you alone if I'm here."

"I don't understand," she said, her eyes pleading with him for an explanation.

He shook his head, angry with himself. "I should have known better. I just thought that we'd be safe out here."

She touched his arm again, and he slowed the horse and buggy. "Alejandro?"

"I have to leave," he repeated abruptly. He pulled the buggy to the side of the road and looked at her. "It's time, Amanda." He paused and turned to face her. "Not tomorrow, not later. But now."

"No," she said softly, her lips pouting.

"What happened back there," he said, gesturing with his hand in the direction from which they had just come. "This will only get worse. They know that I'm here."

She shook her head. "Why do they do that to you? Why do they care?"

"You can't understand, Amanda," he sighed. "I'm a product." He hesitated. How could he explain this to her? An idea came to him. "Every year, you see hundreds of thousands of people come to your town because they are curious about the Amish, *sí*?" She nodded. "They come to learn about you, to buy things in stores that are Amish, to take your picture. That is no different with me. Except, in my world, I have to permit that and welcome it."

He could see that she was digesting what he said. Slowly, she understood and lifted her sorrowful dark eyes to look at him. Gone was the sparkle that he had grown so used to seeing. "I don't want you to go," she whispered.

He placed a finger on her lips and nodded his head. "I came here to make certain you were all right. I also came here to escape, Amanda," he said. He hated how he saw the pain return to her eyes. If only he could make it go away. But the truth was what was needed. "You knew that I couldn't stay forever, Princesa. That was never part of the plan. This is your world," he said gently. "Not mine." He wiped the tear that fell from her eye. "It's time, *sí*. I have to go to Los Angeles for some work before my trip to Europe. You know I have concerts there." Six countries in ten days, he thought. He dreaded it, especially now. Being shuffled from one country to another, never having a good night's sleep, always being hidden in a hotel room until it was showtime. It wasn't the life he had imagined when he started this game.

"Will you return?"

He laughed. "Eventually. I don't plan on staying in Europe forever." Then he sobered, realizing that she meant more than returning to the country. She sounded so innocent when she asked. He almost forgot that she was a grown woman. It dawned on him that she was actually asking if he would return to Pennsylvania. To Lititz.

He sighed, trying to find the right way to tell her the truth. "I have six concerts in different countries through ten days, Amanda. It will be a very strenuous couple of weeks." He looked around the farm. "Not like this week. I needed this break," he said. She was looking away from him, trying to hide the tears that were starting to flow freely from the corners of her eyes. "No, no, none of that, Princesa."

"You won't come back," she said, immediately understanding what he was saying, despite the fact that he didn't say it.

The story of his life, he thought. And then, the words slipped from his lips, "I'll come back. I promise." At that moment, he felt as though he meant it, but in reality, he knew it was impossible. The past few days had been a present, arranged for him by his manager, Mike. He'd never have that amount of time again, not without his entourage and his endless commitments. Not if he wanted to remain on top of the music charts and in the minds of his fans. "I'll try," he said quickly, trying to correct himself but not believing the words as he spoke them.

"It won't be the same . . ." she started but stopped midsentence.

"What won't be the same?" he asked gently. Her eyes, wet with tears, were hurting him. He had always been weak against tears. It reminded him too much of the pain that his own mother had gone through during her years as a single mother, struggling in Miami to raise him.

Amanda lifted her eyes to his, and he was immediately engulfed in the depth of her brown eyes. So dark, so beautiful. "Alejandro, how can I court any Amish boy after having this experience?" she asked, the candor of her words cutting through the unspoken but rising tension in the buggy. She bit her lip, then added what she really meant to say: "After having this experience with you?"

Courting? The word echoed in his mind. Was that what she thought? That he had been courting her? *"Ay, mi madre,"* he mumbled but not unkindly. Instead, he realized how unfair he had been to Amanda. He was used to such a different world, a world of fast women and easy living. Amanda, however, was so pure, so innocent, and so prone to a broken heart. "I'm so sorry, Amanda," he said. He reached for her hand and held it in his. "I never meant to hurt you," he whispered as he raised her hand to his lips and kissed it. "A courtship between us cannot happen, Princesa," he heard himself say, hating the words as they fell from his lips. "You know that."

"Why not?" she asked.

"I could never be Amish," he said, his voice flat and matter-of-fact. She needed to hear the truth; there was no way to sugarcoat it.

Amanda blinked her eyes rapidly as if to force back the tears. He could see that more were on the brink of falling. "I want to experience more, Alejandro. I want to know what it would be like," she whispered.

This was the moment, he thought. She was staring at him, the sparkle in her eyes dimmed by tears. Yet her lips were pouting enough to make him forget himself. He forgot that he was seated inside a buggy, an Amish woman sitting next to him. Instead, he saw just the pure beauty of a woman. He glanced around to make certain that they had not been followed before he held the reins of the horse in one hand and leaned forward. He put his arm around her neck and pulled her closer, letting himself get lost in the moment. Of all the exotic women he had known in his life, he knew that none of them matched the passion of the woman who was sitting next to him.

He let his lips brush gently against hers, hating himself the moment that it happened. Don't, he heard his inner voice screaming. But he couldn't help himself. Instead, he murmured, "Dios mío." Amanda's inner beauty had a stronger pull on him than his own moral strength. Once his lips touched hers, he was no longer able to hold back. He pulled her closer and crushed her against his chest. He could feel her petite body pressed against him, and he knew that he was beyond stopping. Rather than try, he held her tightly and let his mouth cover hers for what he would forever remember as the most passionate kiss of his life. She gave back in a way that was innocence and passion wrapped into one.

Her hands pressed against his chest, and she squeezed his flesh, a return gesture of his desire. He let a low groan escape his mouth as he trailed his lips across her throat and tasted her skin. She was fresh and salty, a perfect blend of country. His hand traveled up the back of her neck and tugged gently at her hair. The pins fell free easily, and before he knew it, her hair hung loose down her back. It smelled sweet like lavender, and he pulled it forward to bury his nose against the scent.

"*Ay*, Amanda,"he moaned. "I can't do this," he said, despite wanting the opposite. Grasping her hair in his hand, he pressed it against her cheek and compelled her to look at him. "It's not right." He forced himself to pull back and stared into her face, pressing his hand against her cheek. "You can't come to my world," he whispered.

"Why not?" she asked, her voice soft and her eyes demanding answers.

Her words echoed in his head. *Why not?* He didn't know how to answer that. There were a thousand wrong reasons why she could come to his world, and he realized, only one very good reason why she shouldn't. He shook his head. "You'd hate me," he offered. "You'd find reasons to hate me for taking you there. It is an ugly world and not worthy of someone as good as you. My world is not like here."

"But I'd be with you," she countered.

Her sincerity and the way that she looked at him could have convinced him. For a moment, he imagined bringing Amanda on tour with him. Everything would be new and exciting to her. He'd get to see the world through new eyes. But then, other images flashed before his eyes. The women, the concerts, the crowds, the parties. Being together was not reason enough, he told himself.

"You wouldn't be *here*," he replied. "And this is where you belong. This is where your life is, Amanda. It is not with me. Not on the road, not with the paparazzi and the fans. You would never survive."

She tensed in his arms and pulled back. A dark shadow crossed over her eyes, and she became tense. "I can survive anything," she said.

He held her hand and caressed it. Her young skin was so soft. In his mind, he thought of the other women who had been in her position.

Wherever he traveled, he surrounded himself with beautiful women who spent their time with one goal in mind: how to remain beautiful. Their days were spent shopping, working out, applying makeup, and fixing themselves up to attract his attention at the clubs or concerts.

He tried to imagine Amanda in such a situation and knew that it would never work. She'd be swallowed up by those women, despite her own natural beauty and innate goodness. Her heart wasn't hardened like theirs. And even though he felt a strong attraction to her, he wasn't going to be responsible for ruining this young woman. Not Amanda.

"Let me take you home," he said softly as he brushed his fingers across her cheek. She reached up and touched his hand, holding it against her skin. The gesture tugged at his heart, and he leaned down, gently touching his lips against hers one last time. "It's time to go," he whispered. He didn't wait for a response before he took the reins in his hands and urged the horse to continue on its way. She sat quietly by his side, staring out the window with tears in her eyes. There was nothing left to say.

Back at the farm, Alejandro helped her out of the buggy. He had his arm around her waist as he led her toward the house. She walked slowly, knowing that this was the end. He was leaving, and despite his promise, she knew that she would never see him again. His kiss lingered on her lips, and she felt as if her heart would break into pieces.

"What happened?" Lizzie asked as she opened the door to let them in.

"I must leave," Alejandro stated. "They know that I am here."

"Who?"

He helped Amanda inside the house as he answered her. "The media. It won't take long for them to find me here, so it is better that I leave before that happens."

"I don't understand what you mean," Lizzie responded, staring at her daughter, who was still visibly upset.

"The people in town," she whispered. "They were crowding Alejandro and pushed me aside." It wasn't a lie, but she knew that it wasn't the truth. How could she tell her *mamm* what she was really feeling in her heart? How could she tell her *mamm* that Alejandro's leaving their farm made her feel as though her life was over?

Alejandro helped her inside before disappearing through the door to the *grossdaadihaus*. Within minutes, he had packed the few items that he had and was waiting on the porch for his driver. Amanda clung to the porch post, watching him with tears in her eyes. Lizzie and Elias stood behind her, not understanding exactly what had happened, but it wasn't in their nature to question his decision to leave so abruptly.

When the black car finally pulled into the driveway, Alejandro turned to Elias and shook his hand. "I cannot thank you enough for allowing me into your lives," he said. "I won't forget my time here."

Elias nodded. "You are a *gut Schaffmann*. Don't forget that." His voice was strained, and Amanda could tell that he was as sad as she was that Alejandro was leaving so quickly.

Lizzie let him embrace her, and she smiled at him when he thanked her for her hospitality.

When he turned to Amanda, he removed his dark sunglasses and gazed at her. Despite the fact that her parents were standing behind her, he reached out and brushed her cheek with his hand. She shut her eyes and felt the warmth of his touch. "From now on, you look both ways crossing the streets, Princesa," he whispered, with a smile not reflected by the sadness in his eyes. He leaned over and gently kissed her forehead, an innocent gesture, but he sensed Lizzie's discomfort.

The driver was waiting for him. With nothing left to say, he picked up his bag and hurried toward the car. He didn't look back as the driver shut the door behind him. He refused. There was nothing more to say or do at the Beiler farm. Alejandro knew that his stay was over and it was time to return to the world of Viper. Looking back would only make the transition that much harder.

Chapter Fourteen

"Elias, something's wrong," Lizzie called out. She was standing at the front door, looking outside at the men who were leaning against a car in their driveway. She looked over her shoulder, her face pale and her mouth pressed together in a tight grimace. "There are quite a few people here, and I don't have a good feeling about them."

Elias came down the stairs. He was pulling up his suspender straps as he walked. "What are they doing?"

She stepped away from the door and let him look for himself. "Englischers. I think they have cameras." She lowered her voice so that Amanda wouldn't hear. "They've been taking photographs of the house."

"What on earth?" he exclaimed. Opening the door, Elias walked outside. "Can I help you fellows with something?"

Amanda propped herself up on the sofa. She had been lounging around all day, tired and bored of not being able to move at will. Her mind continued to replay her last moments with Alejandro. On more than one occasion, she had hidden her face into the side of the sofa and wept, as softly as possible so that her mother wouldn't hear.

Now, with her mother staring out the window and her father calling out to strangers, she found something to divert her attention. *"Wie gehts,* Mamm?" she asked.

"*Nichts* for you to worry about, Dochder," Lizzie replied gently as she stood at the door and watched Elias call out to the men by the car. But the men didn't respond. Instead, they simply pointed their cameras in his direction and started taking more photographs. One of the men even approached the house and called out something that Lizzie couldn't understand. But that was all that Elias had to hear before he quickly turned around and hurried back into his home.

As he shut the door behind him, he glanced at Lizzie, then looked over at Amanda. "Seems like it might be a hot day today," he said, hurrying over to the window by the kitchen sink and pulling down the green shade. The room was immediately enveloped in darkness. "Might want to shut those other shades to keep the sun out."

"Who are they?" Lizzie whispered.

"I don't know."

Amanda watched her parents move about the room, shutting window shades. She knew that something was happening outside and that they were trying to shield her from knowing what it was. But she had her own secrets.

Amanda had not told her parents the true extent of the scene at the village just the day before, neglecting to mention that a mob of Alejandro's fans had shoved her and that she had fallen to the ground. Nor had she told them the real reason why Alejandro had left so abruptly. She shut her eyes and leaned back against the sofa, remembering the kiss that they had shared. For a moment, she almost felt the tears come to her eyes once again. Her heart fluttered in her chest as she wondered if she'd ever hear from him again.

For the rest of the afternoon, Lizzie and Elias seemed to hover nearby. They were looking outside on a regular basis and continued to frown, their expressions showing concern when they lowered the shades. Amanda tried to take a nap but couldn't. She was too distracted by her thoughts and her parents. When it was close to the hour for evening chores, Amanda watched as her father left the house, his hat pulled over his head and his shoulders hunched over as though he was dreading leaving the house.

"What is it, Mamm?" Amanda asked once again.

Lizzie didn't answer, her silence indicating that Amanda didn't need to know.

"May I at least help with supper, then?" Amanda asked, pushing herself up and reaching for her crutches. It took her a few seconds to steady herself on her feet before she hobbled over to the kitchen counter.

"You're supposed to be resting," Lizzie scolded.

"I've been resting all day," she replied. "It's boring. I need to move around."

A deep sigh and a gentle shake of the head showed Lizzie's displeasure, but she didn't say anything else. She knew it was impossible to stop Amanda when she had her mind set on something. "I'm going to get some canned beets and chowchow in the cellar," Lizzie said. "You can pour the applesauce into bowls."

Amanda waited until her mother left the room before hurrying over to the door. Slowly, she opened it, careful not to hit her leg with it as it swung backward. She peeked her head out first, looking around, and quickly noticed the strange car in the driveway. Englischers? That surprised her. Englischers never visited, and from what she quickly surmised, they had been there for a while. She wondered if that was what had bothered her *mamm* and *daed* all day. If they didn't want anything, why didn't they leave?

Curious, Amanda used the crutches to help herself walk down the porch steps, moving along the path toward the car. No one was in it. She imagined they were in the barn with her *daed*. She started to move toward the barn when she heard her *mamm* call her name from the door. "Get back inside, Amanda!" Lizzie yelled.

That was when the two men quickly emerged from around the side of the barn. They ran toward her, taking pictures and following her as Amanda quickly tried to get back into the house. They walked alongside her, the cameras pointed into her face. They were so close that she could hear the click, click, click of the photos being taken. And then they began to ask her questions.

"When did Viper leave?" the one man asked.

"Can you tell us why he stayed here?"

The questions seemed to attack her faster than the clicking of the cameras.

Amanda shook her head and tried to look away, but they stood in her path. "Leave me be," she whispered.

"When is Viper coming back?"

Amanda felt a hand on her arm and was relieved to see her father. He guided her away from the men, sternly telling them to get off his property. But the men didn't seem to care. They continued taking photographs and following them. Elias was strong enough to push his way past them and managed to get Amanda back into the house.

Once inside, she sank down into a chair at the kitchen table. Her hands were shaking, and the blood had drained from her face. For a moment, she thought back to the day when Alejandro had taken her from the hospital to the waiting car in order to return to Lititz. The photographers had been just as invasive and persistent. She hadn't understood it then. She understood it even less now. But the overwhelming feeling of fear overcame her, and she started to cry. When Lizzie hurried over to hug her, Amanda pressed her face against her mother's shoulder and sobbed.

Lizzie looked up at Elias, her eyes wide and desperate. "What do they want?"

Elias shook his head. His face was pale and his eyes worried as he glanced at his daughter. "I think they want Amanda."

A shocked look crossed Lizzie's face. "Why?"

"They were asking her about Alejandro," was all that Elias could think to reply. He rubbed his hand on his forehead and glanced at the door. It was shut and locked, something that they never had to do before. He walked over to the window and moved the curtain slightly in order to peer outside. "I've never seen such aggressive Englische! They won't get off the property."

"What do we do?" Lizzie asked, rubbing Amanda's back to help calm her down.

"If they don't leave, we may have to get help," Elias said.

By late morning the next day, there was no sign of the car in the driveway, but Elias still seemed tense. It was clear that neither Lizzie nor Elias had slept much during the night. They had even insisted that Amanda sleep back upstairs, despite the stairs and the heat. She hadn't minded. In fact, she had taken comfort knowing that she was in the room next to her parents. The two men with the cameras had upset her, and she didn't want to be alone downstairs.

Amanda decided not to go outside, insisting on working on a quilt instead of helping with the outdoor chores. Even with her broken leg, she could have helped her *mamm* with hanging laundry or even weeding the garden, but neither of her parents seemed intent on asking her to do much of anything. It was clear that everyone was on edge from the invasion of privacy. It would take some time for them to return to feeling comfortable and safe.

During the noon meal, Lizzie shared a letter that had arrived that morning from Anna in Ohio. The mood started to lift in the room as they speculated that Anna would not be returning at all. It was clear that she had begun courting someone, although Anna never came right out to admit that. Instead, it was implied. What would have been a joyous occasion seemed sullied and overcast by the events from the previous day.

By early evening, when the tension was beginning to lift from the house, Lizzie sat down with Amanda to look at the quilt that she was bent over. A simple nine-patch for a wall hanging. "Your quilting stitches are quite fine, Amanda," Lizzie said approvingly.

Compliments like that were rare, and Amanda forced a smile. But she didn't feel like smiling. She also didn't feel like quilting. She didn't feel like doing much more than staying in bed and feeling sorry for herself. She missed the life and vitality that Alejandro had brought to the farm. It had been far too long since the house had felt so alive. The death of Aaron had drained the farm of laughter and life. Alejandro had returned it. But now that he was gone, it seemed he had taken it away with him.

"They're back," Elias said as he hurried through the door. He shut and locked the door behind him, his eyes scanning the room to see if the windows were open. "Shut those windows and blinds, Lizzie."

"Who's back?" Amanda said, setting the needle and thread down on the quilt. "Those men?"

"*Ja,*" Elias replied as he pulled the green shades down over the windows by the kitchen counter. "And there are more of them."

"More?" Amanda asked, her eyes wide and the color draining from her face.

Lizzie stood against the counter, wrapping her arms around herself. "How many?"

"Six, I reckon," Elias said.

"What do we do?"

The question was simple, but the answer far too complex for anyone to answer. Elias stared at Lizzie, the silence speaking far more of the challenges that faced them than if he had tried to respond. Without going to the authorities, there was no stopping the photographers. Amish didn't press charges. Amish didn't use the police. Clearly, the men in the driveway knew that and felt safe trespassing. Yet Elias couldn't continue to allow these men to trespass and disrupt their lives. Something would have to give.

"Mayhaps I need to seek out the bishop," he finally said.

The thought of being left alone at the farm with those men lingering and lurking outside did not sit well with Amanda. Without her father, it would only be her *mamm* to protect them both from the intruders. It was apparent that the men were not shy about being overly aggressive. "I suppose we couldn't all go," she mentioned.

"You'll be all right here," her *daed* said, although everyone in the room knew that he was not as convinced as he sounded.

When Elias went outside to hitch up the horse and buggy, Lizzie peered through the window and watched. She refused to let Amanda see what was happening. Instead, Lizzie shook her head and gasped more than once, tsk-tsking, with tears falling down her cheeks. When the buggy finally rattled down the driveway, she hurried to the door to double check that she had locked it properly.

"Why are they here, Mamm?" Amanda asked.

"I just don't know, Dochder," Lizzie responded. She was shaking and tense, clearly anxious about being alone without Elias at the farm.

For the next hour, they sat quietly in the kitchen. It was dark with the shades drawn, and Lizzie didn't make a move to light the lantern. Amanda tried to quilt some more, but she kept unthreading the needle or missing the quilt lines. Giving up, for she didn't feel like quilting anymore, she shut her eyes and tried to rest. She hadn't slept well the night before and was tired. But even now, she was too tense to nap. Her *mamm* alternated between trying to read the Bible and peeking out the window. Amanda didn't need to ask whether the men were still out there. She could tell by the tight expression on her *mamm*'s face that the intruders were still in the driveway.

By the time they heard the buggy return, Amanda couldn't help herself from scurrying to her feet and reaching for the crutches. She moved over to the window and peeked outside as she stood next to her mother. Three buggies rolled into the driveway, and to Amanda's horror, she also noticed that there were more than six men out there now, all with their cameras pointed at her father, the bishop, and one of the ministers. They ignored the photographers as they hurried to the porch. Lizzie quickly unlocked the door and let them inside.

The bishop's face was tight and drawn. Clearly, he was displeased. He removed his hat and stared at Lizzie and Amanda. "I am sorry for your troubles," he started. "Elias told us what has been happening here." He glanced at the other man, David Yoder. "I wouldn't believe it if I hadn't come to see for myself."

"How do we get them to leave?" Lizzie pleaded, her voice cracking with emotion.

The bishop pursed his lips and shook his head. "I hesitate to say it, but I feel that we must contact the Englische authorities to have those camera people removed from the property. That is all that we can do," he said.

"Perhaps having their law enforcement chase them away will be enough," David Yoder added hopefully.

Elias merely shook his head. "I just don't understand why they are here," he said.

The men decided that David Yoder would leave to visit a neighboring farm that had a telephone to contact the police. When he left the house, they could hear the noise of the crowd that littered the driveway outside. It wasn't until they heard his horse pull the buggy down the driveway that everyone seemed to exhale in relief.

Still, there was a tense silence in the room while they waited. No one knew what to say or do. Lizzie and Amanda sat on the sofa, holding each other's hands, staring at the bishop. He felt their apprehension and moved over to a nearby chair.

"Perhaps we should pray together," he said.

Elias stood by the table, his head bowed as he listened to the bishop recite from the Ausbund:

> *With fear and distress I call unto you,*
> *O God, be my Grantor now,*
> *And stand by me securely,*
> *Through Jesus Christ our Lord,*
> *Because I am put to the test.*
> *The kingdom suffers violence,*
> *The way, O Lord, is narrow,*
> *Whoever would receive it,*
> *Must indeed pray and fast.*

It was almost thirty minutes later when two cars pulled into the driveway. Amanda could hear the tires spinning against the gravel and a whooping sound from outside. Police cars. The bishop and Elias hurried to the window, blocking Amanda's view of what was happening. Her heart raced inside her chest. She wished that she could see, too, but that was impossible, especially with the bishop in the room. It would be too disrespectful for her to join them at the window or ask them to step aside.

Patiently, she waited while she sat next to her *mamm*. Time seemed to stop. Amanda glanced at her mother and saw that her eyes were squeezed tight. She was rocking slightly, and her mouth was moving. She was reciting a prayer, but Amanda couldn't tell which one. The bishop and Elias remained positioned at the window, watching without saying a word.

Almost twenty minutes passed before they heard the footsteps on the porch and a brisk knock at the door. Elias was the first to move toward it. The door creaked as he opened it and invited the two officers inside.

Their presence seemed to fill the room. Amanda felt her chest tighten at the sight of the two uniformed officers standing in the kitchen. Her glance fell to their sides, where each wore a holster and a pistol. The scene was surreal, and she reached for her *mamm's* hand again.

The taller officer nodded his head at the ladies but spoke directly to Elias and the bishop. "The men are moving off your property. We have instructed them that they are trespassing."

"Why are they here?" the bishop demanded.

The second officer glanced in the direction of the two women and cleared his throat. Clearly, he was uncomfortable. "It appears that your daughter has become a person of interest to the media."

The room seemed to spin around Amanda, and for a moment, she thought she might faint. *Person of interest?* The words ricocheted in her head. She had no idea what that meant, but it was obvious that it was not a good thing. Why would anyone be interested in her? How on earth could she, a plain Amish woman, be a *person of interest?* And to whom?

"I don't understand," Elias admitted.

The first officer tried to explain. "Apparently, she has some sort of relationship with a celebrity. A singer named Viper."

"There's no relationship!" Lizzie said.

"He's no longer here," Elias added quickly.

"Yes, but the media is here, and that's the problem," the officer said empathetically. He paused and glanced at Amanda again. She was staring at him, her eyes wide and frightened. "Your daughter's *association* with this singer has elevated her to quasi-celebrity status." The way he said the word *association* irritated Amanda, and she caught her breath.

Lizzie squeezed Amanda's hand. "There was no relationship!" she repeated urgently. "He just brought her back from that New York place after she was in the hospital."

"I understand that," the officer said as he took a deep breath. "However, the association between Viper and your daughter has gone viral, I'm afraid."

Elias and Lizzie looked at each other, then back at the officer. "Viral? A sickness?" Elias asked.

"Not like that," the office said gently. "I don't want to alarm you, but there are photos and stories being published in the news, on television, and all over the Internet." He shook his head apologetically, then turned his attention back to the men. "There isn't much we can do about the attention. Just hope that it dies down, Mr. Beiler."

"You mean this will continue?"

The bishop frowned. "You told them to leave the property. They must go away, *ja?*"

The officer lifted his hands, a gesture of uncertainty. "We can hope they will go away. But the law is clear. As long as they are not trespassing on private property, there isn't much we can do."

From the expression on the bishop's face, Amanda could tell that he was angry. "They cannot just keep printing their stories!"

"Actually, they can."

"That's an invasion of privacy!" Elias said.

"She has turned into a quasi-celebrity," the officer repeated. "The laws are different. She has become a limited public figure, and as such, the media can publish stories and her photo."

"The stories aren't true, if they say there was a relationship!" Lizzie replied, shaking her head from side to side.

The officer raised his hands, palms up in defeat. "Unless you wish to file a lawsuit, they will continue to publish whatever they feel will sell their papers. And, again, the laws are different for quasi-celebrities. Once you are in that category, they can basically say anything they want. It's the bad side of freedom of speech," he explained.

Amanda felt the tears start to flow down her cheeks. She lifted the edge of her black apron and dabbed at them. "They don't have my permission," she whispered, her voice cracking as the words escaped. "That's not right."

The officers stood there, uncertain of what to say. For a long moment, the room was silent. The clock ticked in the background, the sound reverberating throughout the kitchen. Amanda felt her chest tighten again and found it hard to breathe. Her heart fluttered, palpitating as she realized that this was exactly what Alejandro had meant when he told her that his world was ugly and not good. She reached up and pressed the palm of her hand over her heart. The pressure helped calm her.

"We will continue to monitor the situation," the officer said. "If they trespass again, you should alert us. Have a neighbor call if you don't have a phone. But short of hiring a lawyer and seeking legal advice, there isn't too much we can do. There just aren't any laws that are being broken. We can only hope the attention disappears quickly."

The second officer nodded. "The interest is likely to die down in a few days or so."

"Days?" Elias gasped in disbelief. He looked at Lizzie. "Will they stay off the property, then?"

The officer shrugged. "Perhaps. They might venture onto the property, then leave again, knowing that the Amish won't press charges. It will be touch-and-go until they lose interest." He reached into his shirt pocket and pulled out two white cards. Handing one to the bishop and one to Elias, he said, "My number is on the card. Please use it if they come onto the property again. I'll have my officers keep an eye on them, see if our presence helps to persuade them to leave." He took a deep breath. "We can hope for that to happen sooner rather than later."

After the officers had left, the bishop stood for a long moment with his back turned toward the Beilers. He was staring out the window, the shade now elevated so that sunlight shone into the kitchen. No one spoke as they watched him, waiting to hear what he would say. As the leader of the community, it was the bishop who would guide them through such a crisis. They were counting on his wisdom.

"Bishop?"

At the sound of Lizzie's voice, he turned around. "I suggest we pray on this. The Lord gives us tests. This is surely one of them." He ran his hand over his face and sighed. "It would have been better if that Englischer had not stayed here. But we cannot undo what has been done." He walked over near the sofa and sat down in the chair. "Let us pray before I leave," he said and lowered his head for a silent prayer, shared with the family.

Chapter Fifteen

Alejandro sat at the table on his patio by the pool, sipping at a steaming mug of strong coffee and staring at the pile of newspapers and tabloids before him. When he was in Miami, his housekeeper always left them on the table so that, while he was eating his breakfast, he could read through them. As a celebrity, keeping up with the buzz within the entertainment industry was important, although it was something Alejandro often neglected when he traveled.

After leaving Lancaster, he had met up with his manager in Atlanta instead of returning directly to Miami. And then Mike sent him to Los Angeles for a string of interviews, meetings, and appointments with his production team. Now he had a few days to relax in Miami before returning to Los Angeles to review the new music video and embark on a series of concerts along the West Coast.

He enjoyed his morning time in Miami. It was usually quiet. The sun was just starting to rise over the majestic view he had of the Atlantic Ocean from his tiered patio. The water glistened and reflected the light, shimmering like a sea of jewels. He had paid top dollar for this penthouse condominium with multimillion-dollar views and even more expensive security. It was his place of respite from the trappings of the crazy life he led.

But this morning, when he picked up the first paper, he froze, his coffee cup barely touching his lips. His eyes scanned the front cover, and he caught his breath. It had been more than three weeks since he had left Lititz and returned to what his manager called the "real world." He had been so busy with interviews and videotaping in Los Angeles that he hadn't given much thought to Amanda and her family. It was an event, albeit a nice one, but just an event: one of many that filled Alejandro's life. Oftentimes he felt that in his life he was simply a moving target with scenes that faded in and out. Once lived, those scenes were replaced with new ones. Similar scenarios, different actors. Yes, he had all but forgotten about Lititz, Pennsylvania. Alejandro was gone, replaced once again by Viper.

But now, as he scanned the headlines and saw those familiar brown eyes staring at him from the cover of the tabloid, he realized that the Alejandro "event" had unexpectedly crossed over into the world of Viper.

"Rodriego!" he called out.

"¿Sí, Alejandro?" A young man, dressed in black slacks and a black polo shirt, walked over to the table. "¿Qué necesitas?"

Alejandro scowled and waved the paper at the young man, who was one of his more seasoned personal assistants. With his blue eyes flashing, Alejandro shook his head. From the muscles clenching in his jaw, it was clear that he was upset. "At what point," he snapped, his words sharp and crisp, his typical gentlemanly tone replaced with anger, "were you going to tell me about this?"

The young man swallowed and stared at Alejandro, uncertain how to respond. "I . . . I left the papers like you wanted. I've been collecting them while you traveled."

Alejandro pushed through the stack of papers and noticed a flurry of different photos on the cover of newspapers and even a magazine.

The headlines popped out at him: "Viper's New Vixen?" "Amish Girl Captures Viper's Heart." "Viper Hibernating with the Amish." "Viper's Secret Affair with Amish Belle Exposed!" Each one was worse than the previous one. There were pictures of the farm, layouts of various photos of Amanda trying to hide her face from the photographers, of her parents, of other Amish people.

"*Dios mío,*" he said as he hung his head in his hands. Why had no one told him? He paid people to watch his image, paid people to keep him informed. Yet not one of them had thought to alert him that the paparazzi and media were still targeting Amanda? "I need you to follow this up, Rodriego. It needs to die down! And I mean now!" He reached for his cell phone, glaring over his shoulder at Rodriego. "I want a daily report on this. *¿Me entiendes?*"

"*Sí, sí,*" Rodriego said and hurried away, more to escape Alejandro and his temper than for any other reason.

Alejandro knew that he needed to diffuse the situation. His heart quickened, and he felt fury race through his veins. He wasn't quite certain how to do it. If he tried to contact Amanda, he knew that would make things worse. The paparazzi would be all over the story, and the media would explode even further. While he knew that time would make the story die, Alejandro felt compelled to try to help it along. The fact that it hadn't died down yet was surprising, even to him.

"Mike," he snapped into the phone when he heard his manager answer. "We have a situation with the Lititz girl!"

He knew that he was telling Mike something that was probably already on his manager's radar. He waited for Mike to jump into a tirade and to start yelling on the other end of the phone, screaming about how he had warned Alejandro and about how bad an idea going to Lititz had been.

But Mike's response actually surprised him. "Alex, Alex!" he said cheerfully. "I heard the LA meetings were great, and the production team says the video is coming along great!"

"*Sí, sí,*" Alejandro said impatiently. "But about this Lititz thing . . ."

"I know," Mike said joyfully. "Brilliant move, Alex. Simply brilliant! I should have known to trust you."

Alejandro frowned and stared at the phone as if he held a foreign object in his hand. No tirade? No screaming? "*¿Qué?*"

"The media is all over you about that girl."

"*¡Exactamente!* And they need to leave her alone," Alejandro said, punctuating the air with his index finger, even though no one else was nearby to see his animated gesture.

"Leave her alone?" Mike repeated, enunciating each word.

"*¡Sí!*" Alejandro stood and began pacing the floor. "Divert their attention. Maybe arrange for some public appearances with some of the girls at clubs to defuse it. Don't you agree?"

There was another long pause. Silence. Alejandro waited for Mike to respond, and for a split second, he wondered if the call had been dropped. He glanced at the phone in his hand, but the signal was fine and the timer was still running. He placed the phone back against his ear in time to hear Mike clear his throat, never a good sign.

"Are you insane?"

Three simple words.

Alejandro was stunned. Speechless. For a second, he stared at the phone in his hand. Had he heard Mike properly? Trying to comprehend what Mike was saying, Alejandro's mind flipped through different scenarios as to why his manager, the very man who hated the idea of Alejandro changing Viper's image, would be asking such an outrageous question.

But just as quickly, it suddenly dawned on him. It was the publicity that excited Mike. The fact that so many fans expressed their interest in Viper and "his" Amish girl was totally unexpected, a true marketing coup. Mike must have known, and as such, he must have instructed people to not distract Alejandro with updates about the media frenzy. His own team was feeding the viral effect of Alejandro's trip to Lititz. Clearly, Mike was not realizing the impact that the media was having on Amanda's life and family, or perhaps he did not even care.

"No," Alejandro said, his voice cold as ice even as he tried to control his temper. "I'm not insane. But perhaps you are."

"Alex!"

"No!" Alejandro shouted into the phone. "This girl did nothing. She had a life, a chance, a way to be a real person. But now that has all changed!"

"It happens, Alex," Mike said, his voice low and slow. "Collateral damage. You knew that when you took her back to her town. Once people knew you were there . . ."

"*Ay, mi madre,*" Alejandro said, his hand flying to his head as though he had a headache. He rubbed his forehead, the words *collateral damage* stinging his conscience. Deep down, he knew that Mike was right: Alejandro should have considered the long-term outcome. Now the thought of Amanda being so exposed, so tormented, and the look on her face from the photos, her eyes in particular, haunted him. "Make this go away, Mike. Please!" he pleaded.

"Alejandro, the media is enamored with her," Mike said. "Don't you see it? Your sales are skyrocketing. They love this. You were right!"

Alejandro rubbed his eyes. He couldn't believe what he was hearing. "I was right about what?"

"The media! They are tired of the bad-boy Viper image. This new side of you is in," Mike said, his voice thick with excitement. "They are thirsting for something different, something new. You gave it to them." He lowered his voice but couldn't contain his delight. "You gave them Alejandro!"

You gave them Alejandro. He cringed at the words. He clenched his fists. Now it is my fault, he thought. No, he would not accept that.

"No, no," he said. "You are wrong! For years, you forced me to be Viper. You can't turn it around now, Mike. You can't say that the public is tired of Viper! He's still here!"

Mike sighed. "Once Viper went to Amish land, he disappeared, Alex. But you found the golden ticket with this girl!"

"Get her out of this, Mike!"

The laughter that came over the line surprised him. Mike was enjoying this, and that angered Alejandro even more. "What would you have me do? I can't shut down social media and gossip rags!"

"Don't give me that crap," Alejandro snapped. "Get me in some clubs tonight with some girls, get the media there, alert the paparazzi." He took a deep breath. "Anything to get their attention away from her."

"Seriously?" Mike said, his voice dripping with disbelief. It was clear that he neither agreed nor could believe that Alejandro was taking the high road. "Ethics over sales? Where is my Alex?" Mike hesitated before asking the one question that was on both their minds: "Did you fall for this girl?"

"Don't go there, Mike!" Alejandro snapped. "I don't know her at all. But I do know she didn't ask for this."

For the rest of the morning, Alejandro tried to think about anything other than Amanda and the photos that he had seen of her, plastered on the tabloids. How could he not have known about this? Why hadn't someone told him? Clearly, Mike had issued a gag order to Alejandro's inner circle, but there should have been other signs. Someone who was loyal enough to him. Yet as soon as he posed the question, he already knew the answer: loyalty did not exist in his world. They knew that he'd be infuriated rather than embrace the media's attention. They chose themselves over him, the very person they were sworn to protect.

And he realized that he had no one to trust, after all.

The club was dark and noisy, packed with several hundred people on the second floor alone. Lights flashed overhead, and the beat of loud music pulsed through his ears. He stood in the VIP section, too aware that everyone was staring at him, both those who were nearby and those who were not permitted entrance to where he lingered by the bar.

He didn't feel like being here, but he knew all too well that public appearances were the only way to create distance between his name and the Amish, especially from Amanda. The more people who saw him at clubs and with other women, the more likely they would share those photos, and the less likely they would remain so fascinated by his week in Lititz at the Beilers' farm.

His arrival at the club had been met with flashbulbs and fanfare. Even Alejandro had to admit that Mike had done a fantastic job with the media. Somehow Mike had leaked the news that Viper would be visiting the hottest nightclub in Miami that night. When his black Escalade pulled up and the bodyguards stepped out to open his door, a mad crush of screaming fans and paparazzi crowded around the vehicle. It had taken five minutes to push everyone back and to control the crowd before Alejandro was able to exit and make his way toward the front doors of Club O. He paused, turning to wave at the crowd, his eyes hidden behind his trademark dark sunglasses.

Inside the club, some of his regular entourage had already been waiting: old friends from growing up in Miami and new friends in the music industry. And, of course, there was the regular crowd of women, dressed in skintight pants or miniskirts with stilettos and tattoos. They stared at him, smiling seductively, each one hoping that she would receive his attention, perhaps a quiet moment and a drink or even an invitation to leave the club with him as the early morning hours rolled in.

Alejandro wasn't in the mood for any of this, however. He hadn't been since his stay at Lititz.

During his European tour, he had been too busy to play at the clubs or socialize with the ladies. Back in Miami, he had been focused on the next round of concerts, starting on the West Coast in just a few weeks. Now, all that he could think about was the photo of Amanda, with such imploring sadness in her eyes, that had greeted him from the paper that morning.

"Hey, you," a soft voice whispered in his ear, followed by the light touch of a perfectly manicured hand on his shoulder.

Switching into Viper mode, Alejandro casually turned to gaze at the beautiful, leggy blonde who started to wrap her body against his. *"Ay, mi madre,"* he murmured. *"¡Qué mujer linda!"* It was a game. He knew it. She knew it. A beautiful woman would approach him, he'd buy her a drink, perhaps they'd dance, and then he'd move on to the next beautiful woman. And there were always plenty of beautiful and willing women to choose from at Club O, or anywhere else for that matter. Plain-looking, unsophisticated women never seemed to show up at these places. It was always the tall, thin, sultry women who made their way inside.

"I thought you'd say that," she replied, her fingers touching the lapel of his white jacket. She lifted her eyes to gaze into his face. He noticed her picture-perfect eye shadow and long, thick eyelashes. He wondered how long it had taken her to get ready for this evening and how much it had cost her. "Now, what about buying me a drink?"

"Sí, sí," he gushed, aware that others were watching. He nodded toward one of his men, who quickly produced a tall glass of bubbling champagne. "For you," Alejandro said as he took the glass and handed it to her, his gesture smooth and fluid. He had done this a thousand times and knew how to move so that every movement flowed and screamed sophistication and charm. *"Salud, mi linda,"* he said, his eyes staring at her from behind his sunglasses as he tipped his own glass at her.

"*Salud,*" she replied, a sparkle in her eyes. The other women in the VIP section were glaring at her. Under different circumstances, Alejandro would have found it amusing. It had always amazed him that, after just a few hit tracks, his world had changed. From singing at smoky, dark clubs to being the main attraction at the hottest concert halls, he wasn't certain he would ever understand the shift. Now, wherever he went, there were women vying for his attention, hoping against all odds to be the one in whom he took an interest . . . even if only for a few hours.

Alejandro kept his eyes on hers as he set his glass down on the bar. "Dance with me," he said, reaching his hand out for hers. She didn't even hesitate, letting him take her glass from her. She placed her fingers on his palm and let him lead her toward the dance floor. Like the parting of the Red Sea, people moved aside to make way for the famous Viper and the lucky lady he had selected to be his dance partner.

Within minutes, every pair of eyes in the club was on them; people watched and whispered about the erotic dance between Viper and the unknown woman. The cell phones were snapping photos, and for those with strong signals, the social media outlets were being flooded with the images. Viper wrapped his arm around her waist and pulled her close, pressing her against his body as they moved to the beat of the music. She smiled at him and said something that only he could hear. He tilted his head back and laughed. Then, while everyone watched, he lowered his nose to her neck and nuzzled her. More photos. More uploads.

She wrapped her arms around his neck and held him close, their bodies still moving together. He placed his other hand on the back of her head, and knowing full well that the next few seconds would produce the image to flood the entertainment news websites and tabloids in the morning, he lowered his mouth onto hers and kissed her. It was a deep kiss that looked full of passion and lust. Just as it happened, he released her and began dancing on the floor by himself, his arms over his head and his hips moving rapidly. He grinned at her and motioned for her to join him. She did. And when the song ended, he pulled her once again into his arms and favored her with yet another passionate kiss.

Holding her hand, he led her back to the VIP section, and then, despite the throng of people staring at him, he whispered to one of his men so that, within seconds, he was whisked out of the club, his hand clutching the woman, who seemed all too thrilled to be dragged along. The rest of the women in the crowd seemed to breathe a disappointed sigh of resignation while the men watched with guarded envy.

The SUV was waiting for him, and Alejandro, ever the gentleman, held the woman's hand as she slid inside and disappeared into the vehicle. Alejandro followed and waved just once to the crowd. And then the door shut, the tinted windows blocking him from the people who were busy snapping photos.

He leaned his head back on the seat and sighed. Taking off his sunglasses, he rubbed his eyes. *"¡Gracias, Maria!"*

She laughed. "Anything for you, Alejandro!"

The driver waited until the bodyguard sat next to him. Then, looking back over the seat, he asked, "Where to?"

Alejandro waved his hand. "Anywhere, but lose the paparazzi." He hesitated. "If they are aggressive, go back to my place. We can escort Maria home later." He reached forward to the ice bucket that was built into the side of the door. "Drink?" he asked as he poured himself one. When she nodded, he handed his glass to her and poured himself another one.

"I was supposed to be in New York tonight," she said lightly. She lifted her glass to him in a silent toast as she added, "My trip was postponed. Mike called me just in time."

"¿Si?" he asked, smiling at her. "How so?"

Maria raised a perfectly shaped eyebrow. "Did you think I would be sitting home alone, Alejandro?" She frowned teasingly, her light hair hanging over her shoulder in loose waves. Her dark, almond-shaped eyes sparkled at him. "Really?"

She was too beautiful to sit home at night. He knew that about her. Laughing, he touched her knee. "No, no, I guess not." He leaned over and planted a friendly kiss on her cheek. "You are good to me, *mi amiga.*"

"Always here to bail you out," she replied teasingly. "Just like back in Cuba!"

He touched her hair. "I like the new color."

"You think I look nice as a blonde? I'm not so sure."

"It's different. Nice for a change, no?"

Maria shrugged, too busy digging into her purse for her compact to check her hair in the small mirror.

For the rest of the drive, they rode in silence. She stared out the window, and he stared at his cell phone, checking the pulse of Twitter and Facebook. Indeed, speculation was running rampant as to who was this mysterious woman. Tweets were flying over the Internet, links to photos of the dancing scene at the club. Viper was back, and his impromptu stint with Maria was a success, he thought. Within days, the haunting image of Amanda would be forgotten, the paparazzi would leave her alone, and they would both get on with their very different lives.

Yet as he monitored the viral action associated with his abrupt departure from the club, the beautiful Maria photographed hanging on his arm, the gossip, and the Retweets, he wondered if all that was truly what he wanted. Was it possible to truly forget Amanda?

Chapter Sixteen

The overcast sky made the day seem even more gloomy as she stood by the window, peering out at nothing in particular. Her cast had been removed just two days before, and she was enjoying the liberty that it finally afforded her. She knew, however, that her freedom to move around was limited by the people who were still stationed near her parents' farm. Even when they had gone to the doctor's to have the cast removed, she had been followed by several cars, and the photographers had taken her picture as she was going into the office and when she left. She had kept her head down and tried to move away from them, but they were too aggressive for her to avoid.

The doctor had smiled at her when she entered his office. "Amanda," he said, "I see you have your entourage with you."

"My entourage?" she asked, not understanding the word.

He nodded toward the window as he lowered the shade. "The people who followed you."

Lizzie had merely shaken her head, dark circles under her eyes. No one at the Beiler house had been getting much sleep these past few weeks.

The paparazzi hadn't left the area. Instead, they seemed to multiply. Their cars and vans were parked alongside the road, and they were constantly snapping photos of any Amish buggy that drove down the road. It didn't take long for the word to spread among the community, and the locals did their best to avoid the area. The family who lived across the road had repeatedly complained to the bishop, but there was nothing anyone could do. The major concern was when the children returned to school. The parents were alarmed about how to protect the children on their way to and from the schoolhouse.

In the first few days, the police had merely stopped by several times a day, shooing the paparazzi away. But the more they chased them, the more arrived. By the second week, police were stationed at the farm around the clock, trying to keep away the photographers who continued to sneak about the property. The situation caused great anxiety.

"Those people are so intrusive," Lizzie said wearily.

Amanda had looked at the doctor, her own face gaunt and drawn. "Why are they so interested in me?" She knew the answer from the perspective of why *her* in particular, but not from the perspective of *why* in general. In her world, private lives were kept just that way: private. Clearly, the Englische had a different perspective of what was off-limits to public scrutiny.

The doctor had shrugged his shoulders. "I don't know, Amanda. But I can tell you that there is a lot of interest in you. People have caught wind of your story, and they seem to be quite taken with you, your religion, and your relationship with that singer fellow."

Now, despite the fact that her cast was removed, her father and mother had insisted that she'd continue to stay in the house. Amanda had protested, but her *daed* was quite firm with her. After all, just the day before, he had found two photographers in the cornfield, trying to approach the house, hoping to get a photograph of the newly healed Amanda. When Elias had tried to chase them off his property, they had proceeded to take his photograph, following him toward the house until Elias had no choice but to flag down the police officer who was stationed at the end of the driveway.

Even the police were annoyed by the media attention. It was a small town with a limited police force. There was no town ordinance about not parking along the side of the road, so the paparazzi and media were within their legal rights to stay there. Yet it was stretching the small town's law enforcement resources to have a car at the farm every single day to ensure that no one trespassed.

Other than that, the farm was quiet. For the past weeks, no one had stopped into the farm for visiting. It was too stressful to deal with the photographers and videographers who crowded around the visitors, taking their images. So, besides being quiet, it was lonely. The usual visitors who would stop in to chat with Elias or visit with Lizzie and Amanda were nowhere to be seen. It was just the three of them, day in and day out.

Even Lizzie and Elias were unable to leave the house without cars following them, taking photos and videos of their every move. They limited their own excursions to the market just once a week and would never leave Amanda alone. Even on Church Sunday, they had given up trying to attend the service. The first Sunday when they attended, the media had blocked the driveway, and then they were caught recording the service from a window. The Beilers hadn't returned since that Sunday.

Amanda tried to ignore the whispers between her mother and father as they discussed how to stop the media from invading their community and private lives. Despite not being included in the conversation, she knew that the discussion focused on Ohio. They whispered that it might be best for Amanda to return there and join her sister, who clearly was not intent on returning to Pennsylvania. Amanda wasn't happy about the thought of going back to Ohio. After all, it was just going to be more of the same, just at another location.

So, as she stood at the window, it surprised Amanda to see the black-box buggy pull up to her parents' driveway. "Someone's here, Mamm," she called out and moved away from the window. "I can't see who it is."

Elias must have heard the buggy's wheels humming against the driveway for he poked his head out of the barn door. When the buggy pulled to a stop in front of the barn, Elias approached it, wiping his hand on his pants and leaning into the open door. Amanda strained her eyes, trying to see who it was. Her curiosity was piqued. Who would have been brave enough to come to their farm?

And then she saw him.

The bishop emerged from the buggy while Elias tied the horse to a hitching post on the side of the barn. Amanda's heart fell inside her chest. Clearly, this was no social visit, judging by the way her father's shoulders slumped as he followed the bishop toward the house.

Lizzie leaned against Amanda, peering over her shoulder. "Well," she said quietly when she recognized the bishop. "I imagine we shouldn't be surprised."

Seconds later, the door opened and the bishop walked inside. He wasn't a tall man, but his shoulders were wide and his presence filled the room. He removed his hat and nodded toward Lizzie. But his eyes bored into Amanda, a piercing look that didn't bode well for a pleasant discussion.

"Would you care to sit down?" Lizzie asked. "Have some tea?"

The bishop shook his head. *"Nein,"* he said, his expression solemn and speaking volumes of what was about to be discussed. "This is not a visit for pleasure, Lizzie."

The air hung heavy in the room, and no one dared to speak. They stared at the bishop, his hat in his hands and his eyes avoiding contact.

"Then let us get right to business," Elias said, his voice heavy and sad. "What brings you?"

"It is the people's concern," the bishop said, getting right to the point. "The Englische are saying some horrible things about Amanda."

"What?" Lizzie gasped.

"It's not true," Elias said simultaneously.

The bishop held up his hand to silence them. "It is the talk," he said. He lifted his eyes and stared at Amanda. There was sorrow in his gaze, but he had a duty to his community. "The papers of the Englische say horrible things, Amanda. They say that you have been with this man, this Englischer. The papers say that you have secretly married him." He paused. "One even claims you are with child and that is why you hide."

Now it was Amanda's turn to gasp. "That's ridiculous!" Her *mamm* clutched at her chest, and Elias hurried to her, holding her up. Amanda's eyes were large and frightened. She stared at her parents. "You know that is all lies!"

"I agree," the bishop said, holding his hand up to stop her and her parents from arguing. "No one in the community doubts you, Amanda. But those lies are fueling the fire of discussion and interest from the Englische."

Amanda moved over toward the table, her leg stiff but her stance fierce. She glared at the bishop, her eyes angry. "I do not know that man in such a way!"

Elias crossed the room toward his daughter. "I can vouch for my daughter. She is honorable and pure."

Sighing, the bishop waved his hand once again. "That is not being questioned, Elias. At least not by me. What is being questioned is what to do regarding the lack of peace among the community: the invasion by these people has created a disruptive lack of peace." He took a deep breath and paused for a moment, gathering his thoughts. "I don't understand this interest in Amanda. I won't pretend that I want to even try. But I have spoken to several Mennonites and even Englische men who are more aware of this media craze."

"What do they say?" Elias asked.

The bishop shook his head. "You won't like it any more than I do," he replied. "They don't think it will stop. They think it will continue. The interest in Amanda is now an interest in the Amish. These Englische cannot get enough of it. If we thought we had too many tourists invading our lives before, it will only get worse. The Englische world is pushing those photographer people for more photos of her. They believe the stories." He shook his head. "It appears that a new generation is enthralled by this . . . this fantasy," he added, waving his hand dismissively.

Lizzie was the next to speak. Her voice was tight and strained. But there was power behind it. She spoke with strength. "What would you have us do, Bishop?"

"That is the question," the bishop said, setting his hat down upon the table and pulling the chair out in order to sit. There was silence in the room as he took his seat and sighed. "I have never been in such a situation before, but I do know that time is not making it any better. As I have learned, the Englische are more interested than ever, and as we all know, it's disrupting our lives. There are news vans in the towns and photographers at every Amish store, taking pictures of Amish, harassing the tourists. It's just terrible what is happening." He took a deep breath and looked first at Lizzie, then at Elias. "The entire community is distraught over this situation, Elias. And the only solution is for Amanda to leave."

Amanda gasped and leaned against the table, both of her hands upon it. "To go where?"

The bishop looked up, his face expressionless. "Anywhere but here."

She couldn't believe that she was hearing this. They wanted her to leave her home and her family? She shook her head. "I won't go!" She looked at her parents, pleading with her eyes. "I have nowhere to go!"

Lizzie moved over toward her daughter and placed her arm protectively around Amanda's shoulders. "We have already lost one child," she said. "You would have us lose another?"

There was a long pause. The bishop avoided Lizzie's and Amanda's eyes. It was at that moment that they all knew the decision had already been made. The elders had decided that Amanda must leave in order to preserve the community. "This was not a decision that we came by lightly," he finally said, glancing at Elias as if seeking support. "But it is clear that we simply cannot continue with such a high level of interest in our community and such interruption of our lives. It is out of hand and far too disruptive." He shifted his eyes toward Amanda. "Far too worldly."

"I don't believe this," Amanda said under her breath. She met the bishop's gaze. "I didn't do anything!"

"You brought that man into the house," the bishop snapped, obviously unhappy with her insolence.

"I'm not leaving!"

Elias spoke next, his voice strong and firm. "The bishop has spoken, Amanda. You shall have to leave, even if just for a while."

Lizzie gasped. "No!" she said and spun around, covering her mouth with her hand and silencing what was clearly sobs at the thought of her daughter being outcast from the community.

"Now, now," the bishop said, standing back up and moving toward Lizzie. "It's only until the fervor dies down. The Englische are prone to fancy things for a very limited amount of time." He looked over his shoulder at Amanda. "Your daughter can return to Ohio for a while, give things time to calm down around here."

"And what if it doesn't?" Amanda retorted, too aware that she didn't want to return to Ohio and too aware that the Englische paparazzi could, and most likely would, follow her there. "Will that solve anything or just relocate it?"

"Amanda!" Elias said, horrified that his daughter had spoken out against the bishop.

"*Nee,* Daed,*"* she said, standing as tall as she could on her weak leg. "Mayhaps I am not yet a baptized member of the church, but the community should be supporting me! I did not ask for this to happen!"

"Now, Amanda," the bishop said, turning toward her, his eyes piercing and dark. "The community did not ask for this, either, and they cannot live with these people . . . these photographers and reporters . . . lurking in their fields and peering into their windows. We have very few options at this point. After all"—he hesitated and leveled his gaze at Elias—"it was not the community who invited the Englischer to stay. I'm afraid the next option would be less pleasant." The message was clear. Either Amanda left or her parents would be shunned. He looked back at Amanda, leveling his gaze at her with a stern expression on his face. "Would you be so selfish . . . ?"

"*Nee!*" she shouted, covering her ears with her hands. Had he truly said the word *selfish* and implied that she was such a vile thing? Did he not understand how much she was suffering? Her heart raced, and her blood boiled. Did he not remember what she had already been through? "Enough!"

Elias took a deep breath and stared at his daughter, clearly feeling the pain that she felt. "Bishop, I will have to ask you to give us some time to consider what you have requested," he said. "It is time and prayer that will help us understand and interpret the will of God in this matter."

The bishop grabbed his hat from the table. His hands were large and chapped, red from having worked in the fields for so many years. The wrinkles and dryness spoke of decades of hard labor and, clearly, a lack of understanding when it came to issues of Englische law. "God has already spoken in this matter," he said sternly. *"Be ye of the world, be ye for the world,"* he quoted. Putting his hat back on his head, he glared at Elias. "I would think you would know the difference, Elias!" And with that, the bishop stormed out of the kitchen, letting the side door slam shut behind him as he left.

There was a long silence among the three of them as the bishop clambered into his buggy and drove down the lane. Even from the house they could hear the cars that revved their engines and began to follow the bishop's buggy. The paparazzi were following him now. Later, of course, they would return to stake out the Beiler farm, hoping to snap a coveted photo of Amanda or her parents. But, for now, they were finally alone.

"What do I do, Daed?" Amanda asked, her eyes brimming with tears.

Lizzie didn't wait for her husband to speak. Her face was pale, and her eyes wide with fright. "You need to contact Alejandro," she said quickly and firmly. "He created this problem. He needs to fix it!"

"Lizzie!" Elias said sharply. "That is the last thing we need to do! It would only make it worse."

But Amanda was no longer listening. Instead, she was mulling over her mother's words in her mind. Could Alejandro fix this? He had, indeed, created the problem. And his involvement was a far more likable solution than being banished to Ohio, she thought. She wasn't certain how she could do such a thing. Without a telephone, she couldn't call him, not that she even had his phone number. She didn't know his address to write to him, either. But she knew that there was only one way to get out of this: through Alejandro.

Chapter
Seventeen

Alejandro sat in the armchair, feeling beads of sweat forming on his forehead. It was hot under the studio lights, and it didn't help that he was wearing his typical black suit. Between the high temperature, the humidity outdoors, and the heat inside Studio 1A from the spotlights, there was no escaping the fact that summer in Los Angeles was hot. Unbelievably hot.

It had been a week since he had ventured into the public eye with Maria. A week of paparazzi and questions, crowds and photographs. But still, the emphasis was on Amanda Beiler, the most famous Amish woman in the world. It was frustrating him that he couldn't distract the media, get them to change course and focus on something else.

The media had barely mentioned his staged encounter with Maria at the club. A few photos made the social media circuit, and he noticed a few comments on Twitter. But an overwhelming majority continued talking about Amanda and the Amish.

Alejandro had tried to step up the distraction. With his encouragement, Maria had staged a catfight with another woman at a club, cleverly timed so that the paparazzi were nearby and it was caught on film. Despite Alejandro swooping in to separate the two women and quickly leaving the building with Maria, there were still more questions about Amanda than about this new, mysterious woman in his life.

Now that he was in Los Angeles again, preparing for his West Coast concert tour, he had insisted that Mike land him a spot on the entertainment news program. One interview, he had insisted. Just one about the music, about Maria, about the tour.

"Come on, Alex," Mike had whined. "They don't care about Maria. No one is buying it." It continued to infuriate Mike that Alejandro wouldn't seize the opportunity of the fans' interest in Amanda by playing on it. "You know it, Alex. They just want more of this Amish chick."

Shaking his head, Alejandro had countered, "It's the idea of Amanda that they want, simply because she is Amish. I'm not doing it. I'm not exploiting her. We have to give them something else to focus on."

Mike laughed. "Marry Maria, and that will stop the rumors."

Alejandro had frowned. While he had known Mike was teasing, the joke stung. "Let's be serious, Mike. That's outrageous and not going to happen." He had tugged at the sleeves of his shirt underneath his suit jacket. "Besides, I'm not the marrying kind." He had looked up at Mike, raising one eyebrow in a perfect arch. "A married Viper is a career killer, no?"

Now, as he sat in the chair, waiting for his turn to be interviewed by Sue Jarrell, the hostess of the top entertainment show in the country, he only hoped that Mike had made the rules of engagement clear. Alejandro had agreed to the interview as long as the questions focused on his latest album, his tour, and, of course, Maria.

"Two minutes, Viper," someone whispered.

He nodded his head and tried to put on his game face: black suit, dark sunglasses, and a half smile as he faced the camera. Mysterious and aloof, a look that he had practiced many times in front of a mirror. He noticed a flurry of activity as the chair was prepared for Sue Jarrell. With one minute to go, she hurried over to sit next to him. She was a leggy brunette wearing a cream-colored suit that showed off her West Coast summer tan, one that he imagined she stretched out throughout the year. Her hair hung over her shoulders in a full wave, and she touched it briefly before looking up at him.

"You ready?" She smiled.

"*Sí, sí,*" he responded.

The cameraman motioned and began counting backward and then, silence. The red light on top of the nearest camera flashed on, and Alejandro knew that they were live. Millions of people were watching him; millions more would watch the YouTube clips over the next few weeks.

"My next guest doesn't need any introduction. He's the Master of Hip-Hop and a truly global sensation!" Sue Jarrell said, smiling into the camera. "And we are honored to have him with us today as he is getting ready to start a three-week tour on the West Coast before heading back to the East and then to Latin America." She shifted her weight in one smooth motion. The camera seemed to follow her every movement. "Viper," she said, addressing him directly. "Tell us about this latest album of yours."

Great transition, he thought. "Well, Sue, I want to start by thanking you for having me here today. It's been a whirlwind of travel since this last album dropped, but the fans have been so responsive. It makes the long days and extensive travel so worthwhile."

"This album has been holding out at number one for six weeks now," she said, but it came out more like a question.

"*Sí, sí,*" he said, nodding his head. "I haven't ever seen anything like it. The songs were all so special to me, so that response from the public means that much more."

"You draw on your own experiences for your songs; isn't that true, Viper?" Sue asked.

"*Sí,* that's true," he said, nodding his head. "These songs are mostly about my experience growing up as a *cubano* in Miami. It's not easy to move to America and learn the language, the culture, the people. The streets give you quite an education." He laughed and added, "Dade County taught me well."

"I imagine that culture is important to you," she asked.

"Of course. My family is from Cuba. It's obviously very different from America. The food, the music, the life," he said. He was relaxing. The interview was proceeding well. Fans loved hearing about his childhood. "Growing up there was quite hard. Long hours of work, and not a lot of payoff. Putting food on the table was a daily struggle."

"You live here now, yes?"

He smiled at Sue. "*Sí, sí.* But I still have plenty of family back in Cuba." He paused, more for effect than because he meant it. "Leaving family behind and not being able to share your life with them is hard, Sue. And I think many Americans can relate to this. If they are not immigrants themselves, then they are likely to be first- or second-generation Americans. They grow up on their own, juggling a lot to survive."

"Are you a survivor?"

He laughed. "I'd like to think so."

"You recently survived a harrowing experience in New York."

Alejandro tried to remain emotionless. He didn't respond. The transition from Cuba to New York suddenly seemed too obvious. How hadn't he caught that?

"Do you want to talk about the car accident?" she asked.

He shifted his weight and leaned forward, his eyes meeting hers. "Not particularly." Silence. "There isn't much to tell."

"Your car ran into a girl, an Amish girl," Sue said. "That's some story, Viper."

"Seems clear-cut to me." No response. The silence was awkward, so he added, "It was an accident, and she is fine."

Sue smiled. "But you spent time in her community back in Pennsylvania. What was that like? Living on an Amish farm?"

He took a deep breath, trying to calm his beating heart. Had Mike told her to avoid these questions after all? Sue Jarrell had an impeccable reputation. She always followed the rules that were set forth by the manager. That was one of the reasons he had granted her the interview. Besides being brilliant and well versed on current events, she was kind and fair. Immediately, Alejandro knew. Certainly Mike had done this to him on purpose.

"I stayed there, *sí*," he began cautiously. "But only to make certain that she was situated and fine before I left for my European shows."

"There's been a lot of talk in the media about this Amish girl," Sue continued. "Is it true that you are secretly dating her?"

Alejandro clenched his jaw and caught his breath. "She's Amish," he said. "That's ridiculous sensationalism."

"So, no songs coming out in the near future about your stay at the farm?"

Despite his best effort to remain expressionless and neutral, he knew that he was frowning. "I'm more focused on my current songs, the ones on my new album. You know that I'm touring the West Coast, promoting this album. In fact, next week, our concert tour opens in Los Angeles." Why won't she get off the Amanda track? he asked himself. "It's the first album where the non-Latino crowd has responded so positively, too. While we are sold out in Los Angeles," he continued, "I heard that our San Francisco, Seattle, and Phoenix concerts sold out in record time, too."

"Should we expect a surprise visit from this Amish girl on the tour?"

Control your temper, he told himself as he rubbed at his face. Why so many questions? he wondered. "I can't imagine an Amish girl would be interested in such a thing."

"Well." Sue laughed. "You *are* Viper."

"Amish don't listen to music. They don't know my songs. And I'm fairly certain that they don't travel," he said, his voice flat and emotionless. "The media made a much bigger deal out of it than was necessary, no?"

"Maybe," Sue said nonchalantly. "But it isn't every day that a major music icon spends so much time with an Amish woman. I suppose the public gets curious. Seems like such an unlikely friendship." The way she said *friendship* made him cringe. It rolled off her tongue, dripping in sarcasm.

He remained silent, keeping a cool demeanor on the outside while cursing Mike on the inside. There was no doubt about it now. Clearly, Mike hadn't given them the rules of engagement. In fact, Alejandro imagined that Mike had encouraged it.

"The interesting thing," Sue continued, leaning forward. "The Amish are a very close-knit community. From what I understand, they don't let outsiders break into their world. Yet you stayed on a family farm and, from what I have read, went to worship with them and even courted the young woman."

He clenched his jaw. "I think it is better if we stick to discussing my upcoming tour, *sí*?"

Sue laughed. "That sounds like a man deflecting the question, Viper."

Silence.

"You know that the media has not left the community, and it has been over a month," Sue continued. "A month." She made it sound like it was years. "Such a long time, don't you think?"

Alejandro inhaled deeply and stared at her. "About my West Coast tour, Sue . . ."

She shifted her weight again so that she was staring directly into the camera. "There you have it, an exclusive interview with Viper about his weeklong stint as an Amish man. While we have no admission of wedding bells, clearly there are sparks flying under these buggy wheels." The red light over the cameras blinked to black, and everyone began moving around. The segment was over.

Alejandro ripped the microphone off his lapel. "Dios *mío,*" he shouted. "What was that?"

Sue Jarrell blinked and looked at him. "Excuse me?"

He stood up and glared at her. "Those questions. They had nothing to do with my tour or music."

Coolly, Sue leaned back in her seat and crossed her legs at the ankle. "No, they didn't."

"What was that about?"

Sue raised an eyebrow. "It was about your fans, Alejandro," she said sternly. It surprised him that she used his given name. Most talk-show hosts and media personnel called him Viper.

"Get off your broom, Jarrell," he snapped. "That was about your ratings!"

She smiled, a nonchalant and cool smile. "I beg to differ. It was about what is on everyone's mind in America . . . everyone who cares about Viper, Viper the Latino Lover with the sharp sting, and his sweet, innocent Amish girlfriend."

"She's not my girlfriend!" he exclaimed, lifting a hand to his forehead in frustration.

"Maybe not in your eyes," Sue smirked. "But America wants to believe that she is, and that's what this was about, my friend." She leaned back, obviously enjoying watching Alejandro try to control his temper. "Maybe you'll find that the American public knows you better than you know yourself. Maybe you'll realize that I just did you a favor."

"That's ridiculous," he snapped, waving away a young man who approached him with a bottle of Perrier water. Instead, he pointed his finger at Sue Jarrell. "You people are the reason she's suffering right now. You need to just leave her alone!" He threw the microphone onto the ground and stormed away, reaching into his pants pocket for his cell phone.

Already there were five text messages from Mike, each one telling him that other entertainment shows had called, demanding equal airtime. Furious, he threw the phone against the wall, ignoring the fact that it shattered into pieces. How could Mike have done that to him? No, he thought bitterly. To Amanda.

For a moment, he hesitated. No one was around to see him stop walking. He stared at nothing, and his mind raced everywhere. It had been a long time since he had cared about someone else more than about himself. Years, he realized. And that had most likely been about his own mother when he had labored to help her improve her life in America. After all of her sacrifices, he wanted to set her up in a nice living arrangement in Miami. She had fought him, stating that she preferred the small apartment in Miami, to stay near her friends and relatives who also had emigrated from Cuba to Florida. But Alejandro had foreseen the future and knew that, eventually, when fame hit, she wouldn't be safe there. It was because he cared that he fought so hard to protect her and prevailed.

Now he found himself in the same situation with Amanda, fighting to protect her, but it was only making it worse. The more he fought it, the more she was exposed. Under normal circumstances, he wouldn't have looked back . . . merely moved along. But there was something about Amanda that clung to him, deep within his heart and soul.

And then it dawned on him.

Dios *mío,* he thought to himself. Could Sue Jarrell have been right?

Chapter Eighteen

His car, a black Escalade with tinted windows, pulled into the farm, the tires grinding against the macadam and gravel. The police had let him through, despite their instructions to block everyone. It was obvious that he was there on important business, and the local police weren't about to argue, especially when he rolled down the window, ignoring the paparazzi that crowded around the car. The police questioned him, recognized him, and, after making a brief call back to the dispatcher, permitted him through their small blockade. Anything to stop the paparazzi and get them to move out of town. Even the police wanted to get on with their lives.

Alejandro ignored the throng of camera people who took photos of him in the black SUV as it was driven down the driveway. The rocks crumbled under the weight of the vehicle that looked so out of place pulling into the farm. He knew they had telephoto lenses and were taking pictures of him exiting the car, adjusting his sunglasses, and approaching the house. This was, after all, the moment for which they had been camping out near the farm for almost a month. They had known that, with enough pressure, it was likely that Alejandro would return.

Indeed, he thought. They had won.

One of his security guards opened the passenger door and quickly blocked the photographers from approaching the car as the driver hurried around to open his door. Alejandro took a deep breath before stepping out of the car. His dark sunglasses hid his eyes from the photographers, and he tilted his head so that they couldn't see his expression. He was annoyed that he had to take the trip from California to Pennsylvania, even more annoyed that he had to take her away with him. Yet there was a part of him that pulsed with new life, an excitement over the unknown that he hadn't felt in a long time.

He could hear the cameras clicking as he walked up the path to the porch. He glanced around, knowing all too well that every movement he made was being recorded and photographed. This was, after all, what they had wanted all along. In fact, he realized, they had orchestrated it by making Amanda Beiler the most famous Amish woman in America. No, he corrected himself. *In the world.*

The paparazzi and media had forced his hand toward this very moment, the moment when he stood on the porch, straightening his black suit jacket before reaching his hand out to knock at the door. He took a step backward, his back to the paparazzi, as he waited for what seemed like an eternity.

And then, the door opened.

It had been just two days ago when he had watched the news report about Amanda. It was Rodriego who had alerted him to the story. Alejandro had been in Los Angeles, recording a new song that he had just written. He was still steaming about the interview with Sue Jarrell, refusing to watch it when it aired the evening before last. All of a sudden, he had been interrupted by a simple text message that flashed across his phone: *Channel 7 News. Now!* If it came from Rodriego, Alejandro had thought, it had to be something important.

Quickly, he had waved his hand to stop the recording session. As the noise died down, everyone stared at him expectantly. If he was at the mercy of his manager and fans while on the road, he was the boss inside the studio.

"Let's take a break," he announced, reaching for a towel to wipe the sweat off his neck. "Got a call I have to take."

He found a television in the lounge and flipped it on to channel 7. It was an entertainment program, one that followed immediately after the evening news. The anchor was talking about the recent breakup of two popular movie stars. With a sigh, Alejandro leaned against the back of the sofa and kept watching, wondering why Rodriego wanted him to see this. Certainly it was about his repeated appearances with Maria. At least he hoped it was. He had made certain to be seen with her repeatedly while in Miami the past week. He had even flown her out to Los Angeles so that the photographers would see her near him both before and after his interview with Sue Jarrell.

The headline for the news segment flashed and, immediately, he caught his breath: "The World's Most Famous Amish Girl." The reporter began speaking, slowly summarizing the past weeks of what was being called "Viper's Romance with the Amish." There were photos of Maria on Viper's arm, but the reporter was stating that a source close to Team Viper confirmed that the relationship was a sham to distract the media and public away from the real story, the one that, according to the reporter, was waiting patiently in Lititz, Pennsylvania, on an Amish farm.

And then he saw her.

Staring into the camera was Amanda, her dark eyes flashing and her face pale. Her dark hair framed her face, and the hint of her prayer *kapp* looked like an angelic halo around her head. Plain, yes. He swallowed and glanced around the room, glad that he was alone. Yes, it was Amanda, so beautiful, with those high cheekbones and plump lips. He had almost forgotten how lovely she really was. Yet there was stress about her. He could see that she looked weary. Her expression was tense, and there were dark circles under those beautiful eyes. Something was wrong, very wrong indeed.

The reporter was talking about Viper's interview with Sue Jarrell, the one that aired just two days before. There was a clip of Alejandro ripping off his microphone and pointing his finger at Sue Jarrell when he had raised his voice and said, "You need to just leave her alone!"

He had groaned, furious that he had fallen for that trick. The cameras had still been rolling, and as usual, the media had taken his statement out of context. The way that it played on the news made it look as though Alejandro was defensive and angry, protective of Amanda. And he had known that it would only fuel the interest in the Amish girl.

The report had then switched to a film clip from the farm. His heart pounding and pulse racing, he had leaned forward to watch the scene unfold before him. He recognized the barn and the fields behind it. Then the camera had closed in on her. Amanda. When she had looked straight into the camera, not trying to hide her face, she spoke slowly and directly. "If you don't leave, I am being sent away," she had said.

Clearly, she had been speaking to the paparazzi. But as Alejandro had watched, he realized something else was being said. She was sending him a message: she was going to be sent away because of the media attention. Because of me, he thought.

He had spent the next two hours on the phone, trying to get a message through to her. It had taken that long to finally locate a police officer who was willing to approach the house in order to find her and hand her a cell phone. Lizzie and Elias were apparently in the barn, milking the cows for the evening chores while Amanda was still trapped inside the house. The police officer had knocked on the door, and when she answered, he merely handed her the phone.

"Hello?" she had said into the small contraption in her hand as she pressed it against her ear.

"Princesa," he had said. Hearing her soft, sweet voice had made his heart swell. "I am so terribly sorry." He had thought he heard her sob, and she was silent for just a few minutes. He let her collect herself. "What is happening out there? *Dígame.*"

It had taken her a moment to compose herself. The relief of hearing his voice made her feel safe for the first time in weeks. She had shut her eyes and, after taking a deep breath, finally whispered into the phone: "They just won't leave me alone, Alejandro. And now the bishop and my *daed* want to send me away." She paused. "I don't want to go to Ohio, Alejandro. It will be just like here. It will hurt more people."

He had rubbed the bridge of his nose with his fingers. *What to do, what to do?* he thought. "I'm sorry, Princesa."

She had paused, and for just a moment Alejandro had thought the call had been lost. Finally, there was a noise, and he knew that she had turned away from the police officer and was trying to hide her voice. "I won't go to Ohio. I can't ruin my sister's life, too. And they have made it clear that they won't let me stay here, Alejandro. My parents will be shunned, and then their lives will be ruined." She hesitated before she asked the final question. "Where am I to go?"

It dawned on him what she was truly saying. "Amanda," he said slowly. "Are you asking me to come for you?"

Silence.

"Is that why you spoke to the reporters?" No answer. "Do your parents know that you did that?" This time, he had waited, letting the silence grow. He could wait all day. It was time for her to answer his questions.

He had heard her shuffle the cell phone in her hand. "Yes," she had breathed into the receiver. "I cannot stay here. It will ruin my parents. I cannot go to Ohio. It will ruin my sister. I have nowhere else to go." She repeated her argument as though trying to convince herself. "My life is ruined no matter what happens. Do I have to drag them with me?"

That had been two days ago. He had spoken on the phone with her for another fifteen minutes before they finally hung up. He was glad that no one else was in the room with him. Sitting alone on the sofa, he leaned against the side and rested his chin on the back of his hand. His mind had cycled through several different scenarios until he finally decided on the only path that the journey could take. And that led him back to the Beiler farm in Lititz, Pennsylvania, just two days after that media story aired on the entertainment channel.

The greeting he received differed tremendously from the first time he had arrived at the farm. Unlike when he had returned Amanda from the city after her accident, this time there was a heavy tension in the house. He could feel it even before he entered. Lizzie looked relieved, while Elias seemed disturbed. He couldn't see Amanda from the doorway.

"I've come for Amanda," he said slowly.

"Alejandro!" he heard her call out from the darkness of the room.

If he hadn't been such a gentleman, he would have pushed past her father to go to her, take her in his arms, and console her. But he knew that there was a right way and a wrong way to approach the situation. "Elias, we both know she can't stay here," he said, reaching up to take off his sunglasses. He slid them into his shirt pocket. "I've dealt with these people for years. I know what they want, and the only way to get the frenzy to die down quickly is to let her come with me. As soon as they have what they want, they'll lose interest and move on."

"She'll be ruined!" Elias said.

"I already am," Amanda retorted, having joined the circle at the door. "If you send me to Ohio, Daed, they will only follow me. Then you will create problems for Anna and her new life. Would you have all of us ruined?"

Lizzie laid her hand on her daughter's arm. "That's not fair."

"Isn't it?" Amanda retorted, feeling a newfound courage. She had grown tremendously in the past few months, the exposure to the world having given her a strength she had never known was actually inside her. "What about what happened to Aaron? I was already ruined because of that!"

Lizzie gasped and turned her face away.

"Amanda!"

She faced her *daed* and shook her head. "You know that his death weighs heavily on my soul. And I know that you blame me."

"That's not true!"

She fought back the tears. "I should have been the one harnessing the horse. I know that, Daed. You didn't have to say it. Your silence during those first months was more than enough to know what you truly thought. It should have been me who was kicked, me who died. Not Aaron! Then you'd still have your son to help you in the fields and inherit the farm. The guilt has burdened me every day since he left . . . has ruined me just as much as this craziness with the camera people!"

"I don't blame you," her *daed* said softly. But his eyes said differently. "You cannot use that as a reason to leave, Amanda."

"Yet I cannot stay here!"

Alejandro cleared his throat and stepped forward. *"Con permiso,"* he said softly. "If Amanda stays here, they will continue to stalk her. If she comes with me, I promise to take care of her. No harm will come to her, and I will end this. Let the paparazzi have their pictures, their interviews. It is better to let them get it out of their system, no? But if you send her to another community, it is likely they will follow her."

"I cannot agree to this," Elias said, his eyes sharp and piercing through Alejandro. Then he straightened his back and lifted his chin. "If you were to go, Amanda, you could never come back."

"They cannot shun me if I leave, Daed," Amanda replied, her shoulders back and her chin lifted as she spoke with conviction. "But they can shun you if I stay, and I will not go back to Ohio. I will not ruin Anna's chance at happiness nor yours." She looked at Alejandro, her gaze steady and determined as if strengthened by the fact that he had come for her. "Besides, I am old enough to make my own decisions and I trust you," she said boldly.

Alejandro nodded his head once, then stood back, his arms crossed behind his back as he waited.

She hurried up the stairs to her room and took a quick glance around, trying to memorize everything. She didn't know when she would return, if ever. But she did know that her heart was pounding inside her chest. She was making the most potentially dangerous decision of her life, but she had been thinking about it for days. She had packed her bag and kept it hidden under her bed. In truth, she hadn't had much to put in it.

The kitchen was silent when she returned. No one had moved in her absence. Her mother had her back turned, but her shoulders were shaking. Her father's jaw was clenched, and his face pale. She wasn't certain what to say or do. She knew that this was a monumental decision, but she also knew that she couldn't keep living with those photographers following her every move and risk her parents being shunned. She also couldn't return to Ohio. What choice did she really have?

"I will write," she said, approaching her mother, who refused to turn around to hug her good-bye. When she moved toward her father, he took a step backward and shifted his body away from her.

For a moment, Amanda felt as if she were floating above herself, watching the scene unfold. How did it come to this? she thought. In her mind, the past few months seemed to flash in snapshots, a quick procession of memories. From crossing the street in Manhattan to waking in the hospital, from the limousine ride home with Alejandro to listening to him sing her a lullaby in the field, and from dancing in his arms to the kiss in the buggy. And then, of course, being stalked by paparazzi. None of it seemed real. Was she really going to leave the only place she had known as home, the only place where she had ever expected to live? She glanced over her shoulder at Alejandro. He had no expression on his face, and his stance had not shifted. The decision was hers, she realized, and she turned back to her parents.

"I'm doing this to protect you, all of you," she said. "If you can't see that today, perhaps you will see it later."

Silence.

Taking a deep breath, she turned and walked toward Alejandro. This time, he raised an eyebrow as if questioning her one last time. She responded by clutching the bag in her hand and moving toward the door. She paused, just once to look over her shoulder at her parents, but neither one looked back. The decision was made; the damage was done. There was no moving backward, only forward. She lifted her eyes to look at Alejandro, and when he looked at her, she nodded and let him open the door.

The paparazzi went crazy, their cameras waiting for this moment. They snapped a rapid succession of photos, a few of them filming with large video recorders. Alejandro took a deep breath and reached down for her bag. Taking it from her, he shifted it so that he could place his free hand on the small of her back.

"You are ready, Amanda?" he asked quietly.

She looked up at him, but he was staring straight ahead. She couldn't get a reading on his emotions at this moment. But she felt the warmth of his touch through her dress. *"Ja,"* she said. She looked ahead, too, mirroring his stance as the photographers pushed toward the SUV, trying to snap their million-dollar photograph.

"I have no choice," she added.

"I will protect you," he whispered.

She smiled and lowered her eyes. "I know that, Alejandro," she replied.

That was the photograph that would be shown across the world, the famous Cuban hip-hop star in his black suit, standing with his hand pressed lightly on the back of the young, petite Amish woman as they came down the porch of her family's farm. The soft hint of a smile on her face and the serious look on his told a story full of speculation and fantasy.

Together, the unlikely couple walked down the steps and hurried to the SUV that was waiting in the driveway to whisk them away from the farm, in the hope that the paparazzi would follow, leaving the Amish community of Lititz in peace, as it had been, in a not-so-distant past.

Acknowledgments

Special words of gratitude follow for two very special people:

First, I must thank fellow author Erin Brady. Through endless (hilarious) texts, e-mails, and an occasional NYC dinner, she has been a true friend, helping me brainstorm and dream about this book. For months, we laughed and strategized over the story line. She continues to be a great asset to me in this series. As a fellow author, she knows and appreciates the hardship of taking a story from concept to publication.

Second, and most importantly, to my husband, Marc, who continues to support me, lets me type until the later hours of the night (despite the clickety-clack of the keyboard and glow of the screen that keeps him awake), and reads, rereads, and rereads again all of my work. He also encourages me to continue my weekend escapes to Lancaster to interact with my Amish friends and "family," while he takes care of the home front. Every writer should be blessed to have a Marc on her team.

Glossary

Pennsylvania Dutch

ach vell	an expression similar to *oh well*
Ausbund	Amish hymnal
Daed, or her *daed*	Father, or her father
danke	thank you
Deitsch	Dutch
dochder	daughter
Englische	non-Amish people
Englischer	a non-Amish person
g'may	church district
grossdaadi	grandfather
grossdaadihaus	small house attached to the main dwelling
gut (guder) mariye	good morning
haus	house
ja	yes
kapp	cap
kinner	children
maedel	unmarried woman
Mamm, or her *mamm*	Mother, or her mother
nee, nein	no
nichts	nothing
Ordnung	unwritten rules of the *g'may*
rumschpringe	period of "fun" time for youths

Schaffmann	worker
wie gehts?	what's going on?
wunderbar	wonderful
verboden	forbidden

Spanish

ay, mi madre	an expression; literally *oh, my mother*
bueno	good
buenos días	a greeting; good day
claro	of course
cubano	Cuban
dígame	talk to me
Dios *mío*	my God
dulce	sweet
gracias	thank you
linda	pretty
permiso	permission
por favor	please
Princesa	nickname; princess
salud	cheers
sí	yes

Plain Change

Book Two of the Plain Fame Series

Sarah Price

Waterfall
PRESS

Chapter One

The sunlight shone through the sheer curtains covering the long windows in the bedroom. It cast a soft and golden glow throughout, painting the thick white comforter on the bed in dancing shades of sunrise. Small specks of dust floated, imprisoned in the sunbeams penetrating the room. But no one saw them. Not yet. The radiance of that particular early-morning phenomenon went unnoticed in the bedroom where Amanda lay, for she wasn't yet awake.

Outside the window, a car horn blasted from the street below. Noise. A fluttering of eyelids. A bit of light. Slowly, Amanda rolled over in bed, lifting her arm to cover her eyes, shielding herself from the morning sunbeams, even if only for a few more seconds. The previous day had been long, and she'd had an even longer night. Sleep had not come easily, and what little she had was fitful.

Everything seemed strange to her as she began to wake up and take in her surroundings. Different indeed. From the brightness of the room to the high, vaulted ceilings with thick white moldings and fancy paintings on the walls, she knew that she was not at home this morning, and all of the memories from the previous day started to flood her heart with emotion.

***

The drive from her parents' farm to Philadelphia seemed to never end. She sat in silence in the back of the SUV, staring thoughtfully out the window, too aware that Alejandro was watching her. His eyes on the back of her neck caused the color to rise in her cheeks, so she kept her head turned away, not wanting him to see the effect he had on her or the tears that were gathering at the corners of her eyes.

As the farmland rolled away and the small meandering roads had turned into a highway, she sighed.

"Princesa?"

She wanted to turn to look at him, but she was afraid.

He reached out and touched her hand. For a moment, she froze. His touch was soft and gentle, reassuring her that he was going to take care of her. When his fingers finally entwined with hers, the warmth of his skin touching hers pushed her over the edge.

The tears fell.

"Princesa," he whispered again and reached out to force her to look at him. He wiped the tears from her eyes, staring deeply into her face. "It's going to be all right, *sí*? I came for you, and you will be fine."

She nodded.

"You believe me, no?"

Again, the simple nod.

He smiled. "You have no words? That is unusual."

She swallowed, wanting to say something, but the feeling of weightlessness hung over her. She felt as if she were floating above herself, watching the two people in the back of the SUV, being driven by a chauffeur who headed toward the big city whose skyscrapers were already visible on the horizon. It was surreal. Certainly this woman who sat here, with a white prayer *kapp* on her head, holding hands with a Cuban singing legend, was not her. Not Amanda Beiler.

"I have left everything I know," she finally whispered.

"You have the future ahead of you," he replied, trying to reassure her. "And there would be no future for you now at home, not with the paparazzi following your every move."

She knew that he spoke wisely. She had known those words to be true. That was why she had finally sent the message to him. Her life was over in the Amish community. No one would ever believe that she had not been romantically involved with Alejandro. No man would want to court the most famous Amish woman in the world. And no community would welcome her to live among them, not with cameras gathering wherever she went.

"What will happen now?" she asked.

"You will change," he said with a shrug of his shoulder, as though it was the most natural thing to do. "And you will live."

She tossed back the covers of the bed and sat up. Looking around the strange surroundings, she caught her breath as she took in the opulence of the hotel room. The high ceilings with thick, ornate moldings painted in high-gloss white with gold layered in between the carvings. There was a brass chandelier hanging from the center of the ceiling with crystal beads dangling from each arm. When the sunlight hit them, rainbow colors danced around the room. It was beautiful and mesmerizing, unlike anything she had seen before . . . dancing colors of red, purple, blue, and gold.

Amanda was wearing her white nightgown, her hair hanging down to her waist. Her small suitcase was on top of a dresser, where she had put it the previous night. It was open, and she could see where she had folded her dress and left it when she had changed. Her black shoes were on the floor, beside the dresser, exactly where she had left them.

Standing in the middle of the room, she turned around, inhaling the foreign ambiance. Once again, she felt that floating feeling, as if she were watching someone else's life. It was surreal, dreamlike, and certainly not happening to her.

The room was magnificent with a large vase of fresh flowers, mostly white roses and lilies, set upon a circular table near the door. There were white roses and lilies. She walked to the flowers and leaned over, breathing deeply. The sweet scent took her back to her parents' farm. She had always loved gardening, spending long spring mornings tending to the vegetables but also to the flowers that Mamm had planted around the porch. Amanda loved to prune back the roses and clip the thorns. Sometimes her mother had even let her keep one or two roses in her own room. Always out of sight of visitors, since flower displays were prideful. Now she was surrounded by dozens of roses.

Indeed, she thought, I will change.

She hadn't expected that the paparazzi would be at the hotel in Philadelphia. She had thought they would still be back in Lititz. So when they pulled up to the hotel, Amanda gasped and shied away from the window. She brushed against Alejandro as the people outside began to crowd around the SUV. Flashes went off as cameras were shoved close to the windows.

"Easy, Princesa," he murmured. "We shall get you inside and settled into a room. Then it will calm down."

"Calm down?"

"You can move about the hotel freely."

She blinked. Hotel, she thought. She had never stayed in a hotel. She was nervous. What if she got lost? What if people stared at her? What if . . .

He put on his dark sunglasses and took a deep breath. "You wait for the doormen to open the doors. They will escort us inside and away from the paparazzi. Don't say anything to those people, and if they touch you, don't respond. Let the doormen handle it. They deal with this a lot," he said.

"Touch me?" The thought horrified her.

"To get your attention," he explained patiently.

When the door to the vehicle opened, Alejandro stepped out and, after straightening his suit jacket, reached his hand down to help Amanda out of the car. Hesitantly, she took his hand. Once outside, she was too aware that there were at least fifteen camera people stealing her image. Beyond them were screaming fans, mostly young girls clamoring for Alejandro's attention. Amanda frowned and stared at them, remembering their visit to Intercourse, in Pennsylvania, a few weeks back when the crowd had started to recognize him.

The girls continued to scream and jump up, waving their arms in the air, anything to get his attention. Alejandro paused, looked at them, and nodded in acknowledgment. But he did not smile or stop to sign autographs or for photo taking. Instead, he placed his hand on the small of Amanda's back and guided her through the crowd. There were five steps, and he held her elbow. He could tell that she was overwhelmed. Between the people and the noise, it was a new and not necessarily pleasant experience for Amanda. And he understood.

She wandered over to the doorway that led to her own private bathroom. It was dark in the room, and she left the door open as she turned on the water. The countertop felt cool to her touch. Marble. The floor was cool, too. No hardwood floors or area rugs made from old clothing to cover them.

She splashed cold water on her face. Her eyes stung. She had cried herself to sleep the night before, hugging the strange, fluffy pillow to her chest. It took an hour, but she eventually found her sleep, although it hadn't been a restful sleep. She had awakened several times throughout the night, listening to the strange noises of Philadelphia that penetrated through the windows.

When she went back into the main room, Amanda took a deep breath, trying to decide what to do next. Get dressed, she told herself. Just like any other day.

The clothing that she had packed the day before seemed inadequate. Just three everyday dresses, her Sunday dress, and a nightgown. That was all she had. So she decided to wear her blue dress. As she pinned it shut, she smoothed down the fabric and glanced in the mirror.

It was a large mirror with a thick wooden frame painted gold. She had never seen a mirror like that before, and as she saw her reflection, she had to catch her breath. Is that really me? she wondered as she walked toward the mirror. With her bare feet and loose hair, she barely recognized herself. Usually, she only looked in the small mirror Mamm had hung in the washroom to make certain her hair was tidy. She hadn't ever seen herself from head to toe. The image took her by surprise.

She was thin, almost too thin. Certainly she had lost weight over the past few weeks from the stress of living under the microscope of the media. When they had taken an interest in her relationship with Alejandro and found her father's farm, Amanda had been too nervous to eat.

Her face looked gaunt, her cheekbones too high, and her skin too tanned. She wasn't certain how that had happened because she hadn't been outside too much during the past few weeks. Her dark eyes looked lifeless and scared, lacking the sparkle that she had always had. For a moment, the image of herself made her want to cry all over again.

Indeed, she realized, I am plain.

When they had first arrived inside the hotel, two men greeted Alejandro and escorted them through the main lobby, away from the peering eyes of the other hotel guests. Amanda stared as they walked, too aware that people were whispering to each other and pointing at her. Only this time, she realized, it wasn't simply because she was Amish. It was because she was Amish and with Alejandro.

She cowered behind him, shielding herself from their gazes with his body.

When he realized that she was no longer next to him, he stopped walking, and she bumped into him. He laughed lightly and turned around.

"Princesa? You are all right?" He reached out and put his arm gently around her shoulder. "I thought we had lost you."

She shook her head and lowered her eyes. His arm on her shoulder felt light yet heavy at the same time. She was too aware that people were staring. She thought she saw someone take a photo. *"Nee,"* she whispered shyly, wishing people would just go away.

Taking off his sunglasses with one hand, he touched the bottom of her chin with his finger and tilted her face so that she had no choice but to look at him. When their eyes met, he smiled. "You will get used to this, Amanda."

She glanced at the people. "I could never get used to this," she replied softly.

He chuckled and tapped his finger against the tip of her nose. "We shall see about that, Princesa. We shall see," he teased. He looked up at the small crowd of hotel guests who stood a safe distance away, gawking at the scene. He smiled at them, a kind smile, but one that also warned them to stay away.

A man began speaking to Alejandro in a language that Amanda didn't understand. Immediately, he put on his sunglasses again and continued walking, talking rapidly in Spanish to the man. Back and forth they volleyed, their singsong words sounding musical and fluid. Ignoring the people who watched them, Amanda tried to listen to the words. She understood nothing.

They stood before an elevator, one of the men pressing a button. When the doors opened, Alejandro escorted her inside the wood-paneled box. The other two men joined them, and the elevator rose up to the top floor of the building.

"Princesa," he said softly, switching back to English. "They will bring your suitcase to your room. I have it adjoining mine so that I am nearby if you need me. It's a secured floor, so only people who have rooms on it can access it."

"Secured?"

He glanced at the two men. "From paparazzi," he explained. "And these two men will also be nearby. They are my security guards when I travel."

"Security guards?" What type of life, she wondered, does he really live? If she had pondered with curiosity about his life at some point, now she knew she was thrown directly into the middle of it. "Are we in danger?"

"No," he replied, a simple answer that needed no further explanation.

When the doors opened, Alejandro took her arm and led her down the hallway. There were mirrors and paintings on the wall. She glanced at them, but Alejandro seemed determined to get her to her room. No time for exploring now. She wondered if she'd have time later to stare at those beautiful pieces of art that hung on the wall.

"This is your room," he said as he opened the door for her.

He stood back and let her walk through the doorway. He did not enter behind her, giving her the privacy that she needed and that he had promised her. "We will only be here two nights. We can talk more tomorrow about what will happen next."

She glanced at him over her shoulder. "What happens next?"

He laughed at the surprise on her face, realizing that she hadn't thought much further than the moment when he had come to rescue her and take her away from the paparazzi frenzy on her father's farm. "Well, we aren't in Lancaster County anymore, no?"

She smiled, glancing around the room. *"Nee,"* she conceded.

"So we must come up with a plan, *sí?"*

"Ja," she answered.

"Now I have some things to do. I will be next door, Amanda," he said, pointing toward a door by the dresser. "It locks on both sides. I will keep my side unlocked in case you need me."

"Need you?"

He raised an eyebrow that peeked up from behind his sunglasses. "In case you get scared or lonely," he responded.

And with that, he shut the door and she was left alone in the middle of the strange room in an even stranger city. Left alone to realize that she had stepped far outside of her world in what she feared was a rash decision. Perhaps she should have left her community for Ohio. Perhaps she should have just permitted the bishop to have her sent away. Perhaps she never should have left with Alejandro.

"What have I done?" she asked out loud, grateful that no one else but herself could hear the doubt in her voice.

The loud ring of the phone on the desk made her jump. She turned away from the mirror and stared at it, wondering who would possibly be calling her. Immediately, she realized that it had to be Alejandro. No one in her family knew where she was yet. In fact, she realized, she herself didn't even know where she was.

She padded across the thick white carpet. It felt soft and warm under her bare feet. The floors at her parents' farm were all made of hardwood with throw rugs scattered throughout, except in the kitchen, which was a cream-colored linoleum. None of their rooms had anything like the plush carpet that tickled her toes right now.

By the fourth ring, she reached for the phone and lifted the handset to her ear. For a moment, she hesitated. It felt strange to answer a phone in a room instead of visiting the phone shanty by the barn. *"Ja?"* she said into the receiver.

"You are up, *sí?*"

She smiled, feeling as if her heart fluttered, and she bit her lip, happy to hear the excitement in his voice. "Alejandro!"

He laughed. "Of course it is Alejandro, Princesa. Who else would call you this early? Who else knows where you are?" Still chuckling, he didn't wait for a response. "Now, Amanda, I imagine you are hungry, no? So I want to take you to breakfast. There is a dining room downstairs with a lovely menu."

Breakfast, she thought. In a hotel, with Alejandro. Now she felt the sensation of butterflies in her stomach. It was all innocent; she knew that. But it would certainly be something to cause raised eyebrows from the bishop and elders at home.

"I . . . I could eat something, *ja*," she replied shyly. She had never had food at a restaurant with a man. Only courting couples did that. She felt nervous, knowing that just because it was courting in Lititz, did not mean that it was courting in Alejandro's world. And he certainly wasn't about to let her starve, so it was only natural that he would ask her to breakfast.

"Bueno! Then I shall knock at your door in just a few minutes to get you," he said before bidding her good-bye.

She hung up the phone and stared at it. Communication is so much easier in the world of the Englische, she thought. With her family and friends, plans had to be made well in advance. Of course, she could use a neighbor's telephone to make and receive phone calls, but the inconvenience of walking to another farm, leaving messages, and trying to connect with people made it easier to just make plans after church service or to visit in person using a horse and buggy. Now, in the world of the Englische, the telephone sat right there, on the desk, and Alejandro Diaz had just called her to invite her to breakfast.

The feeling of butterflies returned to her stomach as she moved away from the phone and chewed on her fingernail. Her eyes wandered back to the mirror, and she saw herself, standing before it. Indeed, she looked Amish in her blue dress held together with straight pins instead of zippers or buttons. Her dark hair was hidden beneath her white heart-shaped prayer *kapp*, the strings hanging over her shoulders. She shut her eyes and waited for the knock on the door, realizing that, for the first time in her life, she wished that she wasn't plain.

About the Author

The Preiss family emigrated from Europe in 1705, settling in Pennsylvania as part of the area's first wave of Mennonite families. Sarah Price has always respected and honored her ancestors through exploration and research about her family's Anabaptist history and their religion. For over twenty-five years, she has been actively involved in an Amish community in Pennsylvania. The author of over thirty novels, Sarah is finally doing what she always wanted to do: write about the religion and culture that she loves so dearly. For more information, visit her blog at www.sarahpriceauthor.com.